"WE WERE AMBUSHED, LIEUTENANT!"

"Really?" Kincaid replied, firing his revolver at a muzzle flash high up in the rocks. "Dismount your troops and have them advance on foot!"

"We're cavalry, man!" Greggory protested. "We're trained to fight on horseback!"

"You're infantry now, Lieutenant! Get off that damned horse and help us bail you out of this mess!"

A mocking laugh drifted down from the timber, followed by the taunting words, "Hear me, Blue Sleeves! You have been beaten by Iron Crow, leader of the Cheyenne! You are no match for us and you all will die! Are you listening, Mandalian, the one called the Snake? You were lucky today, but you will not be so lucky next time we meet! Your scalp will hang from my coup belt!"

EASY COMPANY

EASY COMPANY
IN THE BLACK HILLS

JOHN WESLEY
HOWARD

A JOVE BOOK

First Jove edition published August 1981

First printing

Printed in the United States of America

Jove books are published by Jove Publications, Inc.,
200 Madison Avenue, New York, NY 10016

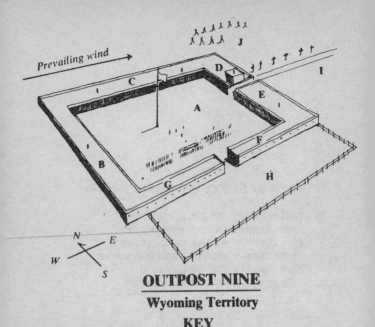

OUTPOST NINE

Wyoming Territory

KEY

A. Parade and flagstaff

B. Officers' quarters ("officers' country")

C. Enlisted men's quarters: barracks, day room, and mess

D. Kitchen, quartermaster supplies, ordnance shop, guardhouse

E. Suttler's store and other shops, tack room, and smithy

F. Stables

G. Quarters for dependents and guests; communal kitchen

H. Paddock

I. Road and telegraph line to regimental headquarters

J. Indian camp occupied by transient "friendlies"

INTERIOR   OUTSIDE

OUTPOST NUMBER NINE
(DETAIL)

Outpost Number Nine is a typical High Plains military outpost of the days following the Battle of the Little Big Horn, and is the home of Easy Company. It is not a "fort"; an official fort is the headquarters of a regiment. However, it resembles a fort in its construction.

The birdseye view shows the general layout and orientation of Outpost Number Nine; features are explained in the Key.

The detail shows a cross-section through the outpost's double walls, which ingeniously combine the functions of fortification and shelter.

The walls are constructed of sod, dug from the prairie on which Outpost Number Nine stands, and are sturdy enough to withstand an assault by anything less than artillery. The roof is of log beams covered by planking, tarpaper, and a top layer of sod. It also provides a parapet from which the outpost's defenders can fire down on an attacking force.

one ━━━━━━━━━━━━━━━

The rising sun spread its golden hue across the vast meadow. The lush grass sparkled with dew-slick vitality while the warmth of a new day swept a thin veil of morning fog from the upper reaches of timber flourishing along the creek. But there was no warmth in the eyes of the two warriors facing each other across the small fire that sent a frail wisp of pale smoke upward to be lost in the cloudless blue sky.

Beside the fire, a war lance had been speared into the ground; its shaft had an odd twisting curve to it that might have indicated a useless and discarded weapon. Such was not the case with this lance, however. The lance was decorated with bright blue striping on the shaft, and twin eagle feathers were attached just behind the partially buried blade. The lance seemed to have symbolic meaning for the two warriors seated nearby in crosslegged silence, and particularly for the one on the left, whose face was marked with jagged lines of blue that crossed his forehead, ran down his high cheeks, and nearly touched at the point of his chin.

A feather hung limply from the rear quarter of his knotted black hair, and his muscled arms were folded across his chest, which was bare in spite of the morning chill. There was a strange handsomeness to his rugged face in spite of its stone-cold expression, and his years would have been marked near the number twenty-five.

The warrior across from him wore no warpaint, and there seemed to be a weariness about his demeanor, as though his forty years of life had taken their toll. He wore a buckskin vest and twin eagle feathers hung from his hair, but the look in his eyes was one of compassion and a plea for understanding.

Seventy-five young warriors, lean, bronzed, and sinewy, were ranged in a circle about the two, and each wore blue

1

stripings of warpaint similar to the younger Indian's markings. They waited in silence for their two leaders to speak.

The younger man continued to stare sullenly across the fire until his hand snapped forward from his chest and a long finger jabbed toward the lance.

"Have you forgotten the meaning of that, Straight Shooter?" he asked without taking his eyes from the other's face.

Straight Shooter's head turned slowly toward the lance and he looked at it in momentary silence before saying, "No, Iron Crow, I have not. It is the symbol of the Crooked Lance Society, the most fierce and brave of all the Cheyenne warriors." Then his eyes drifted back to Iron Crow's face. "Have you forgotten that the Society no longer exists?"

"I have not forgotten that I am a Cheyenne warrior and that I was a member of the Society before the elders like you caused us to flee our hunting grounds and hide like squaws and little children," Iron Crow snapped, his eyes ablaze with anger. "The Society will be reborn, and we"—his arm swung in an arc to indicate the braves standing around them—"will give it meaning again. I have scars on my chest from battle and I fear no white man."

Straight Shooter smiled almost patiently. "Then you are a fool, Iron Crow. The white men are many, and more come each day. We can no longer beat them in combat."

"And what would you have us do, Straight Shooter? You were once a great warrior of the Society and a chief of the Cheyenne. What would you, in all your great wisdom, have us do while our hunting lands are stolen from us?"

"I would have us go north and join with Sitting Bull and abide by whatever decision he makes."

Iron Crow threw his hands up and a sneer curled across his lips. "Sitting Bull is a Sioux, and cannot even lead his own people, let alone Cheyenne warriors of the Crooked Lance Society! His spirit is broken and he cowers here in Canada and moans about the loss of his land and his treatment at the hands of the white people. Eventually he will become even more frightened and turn his people in to the Blue Sleeves and beg for their mercy."

Straight Shooter nodded in agreement. "Perhaps, and that might be the best thing for all of us to do. The great days are

2

gone and we cannot stay here forever. We must accept our fate and live with what we are given."

"Accchhhh!" Iron Crow snarled while spitting viciously toward Straight Shooter's moccasins. "The great days are not gone, only great warriors! Look what we did to Yellow Hair at the Greasy Grass! We defeated the finest soldier they had and destroyed his entire army. It was a great victory and one we will live again one day."

Straight Shooter shook his head. "You are wrong, Iron Crow. It was a great mistake. We took Custer by surprise and our warriors outnumbered his soldiers by four to one. What we did at the Greasy Grass will haunt us for the rest of our lives. The White Mother in England has ordered us to leave Canada, but Sitting Bull is the one the Blue Sleeves want, not you and me. We are nothing to them, and once they have him and the other Sioux, we will be taken one by one until we are all dead, if we do not surrender with the great Sioux chief."

"You speak the words of a dying woman, Straight Shooter. We, the Crooked Lance Society, will return to the Paha Sapa and take what is rightfully ours. We have great medicine and the Blue Sleeves will run from us in fear."

A humorous, quizzical look crossed Straight Shooter's face. "You have great medicine, Iron Crow. From where do you get such medicine?"

Iron Crow smiled in cruel triumph. "From him," he said, pointing to a man standing just behind the elder Cheyenne. "From White Claw, our medicine man. He has spoken with the gods and they have told him of our great medicine. White Claw! Tell the old woman what you have told me."

The ring of warriors moved to one side to allow passage for the medicine man, and a tall, almost emaciated Indian stepped forward. He too was in his mid-twenties, but in that lay his only similarity to the others. The right side of his face was splotched with pale, cream-colored markings, and his right eye was pinkish in color, in contrast with the deep brown of his left. His right arm was held stiffly by his side, and it too was a tapestry of white and brown that led to a hideous, grotesquely disfigured hand. The fingers of that hand were joined together and drawn in to form a permanent, curling hook that was nearly pure white. A medicine bag hung from his neck, and a long stick encased in rattlesnake skin was held in his left hand.

3

A singsong chant escaped White Claw's lips as he moved forward, and its sound was something like that of two coarse rocks being scraped together. His countenance and manner were trancelike as he stopped beside the fire, and his eyes were locked in the distance, as though a vision were there for only him to see.

Straight Shooter looked up at White Claw; there was no respect in his eyes. "This is your medicine man?"

"Yes he is. White Claw has great powers and he was sent by the gods to protect our people."

"I know of White Claw," Straight Shooter said, ignoring the medicine man. "He is the son of a white trapper and a Cheyenne woman. The white people would call him an albino, and they would know, as I do, that he has no powers. He is nothing more than the product of bad blood and he has been crazy since the day of his birth."

"He is not crazy, old man! He is a visionary and he has great powers with the snake stick in his hand. Show him, White Claw, and then he will know."

Slowly, as if he had heard a distant voice, White Claw turned toward the fire while the sound of his increased chanting fractured the still air. His body hunched over and his legs began to move in a shuffling dance and the feathers attached to his calves rose and fell in rhythm to the chant. As the volume of his singing increased, so did the speed of his dance, until he suddenly straightened and screamed while thrusting the stick toward the fire. The flames burst into a flash of light that lasted for several seconds before dying again, while White Claw stood frozen over them with shadows playing across his twisted face.

Straight Shooter watched in silence, obviously unimpressed, then turned again toward Iron Crow while the startled murmur of the warriors surrounding them slowly died. "May I have a look at the snake stick with which White Claw performs such magic?"

"No, you cannot," Iron Crow snapped. "No one touches the snake stick but White Claw. Silence now, old man, the great medicine man is hearing words from the gods."

Straight Shooter looked up again and listened while the medicine man threw his head back and stared up at the sky and intoned: "Maheo, the Great Spirit, we listen to you and do as you command. We will return to the land of our birth and take

4

the Paha Sapa from the evil whites. You will protect us from Wendigo, the Great Evil One. Turtle, the great God of Life, will be with us, and Owl, the God of Death, is on our side. The white man has stolen from us and we will kill him as you have said we should. You have given us great medicine and your children will do as you command. You will guide us to victory, and the white devils will feel the wrath of Wendigo and Owl. We will have vengeance, and victory will be ours!"

And then White Claw was gone, moving through the warriors, who stood aside, watching him in awe as he walked alone across the meadow.

Iron Crow folded his arms across his chest once more and stared again at Straight Shooter. "White Claw has great medicine and we will do as the gods have told him we should do."

Straight Shooter stood and turned to face the warriors nearest him. "Now hear me!" he said in a strong voice. "White Claw is nothing more than a liar and a fake. He would lead you to your deaths against the white man to avenge his own hatred of the white father whose blood has disfigured him. White Claw is crazy, a liar and a fake, as is Iron Crow. I have come to lead you back to—"

Iron Crow's shoulder slammed into Straight Shooter's ribcage, and the older man sprawled onto the grass. Iron Crow stood over him, and his face was livid with hatred. "You have challenged my honor, Straight Shooter, and for your words you will die. You will fight me in the tradition of the Crooked Lance Society, and if you win my warriors will follow you. If you lose, they will go with me to make war on the white man and reclaim our hunting ground in the Paha Sapa. Get up now, and die like a Cheyenne warrior."

Straight Shooter scrambled to his feet while Iron Crow snatched the lance from the ground and held it horizontally across his chest with his hands spaced on the shaft. The older warrior hesitated, then wiped his hands on his leggings and stepped forward to grasp the lance. He flexed his fingers on the rounded wood and stared into Iron Crow's hate-filled eyes.

"You are a coward, Iron Crow, and you are crazy. No matter what happens here, the others will know and they will follow you out of fear, not respect. If I were twenty years younger, you would be dead before you could draw your next breath."

"Those are brave words, Straight Shooter," Iron Crow said

while the sneer returned to his lips again. "But you are no longer a warrior and you deserve to die."

"I am prepared for that," Straight Shooter replied, and his lips pressed tightly together while he braced his feet. "Whenever you are ready."

Their hands were locked to the shaft, and the muscles bulged in their arms with the testing strain. Then, suddenly, Iron Crow twisted the lance while kicking out with a foot to trip his opponent. Straight Shooter checked the sudden surge and stepped to one side while twisting the lance in the opposite direction. The sun was well up now, and sweat glistened on their bodies while they struggled on the matted grass for control of the weapon. They fought in silence, with only their grunts breaking the calm, while the other braves watched from the circle surrounding the two combatants. Nearly fifteen minutes went by before youth began to take its toll on age and the lance moved more easily in response to the urgings of Iron Crow.

"You are getting weaker, old man," Iron Crow panted as he sidestepped the thrusting blow directed at his legs by Straight Shooter's instep. "Your time has come."

Straight Shooter did not reply, but he could feel the strength draining from his arms, and the sweat on his palms was making it increasingly difficult to control the violent twisting of the lance. Another ten minutes passed and Iron Crow was beginning to tire as well; the determination on his face had replaced taunting words. He was surprised by the strength of the old warrior, who was fighting now on nothing more than courage and pride. A plan was slowly forming in Iron Crow's mind, and even though he knew it was a violation of the unwritten rules of the Crooked Lance Society, he also knew he could not afford to lose a test of strength to the old warrior.

In one sudden motion he jerked the lance toward his chest, drawing Straight Shooter inward. Then, dropping to his back on the grass, he curled his legs up and caught his opponent in the stomach with his feet. He pressed upward and back, and Straight Shooter catapulted over his head to land sprawled upon his back.

Iron Crow leaped to his feet and whirled just as Straight Shooter scrambled to one knee. He swung the heel of the lance to crack the weapon sharply across the other man's jaw. Stunned, Straight Shooter flipped onto his back and Iron Crow closed in with sweat streaming off his face and streaking the blue paint that dripped onto his chest. His chest rose and fell in gasping heaves, and he stared down at the man lying at his feet while raising the lance to strike a killing blow.

Straight Shooter's eyes cleared and he looked upward with no indication of fear as he drew in tortured breaths.

"Do you . . . wish to . . . beg for your . . . life . . . old man?" Iron Crow gasped.

"Never. You . . . are not only a liar and crazy . . . you are also a coward. You don't deserve to . . . be called a . . ."

The lance blade flashed in the sunlight an instant before slamming through Straight Shooter's throat and sticking into the ground behind his head. The old warrior opened his mouth to speak, but his jaw hung down and his eyes slowly closed.

Iron Crow turned away to rest his hands on his knees and gulp in several breaths. When his strength returned, he pulled the lance from Straight Shooter's neck and brandished the blood-red weapon high above his head as he turned to face the warriors, who watched him silently and with a hint of disgust.

"We will kill the whites and take the Paha Sapa!" he screamed. "We will kill them with no mercy, as Straight Shooter was killed! Any warrior who wishes to challenge my leadership, step forward now!"

His cold, taunting eyes searched out the faces of each man before him until they all slowly shook their heads and turned away. Iron Crow smiled in triumph. "That is good. Get to your ponies now! We go south to take what is ours!"

As Iron Crow walked toward his mount, a man, heretofore unheard from, lowered the brass object he had been polishing in his hand and stepped toward the warrior. "Nice work, Iron Crow," he said. He was a man of stocky build, medium height, and wearing fringed buckskin trousers tucked inside his boots. A tattered blue army coat covered the woolen undershirt across his chest. A Schofield Smith & Wesson hung from his hip, and the black belt and holster around his narrow waist matched the color of his skin. There was a pleasant, unperturbed look on his ebony face while he placed the brass object comfortably beneath his left arm before adjusting the broad-brimmed hat to a more comfortable position over his kinky hair.

"I won, that's all that matters, Black Devil," Iron Crow

returned. "Are you sure you know how to use that thing?" he asked, nodding toward the man's left arm.

Willy Harper smiled at the Indian's reference to his adopted name. Having served his time with the Union Army during the Civil War, he had seen his share of battle and rather liked being called Black Devil.

"I do," he replied in response to the Indian's question. "If I didn't, I wouldn't be here."

Iron Crow studied him more closely. "We are depending a lot on you and what you say you can do for us. You and your Blue Sleeve sergeant friend. Are you sure his information is correct?"

"You mean about the new outpost being built near Eagle's Nest Pass?"

"Yes, that is what I mean. Is it?"

"Absolutely. It's being manned by a greenhorn cavalry outfit that hasn't ever looked down the workin' end of a barrel. If just plain scared ain't enough, we'll have them so confused that they'll cut and run, and you and your braves will have no trouble pullin' off another Little Big Horn. And as far as the outpost itself goes, it'll burn like a tipi in a pitch fire. The folks that built it didn't know a hell of a lot about what they were doin'. The ones that are garrisoned there know even less."

Iron Crow cocked his head and a curious look came into his eyes. "Why do you want to become involved in this?"

"You know the reason. Me and Sarge already made a deal with you on that."

"The gold?"

"The gold."

"I don't know why the yellow metal is so valuable to your kind, but we do have an agreement. But what I want to know is, why do you wish to make war against your own kind?"

Harper grinned, and white teeth flashed in his black face, which was partially covered by a scruffy beard. "Them ain't my kind. I'd wager I got more reason to hate the white man than you do, but you could never understand my reason why. Let's just say I got tired of pickin' cotton, bein' called a nigger, and takin' orders from white folks. The only thing they respect if you're a black man is money, and when this deal is through, I'll have plenty of that."

"Money? What good is money? The hunting land of your father is the only important thing."

Now the grin widened. "My father ain't never had no land. And the only thing he ever hunted was possum. There ain't many of them 'round here. Now, what say we cut a fat hog in the ass and head south?"

A puzzled look filled Iron Crow's eyes in response to Harper's last statement, and he watched the black man for several seconds before shrugging and swinging onto his pony's back.

Harper was still smiling while his foot found the stirrup to his McClellan saddle. A Spencer repeater hung from the spider attached to the right front swell of the saddle, and a shiny saber was attached to the left. As Iron Crow urged his horse to the front of the mounted warriors, Harper took up the rear and softly blew an old Southern ballad on the gleaming brass bugle in his hand.

two _____

The last plaintive strains of a bugle call still hung in the flame-red evening sky over Outpost Number Nine as the limp flag was lowered from its staff in the center of the parade. There was a haunting quality about the music wafting over the sod-and-timber walls of a lonely outpost situated in the northern plains. It was a sound that might have bespoken a cry for civilization, a yearning for companionship, and a release from the harsh rigors of life that were an integral part of the frontier existence. And as the sun sank beneath the horizon, the parade emptied, the gates closed, and the only beings left to gaze into the chilling night sky were the sentries posted on the walls and prepared to endure the loneliness of walking guard mount while surrounded by empty, vast prairie.

Inside the commanding officer's quarters an exceptionally beautiful woman, her cheeks showing pink from the heat of the stove, worked over the evening meal and paused to brush a wisp of hair from her forehead before stooping to check the biscuits in the oven. Flora Conway, the captain's lady, was in her mid-thirties, and even the arduous years of following her husband from post to post had not dimmed her enthusiasm for life nor her devotion to her husband. Even though her position as the commanding officer's wife would have given her social status above the other wives' on the post, Flora would have none of it, choosing instead to be nothing more than an equal and often a mother figure to lonely soldiers thousands of miles from home.

Retrieving the biscuits from the oven, Flora placed them on the stove top before carefully placing a finger between her full lips to soothe the slight burn she'd received from the hot metal. While she did so, she surveyed the table set for three and was proud of her china and silverware, even though she had known much finer things before coming West. At the sound of boots stomping away dust outside, she touched her hair almost nervously and adjusted the apron over her ample bosom as she turned toward the door.

Two men stepped inside, each dressed in a dark blue uniform with light blue piping, and they were the commanding officer and executive officer of Easy Company. Flora looked at her husband and marveled, as always, at the striking appearance he presented. Tall, broad-shouldered, and slightly graying at the temples, Captain Warner Conway was a Virginian who had served under General Grant during the Civil War and should have been a major but, due to the isolation of his post, had been passed over by the promotions board again. But Warner Conway was not bitter, choosing instead to direct his energies toward the welfare of the men under his command. Without doubt, Conway would have liked to be promoted, but he had other things on his mind, such as getting his outfit paid on time and properly equipped and supplied, securing promotions for the men who were due for increased rank, and attempting to get competent replacements for his men who had died or been wounded in battle.

Standing beside the captain as they placed their hats on the hat tree inside the door was First Lieutenant Matt Kincaid, the company adjutant and second-in-command of Easy Company. He was perhaps ten years younger than Conway, but there was a distinct similarity about them; Kincaid was equally broad of shoulder and matching his commanding officer in height, with a slim waistline and straight military posture. There was a glitter about his gray eyes, as though he were bemused rather than bitter about his having been passed over for promotion just as the captain had been, and there was a fullness to the lieutenant's brown hair, through which he was now sweeping his fingers. Kincaid, a Connecticut Yankee, was a regular-army man, graduate of West Point, class of '69, and was now serving his second tour of duty on the frontier. He had been too late for the Civil War, but his military record showed a citation for bravery on the Staked Plains in the campaign against the Comanche.

Flora Conway smiled brightly, and as they turned toward her she gestured toward the table. "Good evening, gentlemen. Would either of you fine officers be hungry enough for dinner?"

Conway crossed the room in three strides and kissed his wife gently on the lips. "God, yes, honey," he said. "Whatever you're cooking sure smells delicious."

Flora smiled again. "It's not very fancy, but it's the best I could do with what was available. I hope you enjoy it."

"I'm sure we will, Mrs. Conway," Matt said with a grin as he moved across the room. "And thank you very much for the invitation to dinner."

Flora curtsied with a devilish glint in her eye. "You're more than welcome, Matt. However many times we invite you, we seldom have the pleasure of your company. I thought bachelors were supposed to yearn for the occasional home-cooked meal."

"We do, but then we don't like to make a pest of ourselves either."

Conway had filled two glasses with brandy, and he handed one to Kincaid while saying, "The only way you make a pest of yourself, Matt, is by turning us down so often. Here, let's have a drink while Flora finishes getting dinner on the table. Did you see Windy this afternoon?"

"Yes I did. He thanked you for the invitation to dinner, but you know Windy. The old reprobate seems to prefer meat cooked over an open fire, and being closed up in a house makes him a little nervous. But he said he'd stop by for a drink after dinner, if that's all right."

"Fine, fine. Not a better scout in the entire army than Windy, Matt. Whatever it takes to keep him that way, he will get from me."

"And myself as well." Kincaid sipped from his glass and watched the captain. "You said there was something you wanted to talk to me about, sir? Would you like to tell me now?"

"No, let's finish our drink and have dinner first. Then, when Windy gets here, we'll go over it thoroughly. I have to admit it's got me a bit troubled, though."

"Dinner is served, gentlemen," Flora said as she placed a gravy boat on the table.

"Come on, Matt, let's eat," Conway said, placing a hand on his adjutant's shoulder. "I'm hungry enough to eat raw snake."

"I'm hungry too, sir, but I'll pass on the raw snake. I'm

sure Mrs. Conway has prepared something a little more to my liking."

Conway chuckled and drained his glass in a single gulp. "She'd better have, Matt. Be kind of embarrassing to have to start eating in the enlisted men's mess hall."

The conversation was light and enjoyable as the evening meal progressed, but Kincaid thought he could detect an air of preoccupation about the captain, and through that he could also sense a feeling of tension on the part of Flora as she cast surreptitious, worried glances toward her husband. When the captain's wife held up the gravy boat and offered the potatoes in his direction a second time, Matt shook his head while touching a napkin to his lips.

"No thank you, Mrs. Conway. That was an excellent meal, but I've still got to hoist this old body into a saddle in the morning. I doubt that I've ever tasted better roast beef."

"Then you've eaten in some rather suspicious places, Matt," Flora replied with an appreciative smile. "But thank you for the compliment."

Both men accepted a refill of their coffee cups and Conway stirred a spoonful of sugar into his while staring at the brown liquid in silent contemplation, then drank without speaking. Flora had begun clearing the dishes away and had just turned down Kincaid's offer of help when there came a knocking on the door.

Conway looked up quickly. "Suppose that's Windy, Matt?"

"Should be. Shall I show him in?"

"Yes, please do."

Kincaid excused himself and crossed to the door, which he opened and stood to one side. "Well, hello, Windy. I was beginning to wonder if you were going to make it. Come on in, the captain's expecting you."

"Thank you, Matt," the tall, lean, slouching man said, pulling the weathered hat from his head and stepping inside. "Never late when it comes time for a drink. Evenin', Mrs. Conway, Captain."

The captain and his wife returned the greeting while the scout hung his hat on the rack beside the other two. Windy Mandalian moved with a coiled deadliness, as though he were a cobra about to strike; the fringed buckskin clothing clinging to his wiry frame indicated not one inch of fat or unused muscle.

13

The aquiline cast of his nose, flanked by high cheekbones on his deeply tanned face, gave him an almost Indian-like appearance, although in actuality he was the native-born son of an Armenian furrier and a French-Canadian lady who might have had a touch of Cree in her bloodline. He was known as "the snake" by the various Indian tribes with whom he had done battle, due to his uncanny ability to escape both their traps and their bondage, and he was regarded by all as the ultimate man of the plains.

"May I offer you something to eat, Windy?" Flora asked from where she stood, halfway to the kitchen, with the plate of roast beef in her hands.

"Thank you, no, ma'am. I took supper with some of the boys out at the tipi ring. Didn't smell nothin' like what you've got, but it was tolerable."

Matt thought about the tipi ring, a makeshift village of semi-reconstructed Indians who were camped just out of rifle shot from the post and most of whom, squaws included, considered themselves friends of Windy Mandalian. He wondered, as he followed the scout to the table, how he could possibly choose that company over the captain and his beautiful wife, but then he allowed that there was a lot he didn't understand about Mandalian, and he accepted the fact that Windy was the most capable, trustworthy man he had ever known.

"Care for a cup of coffee or maybe a brandy, Windy?" Conway offered, rising from the table.

"Thankin' ya, Captain," Windy replied, taking out a chair and turning it backward before sinking down to place his arms on the backrest, his massive bowie knife hanging from one hip and his revolver from the other. "I could never forgive myself if I drank up all your coffee, but your brandy's another matter. Thank ya, I could stand about three fingers of that."

"Matt?"

"Yes, please."

"Flora, would you care for a little sherry?"

"Yes, dear heart, that sounds nice. Why don't you gentlemen make yourselves comfortable in the living room while I finish clearing the dishes. I'll join you in a few moments."

After Conway had poured the drinks and they had retired to the other section of the quarters, he offered cigars around, which Windy accepted and Matt declined with thanks. Then

14

the captain seated himself on a padded leather chair and pulled a large brown envelope from the inside breast pocket of his tunic. He tapped the envelope absently on his thumbnail and said, "This is why I've asked both of you to come here tonight."

Matt studied the envelope curiously. "What's it have to do with us, Captain?"

"I'll get to that in a minute, as soon as Flora joins us. Strangely, she seems to be involved as much as we are." Conway turned toward Windy. "Are you familiar with the Black Hills, Windy?"

"Yup. Dakota Territory, about a hundred miles northeast of here. We call 'em the Black Hills mainly because of the dark pine trees growin' every damned where. The Sioux call it the Paha Sapa, and so do the Cheyenne."

"What kind of terrain is it?"

Windy scratched the back of his neck before replying. "Well, Captain, you might say whoever made the Rocky Mountains made the Black Hills as a toy for his kids. Roughest piece of ground in the High Plains. Canyons, draws, gullys, rivers, and creeks all leading away from a central highlands, although it sure as hell ain't flat. Rocks, boulders and trees. If the Dakota Confederacy had had any idea of our type of warfare, they could have holed up in the Black Hills until hell froze over, which ain't happened yet, to my recollection."

"They didn't do bad with Custer, Windy," Matt threw in as he took a sip from his glass.

"Right ya are, Matt. But the Little Big Horn is about a hundred miles west of there, and it's rolling plains pretty much like we have here." Windy paused to puff on his cigar. "To my way of thinkin', old Georgie kinda got blamed for somebody else's ignorance on that one."

Conway nodded. "I'm in agreement with you, Windy. His mission was not to engage the Indians in battle. His company was merely intended as a recon patrol. That's why he sent Reno off to the left and Benteen off to the right so they could cover more ground. Once they found the main body of the Dakota Confederacy, he was supposed to notify General Terry, who was bringing up the rear with artillery and Gatlings. What happened, though, was that they stumbled onto Crazy Horse and all his people quite by accident. The rest is history."

"And in my opinion, sir, it's history that will be argued for the rest of history," Matt said.

"I imagine so. And oddly enough, what happened at the Little Big Horn is now affecting us in a limited way. This morning . . ."

Flora walked into the room carrying her glass of sherry in her hand. She nodded her thanks as the three men rose, waited until she had taken a seat by her husband, and then sat down again.

"I'm glad you're here, Flora," Conway said, patting his wife gently on the knee as he resumed his seat. "What Windy, Matt, and I were just talking about includes you as well." He looked again toward the other two men. "As I was saying, the Little Big Horn is in some ways relevant to the orders I have here in my hand. With the discovery of gold in the Black Hills, there has been quite an influx of civilians, miners, feather merchants, all around troublemakers, and the like, into the Black Hills region. Because of that—"

"Excuse me, sir," Kincaid interjected, "and correct me if I'm wrong, but weren't the Black Hills given to the Sioux by the terms of the Treaty of Fort Laramie?"

The smile on Conway's face was one of patient frustration. "You're right, Matt, they were. But, as has been the case with many treaties signed with the Indians, it has proven far easier to keep the Indians under control than to attempt to keep the white people out. We all know General Sheridan's attitude regarding the red man, even though none of us share that view. At any rate, we follow orders from above and issue them below. It seems that with the influx of civilians into the Black Hills and the establishment of two major mining communities, Deadwood and Lead, a new outpost has been built in the Pine River valley a few miles north-northeast of Deadwood."

Conway drew the documents from the envelope and flipped through the pages quickly. "It is to be commanded by one First Lieutenant Steven Greggory, who should have arrived at Outpost Number Thirteen about a month ago. He will be in command of a full company of cavalry. For the most part, the entire command is green both to the region and to Indian fighting in general. The outpost was built to protect gold-mining interests in that area, which, as I understand it, are pretty important to the government."

16

When Conway paused to sip his brandy, Kincaid asked, "Where does your reference to the Little Big Horn fit in, Captain?"

"As you know, five troops of the Seventh Cavalry were wiped out in that fight. The War Department is a little nervous about having another cavalry outfit so close to the scene of the slaughter, especially a greenhorn outfit. Most cavalry outfits are still a little hot under the collar and itching to square accounts. That's where we fit in."

"How's that?" Windy asked.

"We're supposed to go north and make sure they are ready and prepared for excursions into the field that won't lead to another massacre."

"Those cavalry outfits are a pretty proud bunch, Captain," Kincaid said, crossing his knees comfortably. "Do you think they'll listen to anything we blue-legs have to say?"

"Haven't got much choice. Lieutenant Greggory has received an identical copy of these orders. The three of us, plus Sergeant Cohen and two full platoons of Easy Company, are supposed to go up there and show them the ropes."

"This place will fall apart without Sergeant Cohen here to ride herd, sir. You know that as well as I do."

Conway smiled his agreement. "Well, we'll just have to trust Corporal Bradshaw to try and keep a lid on things until we get back."

"Four Eyes?" Windy asked in surprise. "If he loses his spectacles, the post is gone."

"We'll tie them to his head."

Flora looked up from the glass in her hand and there was a curious look in her eyes. "You mentioned my involvement somewhere along the line, Warner. What have I to do with all this?"

"This is the part I like least of all. Lieutenant Greggory is bringing his new bride with him. It's her first exposure to military life and it is requested that you accompany us to help her adjust to the ways of the frontier. Now, they say in this briefing report"—Conway slapped the papers with the back of his hand—"that there is absolutely no danger from Indian attack and that the region is entirely settled, with the exception of Sitting Bull up in Canada, whom they see as no threat."

"Ain't that a crock of . . ." Windy caught himself with an

apologetic glance at Flora. "...beans. The massacre at the Little Big Horn ain't but barely a year old and some of Crazy Horse's warriors, especially the Cheyenne, are strutting their stuff pretty good and are anxious for another chance at those green cavalry troops you mentioned. That area is just about as settled as an Indian's stomach after drinkin' a quart of bad booze, and if you don't mind my sayin' so, Captain, I don't think the Paha Sapa is any place for a lady like Mrs. Conway here."

Flora smiled pleasantly. "Thank you for your concern, Windy, but I can certainly take care of myself. It sounds like a grand adventure to me, and if Mrs. Greggory could use my help, I'd be glad to give it." She turned to Conway and placed a hand on his arm. "Please let me go, dear. I'd love to get away from the post awhile and it should be a beautiful ride."

"Five days in the saddle takes a little of the beauty off anything, Flora. I agree with Windy, I really don't think—"

"Please, Warner. I'd love it and I'm sure I can be of some help once we get there." The concentrated look of excitement in her eyes brought an even greater depth of beauty to her face, while her hand now massaged the captain's arm.

It was obvious that Conway's resolve was melting rapidly, and he looked quickly to Kincaid for support. "What do you think, Matt?"

"Excuse my taking sides, Mrs. Conway, but I'm with Windy. The War Department happens to be located in Washington, D.C., and they've got just about as much idea of what's going on out here as I have of ballroom dancing. The Cheyenne and the Sioux are the two fiercest tribes of all the Dakota Confederacy, and this outpost is being built right next to, if not directly on, their ancestral hunting grounds. Whatever warriors there are left won't take kindly to whites settling in the Black Hills."

"So!" Flora said huffily. "Three men against one woman! Are you all trying to say that I am some weakling who will hold back a major army campaign? Those papers have already said that it is a peaceful excursion to help settle another company into its new quarters. What could be dangerous about that?"

"Everything," Windy said laconically.

Kincaid shrugged helplessly and glanced once at Conway

18

as if to say, *Sorry, pal, you're on your own.* "We're not taking sides against you, Mrs. Conway. We're only concerned for your welfare. If the captain decides you should go along, we'll protect you the best we can."

"Protect me? From what? Saddlesores?" Again she turned to her husband. "Please, Warner. I want to go."

"Thank you, Lieutenant," Conway said with a derisive smile at Kincaid. "I can see you'll do well as a husband. All right, Flora, you can go. We'll be leaving in two days, and please don't bring along your entire wardrobe. We'll prepare an ambulance—"

"Thank you, sir, but I'll ride a horse just like the rest of you."

"You *are* the stubborn one, aren't you?" Conway said, pecking Flora's cheek lightly. "Have it your way. But it'll be a rough ride and we'll be covering a lot of ground every day."

"Did the settlers' women come out West on a magic carpet, dear?" Flora asked with a sweet smile. "I'll be just fine, you'll see."

"Yes, I guess we will."

"Captain?"

"Yes, Matt? What's on your mind?"

"I was just wondering, why was Easy Company chosen to go up north and break in this new outfit? Seems like we've got about all we can handle around here."

Conway picked up the documents again and shuffled through them until he found the page he wanted. "You'll get a laugh out of this, Matt—I know I sure as hell did," Conway said while he searched the print for the paragraph he wanted. "Ah yes, here it is. I'll read it to you. '. . . Your company has been chosen for this assignment due to its superlative combat record in the field and in full knowledge that it is one of the finest mounted infantry units west of the Mississippi. In addition, due to your proximity to the Black Hills region, and in light of the fact that your designated control area is relatively peaceful . . .'" Conway looked up with a knowing grin. "Heard enough?"

"Relatively peaceful?" Kincaid exploded. "If things are so damned peaceful around here, why are we constantly requesting replacements—which seldom arrive!—for our dead and wounded?"

"They figure it's swamp fever we're puttin' up with out here, Matt," Windy said dryly. "Seen any swamps lately?"

"There's not a swamp within five hundred miles of here, Windy."

"Pleased to see ya got my point."

While Kincaid did not have a quick temper, he did harbor a smoldering anger toward the War Department, which he now expressed. "If we're so almighty valuable to them, then why don't they fill our supply requests, issue repeating Spencers to our men, procure boots, saddles, and blankets, and send our pay on time? Easy Company is the most poorly equipped, underpromoted, overlooked outfit—"

Conway held up his hand with a hearty laugh. "I understand how you feel, Matt, and I concur entirely. But I guess since we're doing so well, they don't think we need the other things that army units expect as routine. I wonder if they've ever seen a copy of the Inspector General's field combat readiness report."

"You mean the one we flunked?"

"One and the same."

Now all three men laughed, and the two visitors rose to leave. "I'd give ten dollars for a copy of that and enough postage to get it back to Washington, D.C.," Matt said. "But of course it would have to be in triplicate."

"I'll throw in another ten if we need it, Matt," Windy said. "I think it'd be worth two months of my pay." Then Windy's eyes turned serious and he looked at Conway. "Captain, in two days we leave for the Paha Sapa. I hope it's the cakewalk those boys back East think it's gonna be, but I'd bet my last chaw of tobacco it ain't gonna be. The Cheyenne don't forget their home ground real easy, and we're about to set up camp right on their doorstep. They ain't real fond of visitors."

"I know it, Windy, but we haven't got much choice. We've got orders to follow."

"So did Custer. Night, Captain, Mrs. Conway."

three ━━━━━━━━━━━━━━━━

"Goddammit, trooper, when I say growl, you'd best be droppin' to your knees and bark! You got that?"

"Yes, Sergeant, I just thought—"

"Nobody asked you to think! Now, growl!"

"What?"

The sergeant's gloved knuckles cracked across the trooper's chin in a backhanded blow, and the young private collapsed in the dust of the parade. "You don't hear so good, do you, boy?" Sergeant Aikens growled. "Now, for benefit of your plugged-up eardrums, I'm gonna say it again. When I say—"

"What's the meaning of this, Sergeant?"

The sergeant, a huge, rawboned man with cold, expressionless eyes, turned on his heel and snapped a hasty, if poorly executed, salute. "Afternoon, Lieutenant Greggory, sir. What's the meanin' of what?"

Lieutenant Greggory, of thin build and medium height, was only thirty years old, and he stared up at the sergeant, who was ten years his senior. "The meaning of that trooper crawling on his hands and knees on the dirt at your feet."

"Oh, you mean Trooper Tipton there, sir?" Aikens asked with a cruel but innocent grin. "He was just tryin' to find a nice soft spot to do some pushups for me, sir. Weren't you, Tipton?"

The young trooper, no more than nineteen years of age, had scrambled to his feet and was standing at ramrod attention in the presence of his commanding officer. He stared straight ahead, looking at neither man, but there was a hint of tears in his eyes.

Aikens watched Tipton closely. "I said you was just gonna do a pushup or two for me. Isn't that right, Tipton?"

"Ah . . . ah, yes . . . Sergeant. That is correct."

21

Greggory looked first at one man and then at the other. There was absolute silence in the parade of Outpost Thirteen as the other soldiers quit their labors to watch. A hint of uneasiness came over the lieutenant, a feeling that his authority was being challenged, and he said finally, "Very well, Sergeant. I want to see you in my office immediately. Dismiss that trooper, have him dust that uniform off, and send him to his barracks."

"Yessir," Aikens replied, watching the young lieutenant stride toward the orderly room and noting the tailored fit of his new, dark blue uniform, trimmed with yellow piping. He waited until the lieutenant turned in the doorway, adjusting the shiny cavalry saber by his side, and stepped inside, before heaping his wrath upon Tipton.

"You, Trooper, are on my shit list. If I ever hear a word about what happened here, you'll wish your mama woulda drowned you with the kittens. Is that clear?"

"Yes . . . yes, Sergeant."

"It'd better be. Now get your ass over to the barracks like the man said. I'll get a piece of you later, but right now I gotta talk to the lieutenant. Move it out! On the double!"

Aikens watched the young trooper sprint across the parade before turning and walking to the orderly room and stepping inside. The first sergeant of Outpost Thirteen was a pudgy man, short of stature and given to constantly pulling the waistband of his pants up over his bulging paunch. He glanced up once and then back down at the stack of paperwork piled on his desk.

"What do you want, Aikens?" he asked irritably.

"The lieutenant wants to talk to me, Top."

"More like he wants to talk *at* you. Knock first and then go on in. I imagine he's expecting you."

Aikens grinned his dirty grin and stepped toward the door to the commanding officer's office. "I reckon he just might be, at that," he said as his knuckles rapped twice on the raw wood before he pushed the door aside.

Greggory looked up from the paperwork strewn across his desk and shook his head wearily. "Don't you wait for permission before entering, Sergeant?"

"Top said—"

22

"Never mind. You're here, that's all that matters. What were your reasons for hitting Trooper Tipton?"

"Well, Lieutenant, sir, I didn't actually hit—"

"Like hell you didn't! I've got eyes!"

"Yes, Lieutenant, sir."

"And knock off this 'Lieutenant, sir' bullshit! Use one or the other, but not both."

"Any way you want it, Lieutenant."

Greggory's eyes narrowed at the hardening tone in Aikens' voice, and he determined at once to bring the sergeant to his knees. "You'd better have a damned good reason for using physical violence on one of my men, Sergeant, or you'll be wearing holes where your stripes used to be."

"I got a good reason, Lieutenant. I'm a Sergeant and he ain't nothin' but a trooper. A fucked-up trooper at that. He ain't worth the piss it'd take to make a yellow hole in a snow-bank."

"That's no reason for striking a man, Sergeant. Why did you hit him?"

Aikens pursed his lips, arched his chin, and scratched his neck lazily. "He was late reportin' for his detail. When I chewed him out, he sassed me back. In this man's army, that's reason enough for a little knuckle discipline."

"Not in my command it isn't, Sergeant. People, whatever their rank, should be treated with respect and dignity. You can lead a horse to water but you can't make it drink."

The grin was there again. "Yes you can, Lieutenant. If you hold its head under long enough."

Knowing his intention to upbraid the sergeant was slipping quickly away, Greggory leaned back in his chair and folded his fingers across his chest in a senatorial manner.

"Sergeant Aikens, we've got a tremendous job on our hands here. Every man is going to have to pull his own weight, and that includes you. You're the only seasoned veteran I've got in my command, with the exception of myself, of course," he added quickly, remembering the two weeks he had spent escorting a payroll wagon to Fort Leavenworth, "and I'll need your help in securing this area for the local gold-mining operations."

Sergeant Aikens was aware of the gold discovered accidentally by General Custer's troops, which had started the rush to the Black Hills, and he said, "That's why I volunteered for this assignment, sir." Then, catching himself, he added, "To help out with a difficult assignment, I mean."

Greggory was weary of the day's travail. As a matter of fact, he was thinking of his wife at that moment and not really listening to the sergeant's words. "I'm glad to hear that. I really am. Perhaps you're taking the right approach in toughening up the troops for what might be a very difficult tour. I'm leaving you in charge of training green troopers for duty in which they are totally inexperienced."

The lieutenant rubbed his knotted brow and looked up again. "It's nearly time for retreat now, so make sure they're all assembled for the lowering of the flag."

"You can count on it, sir," Aikens said, saluting listlessly and turning toward the door.

"Oh, one more thing, Sergeant." Greggory dug a folded set of orders from somewhere beneath the litter on his desk and held it up to the light. "There's a mounted infantry outfit, Easy Company from Outpost Number Nine, on its way here to help us with our organization. They should be here within a day or two."

"Mounted infantry?" Aikens said disgustedly. "Hell, sir, them ain't nothin' but footsoldiers too lazy to walk. What the hell could a cavalry outfit have to learn from them?"

"I don't know, Sergeant, but they're on their way and there's nothing we can do to stop them. When they arrive, I'll want the entire troop standing tall and prepared for inspection by"— he paused to search for the names—"yes, here it is, Captain Warner Conway and First Lieutenant Matthew Kincaid."

"Did you say in a day or two, Lieutenant?"

"Yes I did."

"Don't you remember that reconnaissance patrol you assigned me to with Third Squad?"

Greggory ran his fingers through his thick, curly hair. "Yes, I remember. What about it?"

"Well, we're leavin' in the mornin' and might not be back in a day or two."

"Very well, Sergeant. I'll have someone else take care of it. You're dismissed."

"Thank you, sir," Aikens said, pulling the door closed behind him and walking through the orderly room, which the first

24

sergeant had now vacated. There was a troubled look on his face as he crossed the parade. It was the expression of a man whose plans had taken a serious turn for the worse.

Greggory stared at the door for several seconds, then made a desultory effort to finish some paperwork before pushing the document aside. Taking his hat from the rack, he mumbled, "To hell with it. I've had all I can stand of this for one day."

When Greggory stepped inside his quarters, he saw his wife of three months working at the cook stove, and what had come to be a familiar aroma reached his nostrils—that aroma being the smell of burned corned-beef hash. But the sight of the young, slightly built girl overwhelmed any repugnance he might have felt. She turned when she heard the door close, and the wisp of auburn hair hanging down over one eye, in combination with the exasperated look on her rosy-cheeked face, made her look like an elf that had just learned it was allergic to the color green. She was pretty in the way that beautiful women often are, prior to maturity, and when she blew upward from pursed lips, the lock of hair rose, then nestled over her cheek again.

"You did marry me for my cooking ability, didn't you, dear?" she asked weakly while holding the singed pan before her with a pair of potholders.

Stepping forward, Greggory smiled and brushed her hair back, then stooped to kiss her tenderly on her slightly pouting lips. "I married you because you're beautiful and I love you. Besides that, I like my food well done."

"Something reminiscent of a lump of coal, I hope?"

"Yes, with lots of ketchup," Greggory replied, reaching for a brandy bottle on the sideboard and pouring a stiff drink. When he turned with the glass in his hand, he watched his wife spoon hash onto two plates and noticed the bouquet of fresh wildflowers in the center of the table.

"Where did the flowers come from, Tina? You haven't been outside the post again, have you?"

Tina turned and offered a weak, guilty smile. "It's all right, honey. No one nor nothing is going to harm me."

"It's not all right," Greggory said firmly. "This is wild country and there are all kinds of things that can and will harm you. Indians, wild animals, white scum, and the like. I've

25

asked you before not to go outside the compound unless you are accompanied by myself or someone else I've assigned to insure your safety. Do I have your promise on that?"

"How about a definite maybe?"

"Tina, I love you and I could never forgive myself if anything ever happened to you." Greggory looked around the log-walled room and sighed heavily. "I regret even having brought you to this godforsaken hole in the first place."

"Honey, don't say that." Tina laid the potholders on the table and crossed the room to reach up and take her husband's face in her hands. "I love you, and I want to be with you. I have never mistaken you for a Philadelphia lawyer; I knew you were a soldier when I married you, and as a matter of fact it was your handsomeness in this uniform that first attracted me to you."

Now it was Tina's turn to gaze about the room, which the setting sun filled with golden twilight. "Sure, this is a little drab, and that's why I collect flowers and other pretty things to cheer it up. But please don't make me a prisoner here. Things will get better, you'll see. Just give it a little time. I know this is your first chance to command and it's difficult for you, but you're strong, brave, intelligent, and—"

"I don't know, Tina, everything is such a mess that I sometimes wonder if it's worth it."

"Sure it is. You're a career officer and a damned—"

"Tina! You know I forbid you to use that kind of language."

Tina smiled up at him, and there was a devilish twinkle in her eyes. "You don't want me to be a brazen little hussy?" she asked, her voice lowering to just above a whisper.

"No. I want you to be a lady."

"I'd rather be a woman," Tina replied, never taking her eyes from her husband's face while her hands went behind her back to slowly untie the apron around her waist. "Is the door locked?"

Greggory watched her almost nervously as she tossed the apron onto a chair and slowly, ever so slowly, began to unbutton her bodice. "Tina, it's not even dark yet. Let's wait until . . ."

She shook her head, moving toward him, and her fingers had found the last button. "I've waited all day for you, and that's long enough. Now I'm going to attack you."

"What . . . what about dinner?"

"It'll never get any worse than it is right now," Tina replied while the pink tip of her tongue traced across her full lips. "We shouldn't wrinkle your uniform, should we?"

The lieutenant couldn't help but feel a burst of heat flashing through his loins as her bodice fell open. He could see that as usual she was wearing no shift or corset and her small, firm breasts pointed upward, their nipples erect. And when Tina took the glass from him and set it aside, then took his hands and gently drew them up her ribcage, a trembling sensation swept through his body. She stood on her tiptoes and kissed him with tender passion while her hands found the buckle to his belt and tugged with increasing urgency.

"Tina, we really shouldn't . . ."

"I know we shouldn't, darling, and that's precisely why we should," she said softly as the buckle came loose in her hands and her fingers went into his thick hair to pull his head toward her breasts. Her breathing was coming faster now, and when his mouth closed gently over her right nipple, a moan escaped her lips and she threw her head backward in ecstasy.

"I want you, Tina," Greggory managed in a husky voice as he pulled his mouth away to trail the tip of his tongue artfully across her chest. "I want you badly and I want you now."

"You mean you want to make love to a brazen hussy?" Tina whispered with a hint of challenge.

"No. I want to make love to a woman, a beautiful woman, and forget I'm even in the goddamned army."

"That's exactly what I want you to do."

"I'll lock the door and close the shutter. Don't move a muscle, I'll be back in a second."

"I'll wait for you in bed, my darling. Please hurry."

With some difficulty, the lieutenant walked to the door and secured the latch before standing back to close the shutter without being seen, then hurried into the darkening bedroom.

Outside, on the perimeter walls, the corporal of the guard had stopped beside the guard on post number four; they both watched the commanding officer's shutter close and no lights come on inside.

"Looks like the good lieutenant is gonna retire a little early tonight, Corporal," the trooper said with a grin. "Damned unfair of him to close the shutter, though. I was enjoying that."

The two men were friends, and the corporal returned the

27

grin. "Why the hell do you think I came up here to check your guard mount, Charlie?" He glanced wistfully toward the darkened quarters. "Lucky bastard. He ain't much of a soldier but he sure as hell picks his women right. I'd give a month's pay and one of these stripes just to see her bare-assed naked in the moonlight one time."

"Yeah, and since I ain't got either one, I'll just stand here and dream about it. You goin' on that patrol with Sergeant Aikens in the mornin'?"

"Hell no, not after pullin' guard duty all night. Kinda glad too, 'cause he's plain crazy at best."

"And powerful mean. Gonna get somebody killed someday."

The corporal leaned away from the wall and started to walk in the opposite direction. "Well, when he does, let's hope the poor bastard's got a feather up his ass."

"Hey, Billy?"

The corporal stopped and turned. "Whatcha got, Charlie?"

"Just wonderin'." The trooper grinned again. "What color ya think the hair on her pussy is?"

"Might be bald, for all I know. Ask the lieutenant in the mornin', if you want to know for sure."

"You bet I will. Right after I go huntin' a grizzly bear with a willow switch. For right now I'll just have that little patch of heaven be dark brown."

"Fine with me. Just keep your hand on your rifle and out of your pants, Charlie. That's all I can tell ya."

"Sure, Billy, sure. Just long enough for you to get your ass out of sight."

It was late afternoon when Sergeant Aikens held up his hand and halted the reconnaissance patrol somewhere deep in the Black Hills. The troopers dismounted to lounge in the shade of the tall pine trees and rest their backs against the huge boulders surrounding them. The terrain through which they had passed was a patchwork of draws, ravines, canyons, creeks, and rivers, and an occasional herd of wild game had scampered from its bed on the forest floor in flight from the approaching patrol. Up to this point they had found no sign of Indians, which was a disappointment to Aikens.

While his unit rested, the sergeant wandered toward a nearby creek and studied the stream momentarily before plunging his hand into the clear, cold water. He trailed a finger through the dark sand in his palm, then tossed the sample away and found another. Again he studied the fine granules intently, as he did with a third and then a fourth sample. Satisfied, he rinsed his hands, laid his hat to one side, and leaned down for a drink.

The rugged image of his face was clearly visible in the still pool, and he stared at it as though he had never seen his own reflection before. He was extremely pleased with what he saw, and he admired the brilliance of a man who could conceive such a letter-perfect plan. And in his self-enthrallment, he remembered how he, Joe Sutton, had come to be leading an army unit on patrol in the finest gold country in the world.

A convicted murderer from Delaware, he had escaped prison just before the start of the Civil War and had enlisted in the Army of the Potomac under the name of Frank Aikens. Fighting hard and motivated by bloodlust, he had risen through the ranks, and by the time Sherman made his march to the sea, Sergeant Aikens was there and had become one of the general's most trusted enlisted men. In truth, he hated the army and everyone associated with it. But to maintain his cover, he had stayed in after the War, and with the news of the gold strike in the Black Hills, he had volunteered to go West and came under the command of Lieutenant Greggory.

The plan was not complete, though, until his chance meeting with Willy Harper in a Deadwood saloon. Harper, a deserter who had been a bugler under Sheridan, happened to be standing beside him at the bar and they struck up a conversation. Their mutual desire for wealth and a common hatred for the army soon became apparent, and over the course of nearly a month they formulated a plan that would benefit them both. That plan was in motion now, and everything was perfect—with the exception of that damned mounted infantry outfit already en route to Outpost Thirteen. But they would be taken care of as well, Harper would see to that.

Sergeant Aikens was grinning openly as he lowered his face to the crisp water and drank deeply. Yes, he thought to himself, it's just a matter of time now. Soon they can shove the army up the good lieutenant's ass, if he's still alive, and California will have a new resident. A civilian with money to burn. When he stood and turned back toward the forest, he froze in position and stared at the trooper twenty yards behind him. "What the hell are you doing here, Tipton?" he demanded in a low growl.

"Nothing, Sergeant. I was just going to ask permission to fill my canteen."

"Permission denied. You'll have to learn to ration your water when you're on patrol. How goddamn long you been standin' there?"

"A few minutes," Tipton replied weakly.

"That's too fucking long!" Aikens snarled, remembering he had only been there a few minutes himself. "What'd you see?"

"Nothin'. Except I thought maybe you'd lost somethin' there for a while."

"I didn't lose nothin' like you're gonna lose, Trooper! Like your goddamned teeth, for starters! Now, get back to the patrol and mount up. We're moving out."

"Yes, Sergeant," Tipton said with a curious look at the stream before he turned and walked away.

With the sun beginning to sink toward the hills and long shadows from the timber stretching across the carpet of pine needles, Aikens halted the patrol once again. He had been leading them in a direction that might have indicated he knew exactly what he was looking for, as opposed to a random reconnaissance mission, and now he turned to the man riding beside him.

"Corporal Stone, we're going to split up here. You take the rest of the squad and patrol to the left of that ridge," he said, pointing toward a dark object looming before them. "We've got about an hour until dark, and we'll rendezvous on the back side and make camp there for the night. If you get there before we do, post a guard and use the password 'cannonball.'"

"Sure, Sarge, but we ain't supposed to split up the patrol, are we?"

"What you ain't supposed to do is ask a sergeant stupid questions. I'm in charge here and you'll do as I say or you'll damned well wish you had."

Tipton knew he shouldn't speak, but he could not contain himself. "Why me, Sergeant?"

"Why not you?"

"I mean . . . well . . . there's others . . ."

Aikens whirled his horse and reined in sharply beside Tipton's mount. His hand lashed out and closed about the young trooper's throat, and he squeezed until Tipton's eyes bulged in his face.

"Because I said you, Trooper," Aikens said through gritted teeth. "Any more questions?"

Tipton shook his head as far as Aiken's grip would allow, and when the sergeant finally released the hold on his throat, Tipton massaged his neck and remained silent.

"That's better," Aikens snarled. "Any more questions from any of you and this whole damned squad will be placed on report! Now move out!"

Aikens watched while the squad angled to the right and disappeared into the timber before riding in the opposite direction, with Tipton following obediently ten yards behind. The stand of trees grew increasingly thick, and the soldiers leaned against their horses' necks to avoid low-hanging limbs. After nearly a half-hour, they could hear the murmur of water once again, and Aikens rode with a renewed sense of urgency and determination. When their horses' hooves finally sank in the sand bank of the stream, he turned west and rode cautiously, as if he were looking for some specific object.

They found it on the inner sweep of a curve in the streambed, and Aikens pulled in to watch two miners working their last panful of material in the failing light. A relaxed mood came over him and he smiled at Tipton almost cordially as he moved his horse forward once again.

"Evenin', fellas," Aikens said in a friendly voice. "How's the huntin'?"

The two miners, both elderly, squat men, looked up in surprise and reached for rifles propped against rocks beside them before relaxing at the sight of two uniformed soldiers.

"Middlin', soldier," one said in a gravelly voice. "How goes it with you?"

"Same old shit," Aikens replied. "Another boring patrol, lookin' for something we can't find. Any luck with the color?"

The two elderly men glanced at each other before the second man looked up with a grin. "Yeah, we had some luck." There was a strange twinkle in his eyes as he pulled a small sack from around his neck. "Ever seen real gold before, son?"

"No, can't say I have. Mind if I have a look?"

"Have at 'er. But let me warn ya, once you've seen real gold, you'll never be able to look at anything else again."

"I'll take a chance," Aikens said, leaning down to retrieve the bag and pouring some of the contents in his hand. A strange look came over his face as he ran a finger through the sparkling dust, and there was a hardness in his eyes when he closed his hand and looked down at the miner again. "This the real stuff?"

"Shore is. Me and Claude there know gold when we see it." He grinned again. "Ain't that right, Claude?"

The other miner matched the grin. "For a fact, Shorty. We've drank up enough gold to fill that soldier boy's hat there."

Aikens watched them closely. "That's fine, mighty fine. But you won't have to worry about drinkin' this up."

The tone of Aikens' voice caused a cautious, startled look to cross their faces. "What you mean by that, soldier?" Shorty asked.

"What I mean is this," Aikens said, whipping the revolver from his holster and snapping the hammer back. "You boys done had your last drink and your last touch of gold."

"Sergeant!" Tipton said with widening eyes. "You can't do that!"

"Watch me."

The man called Claude lunged for his rifle and the revolver belched flame and the old man slammed against the rock with flailing hands clutching at his chest.

"You bastard!" Shorty yelled. "Claude didn't do nothin'—"

The words died in his throat as the revolver jumped in Aikens' hand again and the miner flopped on his back in the water with a bullet through his stomach. Then Aikens turned the weapon on Tipton. "Get down."

Tipton rose on his stirrups and then hesitated. "Why'd you do that to them two old men, Sergeant?"

"You're a question a minute, aren't you, Tipton? Because they had something I wanted. Now get down off that horse!"

Tipton stepped down while Aikens hung the bag around his neck with one hand and trained the revolver on the trooper with the other. "Throw your revolver to one side and tie your horse to that tree over there," Aikens ordered.

Tipton did as he was instructed and Aikens dismounted. "Now wade out in the middle of that stream and wait there until I tell you otherwise," Aikens said, waggling the barrel toward the creek.

Again the young trooper complied, and Aikens moved toward the two miners, who were now surrounded by blood-red water. He jerked the knife from Claude's belt, and laying his weapon on the rock with a cautious glance at Tipton, he deftly gripped the man's hair at the forehead, traced the sharp knife blade around his skull, then slit the skin at the hairline and jerked the scalp away.

Tipton stared at him with horror-filled eyes and tried to speak, but no words would come. Aikens grinned and moved toward the second man and repeated the procedure. Then he held the two bloody scalps up for Tipton to see.

"Ain't a featherhead in the country what coulda done a better job," he said proudly.

Protesting words formed on Tipton's lips and he started to speak before doubling over at the waist and emptying his guts in the swiftly moving water.

Aikens laughed and waited while Tipton retched again, then he motioned toward the bank with the revolver barrel. "That's enough, boy. Now get your ass outa there and up on dry land."

Tipton stumbled on the slippery rocks, went facedown in the icy water, scrambled to his feet, and struggled onto the shore. Aikens tossed the scalps aside and snatched the trooper by the hair.

"That wasn't a pretty sight, was it, boy?"

Tipton tried to shake his head.

"Want the same to happen to you? That's kind of a handsome head of hair you got there."

Again Tipton shook his head.

"That's smart. Real smart. Now, I've got me a partner back at the post, see? You don't know who he is, and you'll never know, but he'll be watchin' you all the time. If you ever breathe one word about what happened here, you'll meet him damned quick. And you'll be just as bald as them two old farts floatin' out there. You understand that?"

Tipton attempted a feeble nod, and tears trickled down his cheeks as Aikens jerked his head back even harder. "I asked you a question, boy, and I want words for an answer. You understand that?"

"I . . . I . . . understand."

"You understand what?"

"I . . . understand . . . Sergeant."

33

"That's better. Now get on your horse and ride ahead of me. We got a ways to go before we catch up with the patrol."

The moon was full up when they neared the back side of the ridge, and there was a silvery illumination to the night, which contrasted with pitch-black shadows stretching from the base of the trees. Tipton's uniform was still wet and he shivered in the chill air, and when he heard the sentry's call he reined in and remained silent, as he had for the entire ride. Twin red patches of bare scalp were emblazoned in his mind and he could think of nothing else but his hatred for Sergeant Aikens.

"Halt! Who goes there?"

"Sergeant Aikens and Trooper Tipton."

"What's the password?" the sentry asked, peering out from behind a huge boulder.

"Cannonball."

"Right, Sarge. Come on in."

They rode past the sentry and toward a small fire that flickered against the wall of the ridge. Aikens urged his horse up beside Tipton's and said in a low, menacing whisper, "Whatever I say, you agree with it. Don't say nothin' unless you're asked, and if you get asked, make it short and sweet. Got that?"

"Yeah, Sergeant. I got it."

"Good."

Corporal Stone stepped toward the edge of the circle of light and watched while the two men stepped down.

"Heard a couple of shots coming from over your way, Sarge. Everything all right?"

"No. How many guards have you got out?"

"Two. One on each flank. Why?"

"Double 'em. Me and Tipton here jumped a war party of Cheyenne. They'd just killed and scalped two miners, but they got away before we could get a shot at 'em. Hard tellin' what the hell they're up to now."

The corporal looked at Tipton, who stared at the ground, his narrow shoulders shivering beneath the cold uniform. "What the hell happened to you, Tip? Look like you seen a ghost and jumped in a river to hide."

Tipton looked up and started to speak, but Aikens silenced him. "Tipton's horse fell and he took a little dunkin'. He'll be all right as soon as he gets his backside close to that fire." Tipton looked up and caught the sergeant's hard stare. "The ghost you're talkin' about was the sight of them two old duffers with a scab where their hair used to be. Ain't no man wants to have that done to him, ain't that right, Tipton?"

Tipton's gaze wavered and he stared longingly at the fire. "Can I go now, Sergeant?"

"Sure, boy," Aikens said jovially, with a resounding slap on the young man's back. "Get yourself warm and have a bite to eat. Do you a world of good."

Tipton shuffled away and Aikens turned his attention again to the corporal. "Sure would've liked to catch them feather-heads in the act. Plum mutilated them poor old boys, that's what they done. Double them guards like I said, and have somebody put up our horses. I got something to do."

Stone began shouting commands and Tipton watched the sergeant move away in the moonlight; he could see him digging in the front of his shirt for the little bag hanging around his neck.

four ———————————————

Captain Warner Conway drew in a deep breath and exhaled slowly, savoring the crisp, fresh air scented with pine. He gazed around with something nearing wonderment in his eyes before turning to Matt Kincaid, who rode by his side at the head of the column.

"It's almost amazing, isn't it, Matt?"

"What's that, sir?"

"These Black Hills. They rise out of the flat nothingness of the plains like the temple of God, and while there isn't a decent tree within a hundred miles of our post, here they proliferate with wild abandon. And look at the rugged beauty of it all. Streams and creeks everywhere, canyons and ravines carved into the earth through countless years of wear and winter storms, the greenish black of the timber outlined against the brown of the soil, and that air, so alive and invigorating."

Matt chuckled softly. "Sounds to me like you should have been a poet, Captain, instead of a mounted infantry officer."

"Mental inspiration does not necessarily lend itself to mastery of the written word, Lieutenant. I'll do the thinking and let the poets handle pen and ink."

"I suppose that's a wise choice, sir. The way I understand it, poets get paid even worse and less frequently than we do." Kincaid turned in the saddle and looked back over the two platoons of soldiers strung out behind them and winding now into the broken land of the Black Hills. His eyes found Mrs. Conway, riding behind Sergeant Cohen and located in the center of the column for maximum protection, and he noticed again the bright perkiness of her face, her immaculate grooming, and the fact that she rode sidesaddle, with a bearskin robe covering her hard leather saddle for extra comfort. Kincaid turned back and glanced toward the captain once more.

"Speaking of things that are 'almost amazing,' Captain, I find your wife to fit into that category, if I may say so."

"Oh? In what way?"

"We're now into five hard days in the saddle and she hasn't complained or indicated any discomfort whatever. She's helped old Dutch with every meal, even though the old goat keeps claiming he doesn't need any help, and she looks like she might have stepped out of a catalog picture instead of spending nearly a week with a mounted infantry unit. There aren't many women I've known who could, or would, do the same."

Conway smiled his appreciation. "Thank you for the approving words, Matt. Flora is a very determined person. If she sets her sights on something, she's willing to accept the consequences of achieving that goal. I guess she thinks this Lieutenant Greggory's wife is some poor little waif struggling with frontier life, and if she thinks she can help, she'd walk through hell barefooted to get the job done."

"Very commendable. I wouldn't be surprised at all to find exactly that. A frail, coddled woman who feels imposed upon by her husband's assignment and bitching every step of the way about life in an army outpost. We've both seen that a dozen times before."

"Could be. We'll find out shortly, I guess." Conway lifted a gloved hand and pointed toward a clearing ahead. "Here he comes now."

Both officers watched the tall, lean man, dressed in buckskin clothing and mounted on a powerfully built horse, disappear from the patch of sunlight in the opening. They caught occasional glimpses of him as he worked his way toward them through the timber. Windy Mandalian rode like he walked, with a fluid, unhurried grace, as though he and the horse were one. He smiled as he neared the column and turned his horse to ride beside Kincaid.

"What's it look like, Windy?" Matt asked.

"Like there's lots of work to do, Matt."

"What do you mean by that?" the captain threw in, leaning forward slightly to see the scout.

"I'd rather have you see that with your own eyes, Cap'n. Suffice it to say they're about as well prepared for an Indian raid as I am for eatin' any more shit on a shingle. There's a bluff overlooking the outpost within easy fire-arrow range. The

37

walls of the post are made of logs, just like I knew they would be, but the roofs covering the interior buildings are made of rough-cut lumber. It's gotta be dry as hell by now, and one shot from even a blind Cheyenne would burn it down quicker'n a horse shits green apples."

Matt's tone was almost incredulous as he asked, "You mean they haven't covered those roofs with a layer of dirt?"

"If they have, it's the cleanest damned dirt I've ever seen."

"How about water barrels, Windy?" Conway inquired. "See any of them on the roofs?"

"Nope. Guess they plan to line up and take turns pissin' in case of fire. Kinda hard to do with an Indian takin' potshots at you. There's more, gentlemen, but you'll see it soon. We're about five miles away and should be there before sundown." Windy's face turned serious and he was silent for nearly a minute before speaking again. "One thing bothers me most of all," he said, staring straight ahead.

"What's that, Windy?"

"Well, in my travels I was up on that bluff I was tellin' you about. I made myself plainly visible and nobody noticed, or didn't give a damn if they did. And I wasn't the only one who'd been there. There's Indian sign all over the place, like maybe ten, twelve braves, right size for a scouting party, and it hasn't been more'n a day since they left. Not a single print of a shod hoof anywhere on the whole fucking hill. Obviously they didn't care any more about them than they did me. Or, just as bad, they didn't see them like they didn't see me."

"What kind of outfit is this, anyway?" Kincaid said, more as a statement than a question.

"It's one that's greener'n a turtle's balls," Windy replied. "Like I said, if I was a Cheyenne lookin' for a place to build a big bonfire, I sure as hell wouldn't waste no time choppin' wood."

"Maybe it's a good thing we're here after all," Conway offered musingly. "The cavalry can't stand a hell of a lot more egg on its face."

When they broke through the trees and into the two-hundred-yard-wide cleared area around the post, the gates swung open and they could see troopers scrambling onto the parade, some tucking in their shirts and others pulling up yellow suspenders. And as Conway, Kincaid, and Mandalian rode into the compound, the ragged lines of a company hastily falling into inspection formation was a sight nearly as humorous as it was pathetic. Lieutenant Greggory hustled from the orderly room and buckled on his saber and adjusted his hat as he crossed the parade with long strides. Embarrassment was obvious on his face when he glanced once toward his command and then turned and saluted Captain Conway. Kincaid held up his hand and halted the column while Conway returned the salute, and then Matt did likewise, even though he and Greggory were of the same rank, because it appeared the young officer would remain in his frozen position until both men returned the salute.

"Welcome to Outpost Thirteen, Captain," Greggory said, now reaching up for a handshake. "I'm Lieutenant Steven Greggory, commanding. I hope your journey was a pleasant one and thank you for coming."

Conway gripped the lieutenant's hand and noticed the man's uncertain grip. "Thank you, Lieutenant, and it was. I'm Captain Conway. This is Lieutenant Kincaid and this is our chief scout, Windy Mandalian."

Greggory stepped toward Kincaid, but stopped when Conway said, "Could we save the formalities until later, Lieutenant? I'd like to get the rest of my men inside the walls. Don't much like to get caught with one foot in bed and the other on the floor."

Greggory's face reddened and he stepped back. "Certainly, sir. Excuse my rudeness. Please, bring your troopers into the post and make yourselves at home."

"They are not troopers, Lieutenant," Conway said with a smile. "They are soldiers, mounted infantry and seasoned veterans all. Move out the column, Lieutenant."

Kincaid made a forward motion with his arm and the column moved forward once again, and when they passed by the formation, the scarred and battered veterans of Easy Company looked down at the cavalry troops. In contrast to the faded blue of Easy Company's uniforms, the uniforms of the cavalry were obviously new issue, their bright blue uniforms contrasting with brilliant yellow piping. Each of them, to a man, had a shiny saber hanging from his waist, and their leather holsters, boots, and belts were the deep black of newly processed and dyed cowhide. There were no indications on their unscarred faces of previous battles won or lost, and the only indication of willingness to fight was the look of superiority in their eyes, a look that was met with nothing more than derision and contempt from the veterans of Easy Company, many of whom grinned openly while others chewed the tobacco cuts in their cheeks in cold-eyed disdain.

When Flora passed by where Greggory was standing, she smiled down at him and nodded graciously while the Lieutenant jerked the hat from his head and glanced nervously over his shoulder toward his quarters, where he hoped his wife would be standing. There was no sign of life and he shrugged his shoulders in dismay.

With his two platoons dismounted and standing at attention beside their horses, Captain Conway walked back to help his wife down and then escorted her to where Greggory stood in the middle of the parade.

"Lieutenant Greggory, I would like to introduce my wife, Flora. Flora? Lieutenant Greggory."

Greggory pulled the hat from his head again and bowed from the waist. "It is my pleasure, Mrs. Conway. Welcome to Outpost Thirteen. I hope your stay is a pleasant one."

"Thank you, Lieutenant," Flora replied, surprising the lieutenant by offering her hand, which Greggory gripped even more gently than he had Conway's. "I'm absolutely certain it will be."

Greggory risked a glance over his shoulder and saw the door to his quarters open and his wife back out with a broom, vigorously whisking dust from the floor. She was wearing a dusty blue dress that had obviously seen better days. A slightly soiled apron was tied around her waist, and her hair was pinned up beneath a tattered scarf.

"Tina? Would you come here a second, please?"

The young woman looked up and a startled look crossed her face as she rested the broom against the doorjamb, wiped her hands on her apron, removed her scarf and touched at her hair, and walked toward the assemblage.

"I'm sorry, Mrs. Conway," Greggory said apologetically. "I don't think she realized you had arrived." His eyes swept over Flora's neatly combed hair beneath a dark brown, wide-brimmed hat, her beige blouse, and her tan riding skirt, which touched the tops of brown, lace-up boots. "Apparently my wife has been cleaning house."

40

"Think nothing of it," Flora replied. "It was rude of us to arrive without notice. And as for cleaning house, it's the accepted assumption that that's what wives are supposed to do. Your wife looks like a charming lady," Flora concluded with another pleasant smile.

When Tina stopped beside her husband, she was obviously embarrassed to be dressed as she was and standing before the elegantly beautiful Flora Conway. "I'm sorry, Steven," she said in a lowered voice. "I didn't even realize we had company. I must look a mess."

"Nonsense," Flora said, stepping forward to link her arm with Tina's. "Is a woman supposed to clean house in her wedding gown? I'm Flora Conway and you're Tina Greggory. Let's leave these men to their military affairs, and if you could arrange it, I'd dearly love to wash some of the dust from my face and hands."

Tina glanced at her husband with a hint of pleasant surprise, then turned away with Flora. "Of course, Mrs. . . . ."

"Flora."

"Of course . . . Flora. Let's go to my quarters. May I offer you a cup of tea?"

"I would *love* a cup of tea! Do you mean one served in actual china instead of a tin cup?"

Tina giggled happily and nodded her head while the two women moved away. "That's exactly what I mean."

Both Conway and Greggory looked after them, and Conway said, "Well, Lieutenant, it looks as though our wives are going to get along just fine. I hope things go as well with you and me."

"I'm sure they will, sir. Would you do me the honor of inspecting my command?"

Conway glanced toward the assembled soldiers. He knew in his heart that inspecting Greggory's troops was the last thing he wanted to do. But in deference to the young lieutenant's earnest look, he smiled patiently and said, "Of course, Lieutenant. It would be my pleasure."

While Conway inspected the troops, Kincaid made sure the horses were stabled and fed, the men billeted, and tents set up in a far corner of the parade for the soldiers that the barracks were unable to accommodate. When the inspection was over, Conway, Kincaid, and Windy followed Greggory into his office and the young lieutenant poured brandy all around, then offered his seat behind the desk to the captain.

"No thank you, Lieutenant," Conway replied. "A commander sits behind his own desk. Besides, I've had enough sitting in the last five days to last me for a while."

"Thank you, sir," Greggory said, taking his seat and waving his hand helplessly toward the papers strewn before him. "Please excuse this mess, gentlemen, but I haven't had a chance to get everything in order quite yet."

Now the smile and pleasant look vanished from Conway's face. "The condition of your desktop is of no concern to us, Lieutenant, but the survival of you, your command, and this outpost certainly is."

"What do you mean by that, Captain?" Greggory asked, obviously puzzled.

"Our outpost is what they call a 'soddy,' built out of prairie sod and lumber and virtually impossible to set afire. We're located about a hundred miles south of here on the open plains, with nearly unrestricted visibility as far as the eye can see. While we are situated on a piece of traditional Indian hunting territory, we are not positioned directly adjacent to what is considered a sacred ancestral tribal ground of two specific nations, namely the Sioux and the Cheyenne. What you are faced with is the exact antithesis of our situation. Not to mention a few other gross oversights that we noticed when we rode in."

"I'm sorry, Captain, I'm afraid I still don't understand."

"That's why we're here." Conway turned toward the two men standing behind him. "Matt? You and Windy jump in here whenever you want to."

Both men nodded and sipped their brandy while Conway turned back toward Greggory.

"There are no more than two hundred yards of cleared land around this outpost. There should be *five* hundred yards at a minimum. That way you would have an open field of fire against anyone who might attack you."

"Don't forget that bluff, Cap'n," Windy said. "Fortunately for the lieutenant here, it slopes down so he could see any buck crawling toward him with a fire arrow. But not until all the timber and brush are cleared away. Dumbest damned thing I ever saw, buildin' an outpost in a way that an enemy could kill you with *rocks* if he wanted to."

Kincaid shifted to a more comfortable position against the wall and looked closely at Greggory. "Where do you get your water, Lieutenant?"

The puzzlement on the lieutenant's face had turned to one of defensive surprise. "There's a natural spring no more than a hundred yards outside the main gate. That's where we get our water. Surely you must have seen it on your way in?"

"We did. There's an old saying among Indian fighters, Lieutenant. 'He who controls the water hole wins the battle.' If you were under siege for . . . let's say thirty days, how would you supply your men with water?"

"Well . . . ah . . . well, we do have a limited supply here within the compound."

"That's fine, but unfortunately there are no limited sieges if the enemy wants your stronghold bad enough."

"Then what do you suggest?"

"You'll have to dig a well within the walls."

Greggory tried to smile the smile of a commandant. "That's impossible, Lieutenant Kincaid. This is rocky ground, and God knows how long it would take my troops to dig deep enough to hit water."

"And God also knows how long it would take for your troops to dig their own graves. You'd better start digging, Lieutenant, while your men are digging for the future and not for the past."

Flabbergasted, Greggory's eyes darted from one man to the other. "This is impossible! I can't—"

"You're going to have to cover your roofs with at least four inches of dirt, Lieutenant," Conway said firmly, ignoring Greggory's protest. "As Windy implied, the fire arrow is a favorite weapon of the Indian. These dry roofs would be his first target."

"I . . . well . . . I . . ."

"Your guard mount is nearly asleep, son," Windy offered almost gently. "Earlier this afternoon I was up on that bluff jumping up and down and yellin' my lungs out, and nobody paid any attention. Some Cheyenne were up there yesterday. Did anyone notice 'em?"

"Cheyenne?"

"Yup. Blue's their favorite color. There was blue warpaint on the pine needles where they crawled forward on their bellies."

"Warpaint? Certainly, sir, they aren't—"

"Never know about the Cheyenne, Lieutenant. Like stealin' another man's wife; better keep one hand over your ass, 'cause you'll be the next one to get fucked."

"This is preposterous! We're doing just fine here, and I feel slightly insulted that—"

Kincaid drained the last of his brandy and placed the glass on Greggory's desk. "Being slightly insulted beats the shit out of being slightly dead, Lieutenant. While you're at it, you better get some rain barrels up on those roofs. Be ready for fire that way, and save you carrying it up there by hand."

Greggory looked directly at Conway, and his voice filled with resolve. "Sir, I am in command of a United States Cavalry detachment, by reputation the finest, most courageous fighting men in the entire army. I thank you, but I don't feel it necessary that I be told what to do by anyone other than my superiors."

Conway turned sharply and anger flashed in his eyes. "Stand at attention, Lieutenant!"

"What?"

"I said stand at attention, mister, and you damned well better assume that position!"

There was no mistaking the tone in the captain's voice, and Greggory leaped to his feet and snapped into a textbook version of the position of attention.

"You are talking to a superior officer, Lieutenant, and don't you forget it. As for your proud cavalry image, the Seventh was also a cavalry outfit, and they died because of ignorance. There is a broad distinction between courage and stupidity, and I didn't ride five long goddamned days to reinforce the latter. Now, you'll do as I suggest or you'll do as I order, but one way or the other, it's going to get done. Is that understood?"

"Yessir."

"Be at ease."

Greggory wilted, and Conway turned his back to him. "Now, your first priorities are to cover these rooftops with dirt and dig that well. Do you want to initiate that as commanding officer of this outpost or as a temporary subordinate?"

Greggory's Adam's apple bobbed as he swallowed. "As commanding officer, sir," he said weakly.

"Fine. Excellent. If we cooperate we can get this thing squared away much more quickly than if we have to rely on military protocol. Easy Company will pitch in and lend a hand. Now—"

Knuckles rapped on the door and Sergeant Ritter poked his head inside. "Sorry to disturb you, sir, but Sergeant Aikens is back from recon patrol and he says he's got somethin' for your ears only."

Greggory looked at his guests and Conway shrugged his shoulders. "We'll leave if you like, Lieutenant."

"That won't be necessary. Send him in, Top."

Sergeant Aikens stepped inside and glanced warily at the three strangers. "Sorry, sir," he said without saluting, "I didn't know you had visitors. I'll talk to you later if—"

"That's all right, Sergeant. I'd like you to meet Captain Conway, Lieutenant Kincaid, and Windy Mandalian. They're the ones from Easy Company I told you about. Gentlemen, this is Sergeant Aikens, my senior noncom in the field."

The men nodded all around and Conway eyed Aikens closely. "Haven't I seen you somewhere before, Sergeant?"

"Don't think so, sir. Maybe in New York, that's where I come from."

"No, it wasn't in New York. I'll think of it as time goes by. Pleased to meet you, Sergeant."

"Pleased to meet you, sir."

"How did the patrol go, Sergeant?"

Aikens turned to face his lieutenant. "Fine, sir, up to a point."

"The point, Sergeant, is what we're after here," Greggory said impatiently. "Please get to it."

Animosity flickered in Aikens' eyes before he could regain his nonchalant attitude. "Well, sir, it looks like the Cheyenne are gettin' set to raise a little hell again. We found two dead miners about a day's ride from here in the Black Hills. It was near sunset when we jumped 'em, but they got away in the dark. They scalped two poor old duffers, sir, who was pannin' for color in a stream. I gotta say, I've seen some horrible things, but that took the cake."

Windy's eyes narrowed while he propped a foot comfortably on the lower rung of a chair. "How do you know it was Cheyenne, Sergeant? Why couldn't it have been Sioux or Arapaho?"

"Blue warpaint, mister," Aikens said defensively. "The Cheyenne wear blue warpaint."

45

"That they do," Windy agreed laconically. "If you were close enough to see that, why couldn't you have shot 'em?"

Aikens hesitated. "Well . . . like I said, it was near dark and they took off in the tall timber."

"I see," Windy replied, nodding. "How about the hands of those dead miners? Notice anything different about them?"

Now a cunning look came over Aikens, like a young boy accused of stealing while having a stolen jackknife in his pocket. "No, no I didn't. They had hands like everybody else. Maybe a little shriveled from all that water, but everything else was the same. Why?"

"Nothing. Just curious, that's all."

"I'll want a full report of your findings in writing, Sergeant," Greggory said. "Have it on my desk in the morning. That'll be all."

"It'll be here, sir. One more thing, Lieutenant. I'm due for a three-day pass tomorrow. Can I pick it up from the first sergeant?"

Greggory waved his hand unconcernedly. "Sure, go ahead, Sergeant. Obviously you've had a rough patrol and deserve a little time off. When you get back, though, we've got some work to do."

"Fine, sir," Aikens said, flashing his dirty smile. "Always happy to help out."

When Aikens had gone, Greggory looked toward Windy. "Why did you ask him about those miners' hands, Mr. Mandalian?"

"For good reason, Lieutenant. He said those miners were killed by Cheyenne, and I wanted to find out for sure if they were or not."

"He said he saw the blue warpaint. Isn't that good enough?"

"No. Because those men weren't killed by Cheyenne."

"How in hell's name can you say that? Are you accusing Sergeant Aikens of lying?"

"I'm not saying he's lying, I'm only saying those men weren't killed by Cheyenne." Windy straightened and drank his last gulp of brandy. "You see, Lieutenant, the Cheyenne usually cut the fingers off their enemies' hands, as well as taking their scalps. That way they can't grip a weapon in the Happy Hunting Ground. They would never have taken the scalp without the fingers. Somebody else killed those miners."

46

Windy was moving toward the door now, and Greggory asked in a confused voice, "Then, if it wasn't the Cheyenne decked out in blue warpaint, who the hell could it have been?"

Windy turned in the doorway and offered a lazy smile. "That's what I aim to find out, Lieutenant. But I know for sure it wasn't Cheyenne." He nodded, turned, and strode out.

five ⎯⎯⎯⎯⎯⎯⎯⎯⎯⎯⎯⎯⎯⎯

It was dusk when Sergeant Aikens rode into Deadwood. He searched the deepening shadows intently as his horse moved down the street at a leisurely walk. The town of Deadwood had been erected hastily in the wake of the recent gold discoveries, and the yellow, freshly cut pine of its buildings took on a golden hue in the dying rays of the vanishing sun. Where once there had been a semi-remote mountain village, there was now a bustle of activity, with new buildings rising almost overnight, and those who depended on the success of the miners hawked their wares and services with greed matched only by that of the nearly maniacal gold-seekers themselves.

But Aikens' mind was not on the birth of a new industry or the sudden appearance of a fledgling town. Rather it was on the man who would help him profit from recent developments, and he studied the shadows one last time before swinging down and tying his horse to the rail in front of the Deadwood Saloon. As he stepped inside, his eyes darted over the faces of the numerous men lined up at the bar, many of whom he recognized, but none of whom he would consider a friend. Friendship was not a thing that Aikens looked for from his fellowman. His only concern was acquaintances who might, however unwittingly, clear the pathway for his own personal success. He was disappointed and slightly angered not to find the face of one such friend among the crowd.

"What'll it be, soldier?" the bartender asked as Aikens moved up to the roughly hewn plank bar.

"Double whiskey. Leave the bottle."

"Payday today?" the man behind the bar asked as he sloshed whiskey into a glass. "Thought that came at the first of the month."

"It does," Aikens replied irritably. "Had a three-day pass

comin' and a little money in my boot." He turned with the drink in his hand and rested his back against the plank while his eyes adjusted to the dim lamplight and he scanned the tables throughout the room. Then a grin split his lips as he found what he had been searching for: an ebony-skinned man seated alone in a corner and wearing a tattered army tunic. After sliding two silver dollars across the bar, he took the bottle in his free hand and angled toward the silent figure who indicated no recognition with the exception of the lifting of a single black finger.

"Glad I found you," Aikens said while pulling a chair out with the grating scrape of wood on wood. "I figured you'd be waitin' outside. A little chancy, ain't it, you comin' in here like this?"

Willy Harper stared at the man across from him and there was a coldness in his eyes. "This ain't Atlanta, Frank. I can drink wherever I damned well please."

"I didn't mean it that way, Willy," Aikens replied, smiling without emotion and filling the black man's glass. "What I meant was, we're damned close now and we don't want any little slip-ups to queer the deal." Now Aikens glanced around cautiously and lowered his voice as he turned back to Harper. "Where's Iron Crow and his braves?"

"Where they said they would be—in the Paha Sapa, waitin' for the next move from you. They found a couple of dead miners. Crow said they was scalped, looked like a white man did it." Harper's milky eyes narrowed and he raised the glass to his lips while saying, "He said they was robbed and any gold they had was missing."

The bag around Aikens' neck suddenly became heavy and he downed a quick shot, then refilled his glass with an air of nonchalance. "That's what I heard too. Serves 'em right for—"

"We're supposed to split everything fifty-fifty, Frank. I want my half."

Aikens glanced over his shoulder and hunched his shoulders closer to Harper. "Keep your voice down, Willy, and your suspicions. Sure I did it, but them two old bastards didn't have any gold. It's part of the setup we talked about, and I did it for both of us, not just me."

49

"Okay, I'll take your word on that," Harper replied, reaching for the bottle again. "But just don't forget we're pardners."

"I know that. I just want to make sure you remember it."

"I do. Have you heard any talk in the saloon tonight about those two miners?"

"No."

"Good. I want it to be a complete surprise when I spread the word."

Harper slowly turned the glass in his fingertips as though deeply engrossed in thought before saying finally, "We checked out the outpost yesterday. Should be a lead-pipe cinch. It'll burn like a tinderbox and we'll have those cavalry troops ridin' into the Black Hills where we want 'em."

"Well, Willy," Aikens offered cautiously, "I'm afraid there's been a change of plans on that."

"What do you mean, a change of plans? Iron Crow wants a complete victory over that outfit, something like Little Big Horn, and he ain't gonna be happy with anything less. We've made a deal to lead them into a trap, and you'll supposedly be killed in the ambush. You'll be out of the army with nobody the wiser, and we'll have all the gold we can carry out of the Paha Sapa. Don't sound to me like that needs much changin', and Iron Crow ain't in a real good mood for listenin' to somebody backin' out on a deal."

"We're not backin' out, Willy, we've just got to make some adjustments and Iron Crow doesn't have any choice but to go along with them."

Harper stared at Aikens with expressionless eyes. "What kind of changes?"

"The payoff will be the same, but we can't do it exactly like we planned. When we're through, though, Iron Crow will have even a bigger victory than he'd planned on."

"I'm listenin'."

"Two platoons of mounted infantry showed up at the post this afternoon—an outfit called Easy Company, from down south somewhere. The men in charge are a Captain Conway, a Lieutenant Kincaid, and a scout named Windy something-or-other. Anyway, they're seasoned veterans, and what Greggory knows about Indian fightin' wouldn't be a drop in a bucket compared to them. I was having a dummy conversation with

50

Sergeant Ritter in the orderly room today, but really I was listenin' to what was being said in the lieutenant's office."

"And?" Harper asked with raised eyebrows.

"And they're gonna do all the things that should have been done when the outpost was built to make it defensible against attack. They've started already, and by this time tomorrow, Iron Crow's fire arrows won't be worth a shit. We're gonna have to lure them into the Black Hills another way, and that's why I killed those two miners. Our plan, once we get them away from the outpost, will go like clockwork, but there's no point in the Cheyenne tryin' to take the outpost."

"And what does killin' two worthless miners have to do with gettin' two army units out where Iron Crow can give 'em all a permanent discharge?"

"Everything. That's why I took their scalps, to make it look like the Cheyenne did it. But you're right, the army ain't gonna hotfoot it up there over two lousy old prospectors." Aikens paused and smiled with satisfaction. "Now, if maybe twenty or thirty miners was killed and scalped, that'd be a whole 'nother matter. They wouldn't have any choice but to go into the Paha Sapa and settle an uprising."

Harper was clearly puzzled. "For sure not, but how you gonna work that?"

"Don't worry about the details. Leave it up to me," Aikens replied, filling their glasses one more time. "Let's finish this drink and then you get back to Iron Crow's camp. Tell him to have his warriors waitin' by White Bluff, where the prairie meets the hills, and to have an ambush set up somewhere around noon." The smile crossing Aikens' face was merciless and cold as he leaned back comfortably in his chair and said, "Tell that hard-nuts chief that he'll get his first taste of white blood tomorrow, and it'll only be the beginning."

"How 'bout you? Anybody gonna suspect you in this thing?"

"Naw. I'm on a three-day pass. Ever'body knows that soldiers get drunker'n seven hundred dollars when they get to town. I'll be clean as a whistle. Better move out now and let me get on with my work."

Harper downed his drink and stood. "White Bluffs? Tomorrow at noon?"

"Yup. In two days we'll have the army chasin' its tail all over the Paha Sapa, and you can play a little tune for 'em."

"Be right glad to," Harper replied, a deep laugh rumbling from his throat. "Been waitin' for that a long time."

Aikens watched the black man work his way unnoticed through the crowd before taking his bottle and moving back to the bar. He squeezed in beside two miners and shoved the whiskey toward them.

"Have a drink, fellas. We'll drink to their memory," Aikens said somberly while raising his own glass.

The two miners looked up at the big soldier and nodded their thanks while pouring generously from the sergeant's bottle. "Proud to drink with ya, soldier," the larger man said. "My name's Duke and my friend here goes by Adams."

Aikens inclined his drink toward them before resting his elbows on the plank and propping a boot on the footrail to gaze into the amber liquid.

The one called Duke watched him quizzically with the glass held halfway to his lips. "You said we was drinkin' to somebody's memory, soldier. Mind if I ask who afore I take likker with ya?"

Aikens turned in mock surprise. "You mean you ain't heard?"

"Heard what?"

"About Claude and Shorty."

Duke turned and searched the room. "They ain't here yet, that's all I know. What about 'em?"

"They were killed yesterday."

Now the two miners stared at each other in stunned disbelief before Adams turned slowly toward Aikens. "How do you know that?"

"Because I'm the one that found them. Me and my recon patrol, that is. They were murdered, scalped, and robbed."

"Scalped?"

"That's right," Aikens replied, speaking a little louder than necessary and pleased with the startled murmurs of the other men standing around him. "I've been a soldier a long time and I've seen my share of dead men, but what was done to the remains of poor old Shorty and Claude was the most brutal, heartless thing I've ever seen. Of course, the Cheyenne ain't known for being kind to dead men."

"The Cheyenne?" Duke asked. "You know for sure it was them what done it?"

"For a fact. I saw 'em clear as all hell, blue warpaint and all, but it was near dark and they got away in the tall timber."

The room had gone silent now and all of the miners were listening intently and thinking of their own claims on the streams and rivers of the Black Hills. "Did you say warpaint?" a man asked from the rear, crowding closer and elbowing his way through the crowd.

Aikens turned toward him. "That's what I said, mister."

"Well, what the hell's the army gonna do about it?" another man demanded. "We all got claims up near where Shorty and Claude was workin'."

"Not a damned thing," Aikens replied with an indulgent smile. "I'll be the first man to admit that those Cheyenne need to be taught a lesson, but there's nothing I can do about it as one soldier. Now if twenty or thirty well-armed men were to ride out and show them featherheads that white men won't be pushed around, then maybe we could do something. You know the army, we've got to wait for orders from the War Department and all that shit, and Christ knows how many more men will die before those come through."

"Well, we don't have to wait for any goddamned orders!" Duke shouted, slamming his glass onto the plank. "And we ain't gonna take any of this kind of shit off a bunch of featherheads! Shorty and Claude was friends of ours and whoever by God killed 'em is gonna pay in kind!"

There was no hesitation from the other men, and the room filled with a chorus of threats and condemnations. Aikens waited before holding up his hands for silence.

"Now listen, boys, don't go gettin' yourselves all riled. This is an army matter and the army will—"

"Will what?" Adams demanded. "Sit on their ass and wait for some magic piece of paper to come out here from Washington? We ain't got time to wait for that, soldier. We got claims to work and a man can't concentrate on the color too good when he thinks he's gonna get an arrow through his back. I say we take 'em now!"

Aikens nodded in agreement. "I can understand how you feel, but I can't get involved. There's only ten, maybe twelve renegades that you've got to worry about, I know that for a fact because I've seen their camp at the base of White Bluffs. But as a soldier in the United States Army, I think—"

"We don't give a shit what you think! Did you say White Bluffs?"

"Yes, where the prairie meets the hills. I'm sure they're the ones that did in Claude and Shorty, but the army needs proof before we can—"

"Fuck your proof!" Duke shouted. "Claude and Shorty are dead with their hair lifted. That's all the proof we need!"

"I know where White Bluffs is," a man farther down the bar threw in. "It's about half a day's ride due west of here. What say we light out now and take 'em in the dark?"

Again, Aikens raised his hands to quiet the clamor. "Gentlemen, gentlemen, please. If you're dead set on doing this, there's nothing I can do to stop you. But if you are going, please listen to the advice of a veteran. Your wisest move would be to leave about six in the morning. That would put you on their camp at around noon. Those Cheyenne know what they've done, and they raid only in the morning and late evening. They lay low during the day to avoid any army patrols that happen to be out, which there's damned few of. If you want to surprise 'em, noontime would be your best bet."

The miners glanced at one another and their voices stilled to murmurs of agreement. Duke watched his compatriots before turning to the bar and slamming his glass down again.

"Okay, it's settled. We ride at dawn. Now let's have a few drinks in Claude and Shorty's honor. They'd've done the same for us. Bartender!"

When the bartender stepped up, Aikens pulled a wad of bills from his pocket and threw them on the plank. "Since you boys are going to do the army's work for us, let me buy a couple of bottles and pass 'em around. It's the least I could do. Then I gotta get me a room and some sleep. It's been a long, hard day."

A chorus of cheers went up and the miners crowded toward the bar with glasses extended while Aikens finished his drink, collected his change, slapped Duke and Adams on the back, and walked toward the door. He turned in the doorway with a casual smile and watched the miners down their whiskey in the sullen atmosphere of a surly mob. Then he turned and left, taking his horse and leading it toward the stable.

After Aikens had been gone for nearly an hour, Duke draped

an arm over Adams' shoulder and leaned toward his ear. "You know, Adams, what I remember best about old Shorty?"

"No, what's that?" Adams asked owlishly.

"Well, you know he was a real practical joker. 'Member how he used to pass that iron pyrite off to dudes as the genuine article?"

Adams chuckled heartily at the memory. "Sure do. He always carried that little sack of fool's gold around his neck and passed it off to every greenhorn he could as real gold. Got more whiskey bought for him that way than with real money."

"And Claude, he always went along with it and they'd both laugh like hell."

"Yup. A couple of real characters they were. Anything for a good joke."

Duke's face turned gloomy once again and he leaned even more heavily on his friend's shoulder. "Gonna miss them two old birds."

"Sure 'nuff. But tomorrow we're gonna even the score."

"Damned right we are. Can't hardly wait till morning."

"You know, that soldier boy was a purty damned nice feller."

"Yeah, he was. For a soldier. Now let's forget everythin' and just get good and drunk."

"I'm for that. As a matter of fact, I think we're doin' that right now."

The two miners laughed loudly and banged their glasses on the bar for more drinks.

Compared to the scene at the outpost, the sun appeared to be a late riser, one who is tardy for work and who leaps out of bed and surges toward the chores of the day. By the time it broke cleanly above the eastern horizon to cast a warming flood of light across the hills, the two army units were swarming to their tasks like honeybees caught unawares by the first early storm of winter.

Buckets full of dirt were being handed up to the roofs in fire-brigade fashion, and spread across dry wood in a cool blanket of moistness. Crews were already spading rock and dirt from the new well, which had already been dug almost six feet, to be sifted and loaded into waiting buckets. Tall trees swayed and fell with a thunderous crash around the perimeter of the outpost while brush and smaller timber were being hacked and chopped out of the area to be cleared. Higher up, dust rose in an increasing cloud from churning hooves as horses strained to pull felled trees from the towering bluff. Mounted units patrolled the surrounding area, and sentries upon the outpost walls walked their posts with vigilant stares into the surrounding forest.

Inside the orderly room, Sergeant Ben Cohen, a beefy man with scarred knuckles from past sessions of behind-the-barracks discipline, leaned over Sergeant Ritter's desk. Taking up a slip of paper, he held it up to the light.

"Now here is a perfect example of what I'm talking about," Cohen said to the beleaguered Ritter, who appeared to be in danger of drowning in the sea of paperwork before him. "You don't need all this shit."

Ritter looked up and his flaccid jowls danced across his chin. "What do you mean, I don't need it? I don't want it, couldn't care less about it, and hope I never see it! But Regimental Supply doesn't see it that way. What in Christ's holy name do I do with four barrels of guncotton?"

"That's just what I mean. Obviously they were supposed to go to some artillery outfit and are being shipped to you by mistake. You find out what outfit it is, or any outfit for that matter, and trade it for something you need, like maybe an extra case of ammunition."

A protest formed on Ritter's fleshy lips. "But orders would have to be cut to make that kind of trade, and I—"

"Bullshit," Cohen replied. "Out here you worry about what you need, not what they think you should have back East. They don't give a damn where that guncotton goes as long as it goes somewhere. Trade it, make firecrackers with it, or use it to blow up some uppity private, but don't try to store it. You haven't got the space, and it's dangerous to keep around."

"If all the shit the lieutenant has ordered, or is being sent, ever arrives, we won't have room inside these walls for a flat cow turd," Ritter said with a helpless gesture toward the stacks of requisitions and invoices. "Somewhere in the pile is a requisition for a hundred cases of corned beef. For Christsakes, we've already got that many cases on hand and that's all we've eaten since we got here! What the hell am I going to do with a hundred more cases?"

56

"Trade it."

"Huh?"

"Trading is the name of the game. You've got some reconstructed Indians around here. Trade the corned beef for fresh game, fruit, and vegetables. They know where the wild onions are, mushrooms, plums, blackberries, nuts, and other things like that. Strike a deal with them—two cases of corned beef for three venison. Throw in a little extra for some onions, maybe a few strips of pemmican for flavor, mushrooms, and whatnot, and your cook can whip up one hell of a stew for your men."

Cohen stalked around the desk and searched out another document, which he held up and slapped disgustedly with the back of his hand. "And this bunch of bullshit," he said, waving the directive regarding the treatment of troops who had overstayed their welcome in town, "should be burned, hung on the shithouse wall, or eaten by the rosy-cheeked little officer who sent it to you."

Ritter smiled uneasily. "That might be fine for you, Cohen, but not for me. Lieutenant Greggory is a stickler for rules, going by the book and that sort of thing. Nothing is to be done around here without his knowledge."

"And once again, that's exactly my point. The lieutenant doesn't need to know about all the little nitpicky shit that goes on here. In fact, it's your job to make sure he doesn't find out about some things. Soldiers are, due to the nature of the beast, going to raise hell and fuck up. But everything has to go through you to get to the lieutenant, right?"

"Yeah, it's supposed to."

"Make damned sure that it does. And when it does, you handle the tedious bullshit. Your commanding officer's got more important things to worry about. If one of your troopers gets drunk and pukes in somebody's lap, does the CO need to know about it? If the man's a straight soldier, give him some little asshole detail to pull. If he isn't, take him out behind the barracks and make him into one. This is the frontier, Sarge. Mostly, you make your own rules out here."

Ritter smiled for the first time that he could remember since having been shipped West. He rubbed his knuckles and the look on his face was of pleasant memories returned. "I used

57

to be a pretty good hand in a scrape, back in the old days. I guess I could still hold my own."

"That's good, but not good enough. You don't just hold your own. Win and win big. Get yourself in shape and earn the respect of the men under you through fairness and a willingness to cover a good man when he needs it. Word spreads fast in an army unit, and it's damned easy to make the worst out of a bad situation. Now that's enough of that," Cohen said, taking up a stack of papers and beginning to shuffle through them, consigning at least half to the wastebasket. "Let's get on with it. We haven't much time to get this deal squared away."

Outside, Windy led his horse to the deepening well and stopped beside Kincaid, who was talking to the work detail. When the lieutenant had finished and turned toward him, Windy said, "Talk to you for a minute, Matt?"

"Sure, Windy. Let's talk while we walk outside. I want to see how things are going out there." They moved away, with Windy leading his horse, and Kincaid took up the conversation. "What's going on? Looks like you're going for a ride."

"Yeah, thought I would. All this work makes me nervous."

"And that's the only reason?"

"Nope. Kinda like to have a little look around. Either Aikens doesn't know what he's talkin' about or he's a flat-assed liar."

"Which way do you lean?"

"I think his ass is flat, Matt."

Kincaid grinned. "I wouldn't dispute you on that. Ever get just a . . . *feeling* about somebody?"

"Yup. And I've been right more'n wrong."

"I know you have. Why do you think Aikens would want to lie about the Cheyenne killing those miners?"

"Same reason as anybody else would; there's somethin' in it for him." Mandalian switched the reins behind his back to the other hand, found a cut of tobacco in his pocket, and tore off a chunk. "I've kinda been talkin' to some of the men who were on the recon patrol with him," Windy said, nestling the cut with a motion of his tongue and lips, and chewing thoughtfully.

"Find out anything?"

"Sure I did. Mainly that they haven't got anything to say." Now he looked directly at Kincaid. "Ever know any soldier to

58

come back from a patrol where they run into a little combat and not talk your damned ear off about it?"

"No, can't say as I have."

"Neither have I. But Aikens' men ain't sayin' a fuckin' word. It's like they never were there. Especially a young feller named Tipton."

"Tipton?"

"Yeah, Tipton. He's a slick-sleeve private and he seems scared shitless. Keeps lookin' around like somebody was watchin' him, and he's prone to gettin' a strange twitch at the corner of his mouth anytime anybody mentions what happened to those miners. Now, either he cut and run and he's ashamed of himself, or he saw somethin' he didn't want to see."

Kincaid pursed his lips and thought a minute before giving any response. "Think I should have a talk with him?"

"Wouldn't be a bad idea. He might tell an officer something he wouldn't tell nobody else."

"All right, I will. First time the opportunity comes up. Where you heading today?"

"Wherever my nose takes me."

Kincaid grinned again, but more broadly this time as he glanced at the scout's aquiline proboscis. "That could be a long ride, Windy."

Windy worked the cut for several seconds and a stream of brown juice squirted from between his lips. "You're a humorous man, Matt," he said, unsmiling.

"I couldn't help it, Windy," Matt replied with a chuckle. "Seriously, when do you think you'll be back?"

"Don't know. Think I might head into the Paha Sapa and see if any Cheyenne came back to visit old bones. Be nightfall at least 'fore I look at everything there is to see."

They had just passed through the gates and the scout stopped to swing up onto his saddle as Kincaid said, "Now don't get yourself into something you can't get back out of."

"Ain't done it yet, Matt. Don't 'spect I'll do it now. See ya."

Kincaid watched the horse canter away and noticed how quickly the dun-colored horse and buckskin-clad rider blended in with the surrounding terrain as they moved into the trees.

"Old bastard," he mumbled with a half-smile as he walked

toward the tree-cutting detail. "Don't know how the hell we'd ever get along without you."

There were twenty-two of them, spread out abreast and riding at a gallop as they left Deadwood. They were armed with rifles, revolvers, and shotguns, and they rode with deadly determination on their faces, deepened by the painful effects of well-earned hangovers. With the rising sun to their backs, they headed west. The miners, to a man, had only one goal in mind: to reach the Cheyenne encampment at White Bluffs by midday and take out their revenge on the people who had killed two of their comrades. There was no conversation among them, only a sense of urgency that caused them to hunch forward in their saddles, as though pressing time and their mounts to a faster pace.

When they had ridden down the main street of Deadwood, none of them had seen a curtain pull to one side in the hotel window, nor did they see it fall when Sergeant Aikens turned away to take up his pistol and saber. With his armament about him, he went out the front door of the hotel, paused to look in both directions, then hurried across the street to the stable. After throwing the riding gear on his horse, he mounted up and turned the bay gelding down the street before cutting into the timber breasting the town and urging his horse to a full run. Sergeant Aikens knew the way to White Bluffs, and he also knew he would be there before the miners arrived.

six _____

With the sound of boots scraping wood and heavy buckets being dragged overhead, Flora and Tina sat in the commanding officer's quarters with a large rectangle of material, divided into two halves, one red, the other white, stretched across the kitchen table between them. Flora's long fingers artfully worked the needle through the large block letters being attached to the material, while Tina worked with desultory lack of interest and a somewhat clumsy lack of skill.

"Your husband is going to be very proud of you when he sees this, Tina," Flora said with a pleasant smile as she smoothed the material with one hand to admire their craftsmanship. "His company will have a guidon to carry on special occasions, and nothing makes an officer more proud than that."

Tina sighed. "I hope he will be, but if he has anyone to thank, it's you. As I'm sure you've noticed, I'm something less than Betsy Ross when it comes to flagmaking. Or any other kind of needlecraft for that matter."

"It'll come to you in time. As of now, you're only doing what is expected of officers' wives."

"That's another problem," Tina said, glancing up with concern in her eyes.

"What's another problem, dear?"

"This business of what's expected of officers' wives. I'm not certain I can live up to it, and even worse, I'm not sure I want to."

"Why wouldn't you want to make your husband proud of you?"

"It's not that I don't want Steven to be proud of me," Tina said, her tone taking on a hint of exasperation. "I love him and want him to be happy. It's just that I want to be happy too."

"And making him proud wouldn't make you happy?"

"Of course it would. Please try to understand, Flora. Please? When I married him, I married him to be his wife, not his social butterfly."

Flora laid her needle aside. Taking up her teacup, she sipped the lukewarm beverage and studied the young girl across from her. "There is something you have to understand about being an officer's wife, and especially the wife of the commanding officer. He can only function if his men are proud of him, respect him, and wish that they were like him. His wife is a very important part of that. If they respect her and regard her as a lady, then they will treat her with deference as a tribute and courtesy to their commanding officer. While you should not act as though you are above them, you should deport yourself in a manner that will make them *want to think* you are above them and they will act in accordance with the belief that you are a special person. That, in turn, will aid in the respect they give your husband. May I help myself to more tea?"

"Certainly. Excuse me, I should have offered," Tina said, starting to rise. "Here, let me—"

"Nonsense. Sit down. There's a difference between the way you should act in front of enlisted men and other officers' wives. Let's just be friends, equals. I'm entirely capable of filling my own teacup. May I get you some more?"

"Yes, please," Tina replied weakly and sat back to watch the steaming brew pour into her cup. "You said we could be friends; may I tell you something?"

"Of course, dear," Flora answered, placing the kettle onto the stove and resuming her seat. "I certainly didn't ride all this way to do all the talking."

Tina studied her thoughts momentarily while listlessly stirring a spoonful of sugar into her tea. "You mentioned being a lady a while ago, and that's my biggest problem. I really don't want to be a lady. Being a lady is so confining, so limiting. Because of my tomboyish ways, I was a constant disappointment to my mother back home in Boston. I always rode astride instead of sidesaddle, I preferred to play roughhouse games with boys instead of little-girl games with dolls, and I always enjoyed chopping wood with my father more than I did learning to cook with my mother. Is that all bad?"

Flora smiled and reached across to pat Tina's hand. "Of

course not, it's marvelous. In fact, it's very much the same way I felt as a young girl."

"You?" Tina asked, her eyes widening in surprise. She couldn't help but stare at the beautiful, elegant lady across from her. "You felt like that?"

Flora nodded. "I not only felt like that, I acted like that. Maybe not to the extreme you've mentioned, but I certainly did envy the boys, who seemed to have all the freedom while we girls were being prepared for bustles and corsets."

Tina laughed happily. "Well, I sure am glad to meet someone who can understand my feelings." Then her face saddened and she looked down at the table and toyed absently with an edge of the guidon. "But you changed and I'm not sure I want to. Steven keeps apologizing for bringing me here, but I love it. I absolutely love it. There is nothing that interests me more than nature, being out of doors, and wandering through the trees with little verses of Elizabeth Barrett Browning slipping through my mind like a breeze in the forest. But Steven won't let me, he says it's too dangerous. Sometimes I feel like a prisoner in my own home."

"Your husband is right," Flora replied softly while taking up her needle again and beginning the final stitches on the guidon. "Why do you think they are doing all that work outside right now?"

"Steven told me, so I know. It's because your husband thinks we might get attacked by some wild band of Indians. Honestly, Flora, I think it's a bit much. And I'm afraid Steven agrees. We've been here over a month now, and the only hostile thing I've seen is a mad yellowjacket."

"Then consider yourself lucky, Tina. There are many frontier wives, some of whom I've known, who would dearly love to say the same thing." Flora glanced up and her gaze leveled on the young woman. "But unfortunately they can't. They have either been killed or raped, or both. They didn't get a second chance."

"The woods are so beautiful and peaceful and I sometimes lie on my back on the pine needles and just stare at the sky. If something happened—which it won't—I could take care of myself. And besides, there are nearly a hundred soldiers here to protect me."

"Tina, my dear, most of the men out here, and especially

in the region of a gold strike, are lonely men who have not seen, nor been with, a white woman in months. Especially a beautiful white woman as you are, and in time those soldiers whom you say will protect you will be in that same category. And that's partially why you have to act like a lady and gain their respect, to place yourself so morally high above them that they would not dare touch you. And it doesn't matter if your husband could court-martial them, have them hanged, or whatever. In the blinding moment of sexual lust, the mind has no conscience. That's why it's so important that you gain their admiration to the degree that they love you only in a protective way in which they would never allow anyone to harm you."

Tina drew a deep breath and exhaled slowly, and there was defensiveness in her face when she looked at Flora again. "You make it all sound so terrible, Flora, like we were living among animals instead of men. All I want is to be able to roam these beautiful hills in the fullest enjoyment of what nature has given us. I just want to be left alone—with the exception of Steven, of course—and be at peace with the world."

As if she hadn't heard Tina's words, Flora held up the guidon to admire the finished product. "There we are. Isn't it beautiful? What cavalry unit wouldn't be proud to ride post parade with this for their company colors?"

"It is beautiful, Flora. Thank you so much. More than that, thank you for listening."

"Listening to what, my dear?" Flora said, gathering up her things. "I think I did more talking than you did. Well, I'd better leave now. It's almost time for your husband's lunch, and no man likes to come home and find two women chatting idly with nothing cooking on the stove."

"Won't you stay for lunch, Flora? You and your husband? I'll have something fixed in a jiffy."

Standing, Flora turned and smiled. "No, but thank you very much for the invitation. I only came here to visit, not to be an imposition. Besides, it's far more pleasant for a man and wife to share that hour in the middle of the day by themselves. In my opinion, that is one of the most enjoyable meals to be served. Don't bother showing me out, I'm sure I can find my way."

When Flora was halfway across the room, the door swung open and Lieutenant Greggory stepped inside.

"Honey?" Seeing Flora, he swept the hat from his head and stood to one side. "I'm sorry, Mrs. Conway. I didn't realize my wife had an honored guest."

"No apologies needed, Lieutenant, and if they are going to be tendered, they should come from me for staying too long."

"Steven?" Tina called, scrambling away from the table and holding the guidon at arm's length. "See what Flora made for you?"

Greggory looked at the guidon in speechless disbelief for several seconds, and there was an unmistakable look of pride and affection in his eyes. Finally he said, "Did you really make that for us, Mrs. Conway?"

"Well, not exactly. Tina and I made it. I hope you like it."

"Like it? I love it! It's beautiful and I don't know how to thank you."

"Then don't thank me. It was my pleasure. I really must go now," Flora said, stepping outside. "Have an enjoyable lunch."

When the door closed behind her, Flora thought she heard the whoop of joy that might come from a young boy getting his first pony. She smiled happily and, lifting her skirts daintily, walked toward her room in the bachelor officers' quarters.

Matt Kincaid approached the young soldier hacking limbs from a felled tree with an ax. He noticed a frail handsomeness about him. There were beads of perspiration across his forehead and on the blond, thin mustache gracing his upper lip. He was giving total concentration to the ax in his hand and didn't hear Kincaid walk up and stop beside him.

"Are you Trooper Tipton?"

Tipton straightened and turned in one motion, and at the sight of the officer he snapped to attention with a hasty salute. "Yes I am, sir," he replied in a slightly high voice.

Matt returned the salute, saying, "At ease, Trooper. It looks to me like you're doing one hell of a fine job there."

"I'm trying, sir."

"That's all that can be asked. Relax and sit down for a moment if you like."

"I'd rather stand, sir, if it's all right."

"Fine with me," Kincaid replied, glancing around the

65

cleared area. "Looks like we should have this done in a couple more days, huh?"

"If you say so, sir."

Kincaid chuckled and continued in a cordial voice, "I appreciate your evaluation of my powers, Trooper, but merely the fact of my saying so isn't going to get a dammed thing done. It's men like yourself that make an army post function."

"Yessir."

"How long have you been in the army?"

"Nearly a year now, sir."

"How do you like it?"

"I like it fine, sir."

"Are you going to make a career out of it?"

Tipton's eyes wavered and the blank expression on his face took on a slightly concerned look. "I . . . I . . . don't know, sir. I thought I would when I joined."

"But now you don't know?" Kincaid asked, watching Tipton closely. "What changed your mind."

"Nothing . . . nothing in particular, sir. I just don't know right now."

"Something must have happened. Would you care to talk about it?"

"Begging your pardon, sir, no. I'd rather not talk about it."

Kincaid stooped to pick up a twig and chewed it in a moment's contemplation. "That's fine, no problem. You were on that recon patrol with Sergeant Aikens the other day, weren't you?"

Tipton's face tightened and a twitch tickled the corner of his mouth. In what appeared to be an involuntary action, he glanced toward the timber yet standing, before his head jerked back to front and center. Kincaid looked in the same direction and saw a soldier leaning against a tree and watching them intently, an ax held loosely in his grasp. When the trooper knew he had been seen, he pulled a file from his boot and began to sharpen the blade as if that were his entire reason for stopping work. Kincaid looked at Tipton again and noticed an increase in the spasmodic twitch.

"Were you?" he asked again.

"Yessir."

"Were you with the sergeant when he found those two scalped miners?"

Tipton flinched noticeably at the word "scalped," but continued to stare straight ahead. "Yes I was, sir. We all were."

"You all were? The entire squad?"

Tipton hesitated. "Yes . . . yessir. We all were."

"I see. Strange, but nobody seems to want to talk about it, which strikes me as a little peculiar. Were those the first dead men you've ever seen?"

"They were."

"Kind of a terrible sight. Men who once were breathing, laughing, and talking, lying there with the life shot out of them. It's unnerving to say the least." Kincaid watched Tipton even more closely. "Especially when they've been scalped."

Tipton closed his eyes and swallowed hard, as if he might be trying desperately to restrain something rising in his throat. He made no effort to reply.

Kincaid had seen all he needed to see, and now he said casually, "Well, I'd better go and let you get back to your work. The death of those miners has me a little curious, though, and I'd appreciate your coming to me if you think of some little detail that might have been overlooked, something the sergeant might have forgotten to put in his report. Would you do that? Come to me personally, I mean?"

"Yessir, I will," Tipton managed to croak in a weak voice. "But I don't know nothin' except what the sergeant said."

"I understand. But if anything does come to mind, anything at all, you can trust me to keep it confidential. I wouldn't want to have Sergeant Aikens getting mad at you for having a better memory than he has. Thanks for talking with me, Trooper."

The two men saluted again, and as Kincaid walked away, Tipton watched him almost longingly. There was the look in his eyes of a man yearning to cry out, to spill his guts to someone, anyone, and he blinked at the moisture forming on his lashes. Then he picked up the ax and began to chop in a wild fury.

When Windy saw the White Bluffs in the distance, his curiosity had been aroused and he had ridden in their direction for nearly an hour. The bluffs were obscured by timber now, and Windy pulled his horse up in a clearing and glanced upward at the hard blue sky. With the sun nearing its zenith, he decided to swing north at the bluffs and then angle east and be back at the outpost before nightfall. He had seen glimpses of the green prairie off to his left and he reined in that direction, then stopped sharply.

The sound of several horses running, mixed with an occasional shout, reached his ears and he tried to make out their number. He knew there had to be at least twenty mounts, maybe more. And then the first rifle shot blasted off the prairie floor and echoed through the timber. Another shot resounded, followed by a third, and Mandalian pressed his horse to a gallop and wove in and out of the trees as he worked his way to the ridge of ground leading down to the valley floor. Staying just within the timberline, he could see the entire expanse of green below, with a clear field of vision to the White Bluffs and the rolling prairie swell beyond.

Maybe two hundred and fifty yards below him, he could see a group of twenty or more men riding hard and firing an occasional shot, and a sickening sensation swept through the pit of his stomach when he saw what they were firing at.

Riding ahead of the pursuers, and just out of rifle range, yet close enough to tantalize, ten Indian braves streaked across the plains, low to their ponies' necks and glancing backward to make sure they did not lose the riders behind them. Windy knew immediately that the twenty men in pursuit were but minutes from certain death. Even worse, he knew there was nothing he could do about it. They were riding as though they might be caught, but angling toward the swell, which revealed nothing on the other side.

Instantly, Windy attempted to calculate how many warriors would be waiting for the unsuspecting pursuers. With ten braves acting as decoys, he knew there must be another forty or fifty lying in wait. Then, with dread in his heart, he tensed in the saddle and waited for the massacre. He had not long to wait.

The miners were pushing their horses hard, knowing they were closing ground, and their ecstatic yells increased, as did their weapons' fire. The warriors, now but a hundred yards from the crest of the swell, slowed their ponies even more, as if their mounts were becoming weary, and Windy knew the pounding joy in the miners' hearts that came with the thought of impending victory. The first brave disappeared over the swell, with the others going over one by one, and there was no more than a hundred yards of distance between them and the miners. Then the Cheyenne were gone and only the miners could be seen closing on the horizon. Just as they hit the crest, an explosion of rifle fire erupted. Horses reared on the skyline before toppling over, and the miners were spilling from their saddles like toothpicks shaken from a box.

While he watched, Windy visualized the placement of the waiting Cheyenne. If the war party was as big as he assumed, there would be at least twenty warriors lying flat on their stomachs, hidden in the grass about fifty yards from the crest. Waiting below, mounted and prepared to charge, the remainder of the band would be waiting. And the braves who had served as decoys would veer to the left, whirl their mounts, and attack from the flank.

Now Windy could see one or two riderless horses galloping away from the scene of the ambush, and the horizon was filled with mounted Cheyenne closing in for the kill. War screams drifted across the plains and he could see several warriors leap from their ponies and bend quickly over prone objects stretched out on the ground. Several more caught up with the two fleeing horses and shot them from the side as they might shoot a buffalo, before turning and racing back to the melee.

And then there was complete silence. The war party moved along the horizon like ghosts quitting a cemetery, and there was no apparent urgency to their movements as they slowly disappeared from view. Windy continued to watch until something blue flashed in the corner of his eye for a split second, below him and off to the left. Jerking his head in that direction, Mandalian strained for another glimpse of what he thought he had seen, but even though he maneuvered his horse for a better field of vision, he caught no other sight of the strange object. He started to quarter down the ridge in pursuit, and then his conscience overwhelmed him. It was doubtful, he knew, but if there were any survivors of the ambush, they would need help immediately. But Windy also knew that he'd better wait until he was certain there were no Cheyenne lying in wait for would-be rescuers.

After ten minutes he cautiously worked his horse down the ridge, and keeping close to the bluffs, he walked his mount toward the horizon. When he did turn his horse onto the prairie, it wasn't until he had crested the swell and could see to the limits of his vision in either direction. With that much distance given, he knew he could outrun any Cheyenne who might return to the scene.

As a renowned Indian fighter and man of the plains, Windy had seen many grisly sights, but what lay before him when he stopped his horse turned his stomach. They were strewn across the prairie swell, some lying on their stomachs and some upon their backs, but all twisted in the final agony of death. Each of them, to a man, had been scalped, and the fingers cut from their hands lay before their stumps like toys just out of reach.

Kneeling by each man one by one, Windy listened for heartbeats and found none. The only indication of life was a single horse, gutshot and attempting to struggle to its feet. Windy pulled the big knife from the sheath hanging from his belt. Grasping the dying animal by its halter, he rolled it onto its side and slid the knife into its throat with one deft thrust. The horse kicked one final time and then lay still while Windy wiped the knife blade clean on its hide and returned the bowie to his belt.

Mandalian could see that the men had been miners, and he knew for certain that they had been hellbent on seeking revenge for their dead comrades. What he didn't know was how the Cheyenne had known they were coming. Even though it was an old Cheyenne tactic, this trap had obviously been pre-planned, which could only mean there was a collaborator working with them who had known of the miners' intentions. The hint of blue flashed through Windy's mind again as his foot found a stirrup and he searched his mind for some part of the puzzle he might have overlooked.

Then, with one final glance at the carnage, he turned his horse and galloped toward the protecting timber on the ridge.

Sergeant Aikens waited until it was dark and he knew the hostler had gone home before he rode into town, staying in the shadows until he reached the livery. The sweat on his cooled horse had dried, and he quickly curried it before turning the hungry animal into a stall. He was pleased with himself as he crept to the doorway and looked in both directions. The hostler had not been there when he put the horse up the night before, he hadn't been there when he left early that morning, and he wasn't there now, so no one could say his horse had been out of its stall.

He sprinted across the street, climbed up the back stairs, and tiptoed down the hall to his room, where he quickly washed and shaved. Then, with his hair freshly combed and still wet, he went back onto the street and angled toward the Deadwood Saloon. He could see there were only two customers at the bar, and Aikens hid in the shadows until they finished their drinks and left before walking into the saloon.

"Evenin', bartender," he said cordially. "Looks like you've got a problem out back, huh?"

The bartender looked up from the polishing rag in his hand in surprise. "Evenin', soldier," he returned. "What kind of problem is that?"

"Well, I just went around back to answer the call of nature, you know, and there's some poor old guy laying out there and gripping his guts like somebody just poisoned him."

"Really? I wonder who the hell that could be," the bartender said, laying the rag aside and wiping his hands on his apron as he headed toward the door.

Aikens hurried to catch up. "Beats me. Here, I'll show you where he is, I might be able to help."

When they stepped through the door, the bartender looked in both directions, then turned sharply at the singing sound of metal swishing on metal. "What—"

The saber in Aikens' hand silenced further words as it slammed through the bartender's upper ribcage and pierced the center of his heart. The elderly man slumped to the ground without a sound and Aikens pulled the saber free, wiped it clean on the bartender's white apron, then sprinted down the alley to the Gold Dust Saloon. He stepped onto the boardwalk, making certain he hadn't been seen emerging from the darkness, and walked inside.

"Evenin', bartender. How 'bout a double whiskey and leave the bottle."

"Howdy, soldier," the bartender replied. "Comin' up."

"Mighty slow tonight, ain't it?" Aikens asked as he shoved some money across and took up his drink.

"It is that. Guess all the boys went back to their claims."

"Might have, at that," Aikens replied casually.

But his mind was not on conversation. He smiled inwardly as he raised the glass to his lips and savored the welcome taste. The bartender at the Deadwood Saloon was the last man alive who could have tied him in with the miners, and he no longer was a problem. Now there would be no more obstacles and the plan was in full swing.

Windy guided his weary horse through the main gates and rode directly toward Lieutenant Kincaid's quarters. Lights glowed dimly in the windows of the buildings surrounding the parade, and night had fallen across the post. When he stepped down from his horse, he rapped his knuckles on Kincaid's door and waited a few seconds before the door swung open.

"Come on it, Windy. I was beginning to think you really were going to follow your nose," Matt said, smiling warmly.

Windy offered a weak, sardonic smile, threw his hat on the floor, and sank tiredly into a chair. "Got a drink around here, Matt? I'm thinkin' the old body could sure use one."

"Of course. Just a second. Let me get a bottle and a couple of glasses." When he handed the drink to Windy, Kincaid said, "You look beat, old pardner. How'd it go?"

"Plum shitty." Windy took a long drink before wiping his bewhiskered mouth with the back of a hand while watching Kincaid closely. "We've got a real problem on our hands now, Matt."

"Oh? How's that?"

"Yesterday we had two dead miners to worry about, right?"

"Yeah, that's right," Matt replied cautiously.

"Well, now we've got twenty-four."

"What?"

"I just watched twenty-two more go down. Only difference is, besides numbers, this time I know it was Cheyenne that done it."

"You do?"

"Yup. Watched it with my own eyes. Couldn't do nothin' to help 'em. They rode straight into a classic Cheyenne ambush."

Windy recounted the massacre while Kincaid looked on in mild shock, and when Windy had finished, Matt shook his head in disbelief.

"Do you think they were out to get revenge for their two buddies?"

"I imagine so, but I've got a feelin' they were put up to it

72

by somebody. Somebody who stands to gain from a war between the Cheyenne and the outfit manning this post."

"Why do you think that?"

"It was just too pat, too damned pat. Those Cheyenne knew they had bacon hangin' in the woodshed before they slaughtered the pig."

"Why would anybody want to see that many men die for any reason?"

"Why don't crows fly backward? Same answer—it beats the hell out of me. How many army fellers do you know of that are off this post right now?"

Kincaid shrugged. "Only Aikens, as far as I know. Why?"

"Just wonderin'. It might've been only my imagination, and then again maybe not, but I thought I saw a flash of Union blue cuttin' trail away from where I was just as soon as there weren't no doubt that those miners was standin' in shit clear up past their necks. Like I said, I only got one glimpse of it, and it might have been a damned blue jay or somethin'. But if it was, that's one bird I wouldn't want to be alone in the hen house with."

"You think it might have been Aikens?"

"Don't know. How long'd he say he was going to be gone? Three days?"

"That's what he said. He had a three-day pass coming, which I wouldn't have given him on a bet, with all the work we've got to do around here."

"Got any more likker left?" Mandalian asked, holding up his empty glass.

"Sure, help yourself," Matt replied, handing the bottle across.

Windy spoke while he poured. "You have any luck with Tipton today?"

"Not much, unless you consider it lucky to be called 'sir' fifty fucking times. Something's really bothering him, and when he knew he was being watched by another soldier, that funny little twitch at the corner of his mouth damned near shook his mustache off. Tell you what my opinion is—I think he knows more than he is telling about that recon patrol."

"No argument there," Windy said, leaning over to refill Kincaid's glass. "He ain't said two words yet, so if we hit him for three, we'd really be shittin' in tall cotton."

73

Kincaid couldn't help but smile. "Yeah, I guess you're right. At any rate I've made myself available to him if he wants to talk. He knows where to find me."

"A blind man could find you in this little four-by-four shit-hole, Matt. Think we ought to tell Greggory about those miners?"

Kincaid studied him for a bit. "No, not just yet. I'll tell Captain Conway, but let's let Greggory slide for a while."

"That's pretty much my thinkin'. Might as well try for two; are you thinkin' what I'm thinkin' one more time?"

"That we should take a little ride into Deadwood?"

"That's what I'm thinkin'. Seems to me Aikens could stand a friendly conversation just about now."

"Right, we'll go first thing in the morning. If nothing else, I'd kind of like to see him do a little of the sweating around here."

"The blood of the honest man, huh?" Windy said with a grin. "If that's the case, he's gonna be drier than a buffalo's hump in mid-July."

"Maybe so. Let's finish this drink and go talk to the captain."

Windy yawned expansively and shoved his boots out in front of him. "Naw, you know everything I do. You go tell him and I'll make love to that bottle of yours till it's gone, then I think I'll get a little shut-eye."

"You mean you're not going to put up your horse?"

"Oh shit!" Windy growled, struggling to his feet. "Gonna teach that son of a bitch to unsaddle itself one fine day."

"And when you do, I'll expect to see those crows flying backward," Kincaid replied with a grin as he stepped into the darkness.

seven _____

Iron Crow looked at the scalps hung on sticks by the fire to dry, his dark eyes shining like black stars. His encampment was located where an inlet of grass flowed like a green sea into the foothills of the Paha Sapa and then flowed out again, providing an escape route on either end. To the right was an isolated mesa, where a vigilant guard now stood watch, and to the left were the Black Hills themselves, into which he and his warriors could flee if necessary. And to the right rear, about a quarter-mile distant, there was a long, narrow meadow that curved at a point out of sight from the entrance and formed a box canyon where a sharp escarpment rose from the prairie floor. That canyon was the principal reason for his choice of campsite and would play a major role in his first battle with the unit from Outpost Thirteen.

Iron Crow stooped and dug a handful of dull gray prairie soil from beside his feet and smeared it across his forehead and chest. "We have returned!" he screamed to the warriors seated about him. "We have returned to the Paha Sapa, ancient hunting grounds of our grandfathers! We come here in war, not peace! The white man felt the bite of Cheyenne knives today, and their scalps now dry by our fires. We are victorious, and we will count coup many more times until all white men are driven from our land. We are the last warriors of the Crooked Lance Society, and we will not be defeated. We will die before we leave our homeland again!"

Willy Harper sat beside the fire and watched the multitude of painted faces around him. From their reaction, he could see that Iron Crow was whipping them into a blood frenzy. Many leaped to their feet and began to dance in circles, with high-lifted knees, to the tune of a war chant and the methodical beating of a skin drum. While the remaining braves joined in, he marveled at the chief's abilities as an orator. He could see why the young warriors had chosen to follow Iron Crow instead of Straight Shooter.

With his face aglow in the firelight, Iron Crow snatched the strange crooked lance from the ground, speared a wet scalp from one of the poles, and held it over his head. *"Aaaaiiiiieeeee!"* he screamed repeatedly, and the wildness of the dancing increased. The chief moved among his warriors, dancing and screaming, and Harper felt a chill run up his spine. Surrounded as he was by wild Cheyenne intoxicated on victory, he thought of Aikens. "Don't let me down, you son of a bitch," he mumbled. "These bastards are plumb crazy, and my old head will be up on that lance the first time we do these fellers wrong."

When the dance had ended, the exhausted warriors sank again to the grass and Iron Crow walked over and hunkered down beside Harper.

"We had a great victory today, Black Devil."

"Yeah, we sure did, Crow. But remember, it ain't gonna be so easy against them army outfits," Harper replied with a cautious smile.

"No, Black Devil. It will be easier. The Blue Sleeves will be wanting revenge for what happened at the Greasy Grass, and revenge is the eyesight of the blind. They will follow where they are led." Iron Crow's face became impassive and he stared at Harper. "It is the job of your yellow-leg sergeant to bring them to me."

"And he'll do it, Crow. He'll do it. Don't worry none about old Aikens, he's a man of his word. But when we made this deal, we hadn't figured on having that other outfit to contend with."

The Cheyenne cocked his head quizzically. "And that makes a difference? We have an agreement and it shall not be broken. Nothing has changed on my end of the bargain, and anything that changes on your end is your problem to deal with."

"I know it, Crow," Harper said quickly. "I know it and we are. We're gonna give you twice as big a victory as we bargained for at the start. That should be worth twice as much gold, shouldn't it?"

"Hah! Gold!" Iron Crow scoffed, and spat disgustedly. "Gold, that's all you and the white men think of. Gold! What is it worth? You cannot make an arrowhead out of it, it won't burn, you can't eat it, it's too heavy for war dress, so what is its value? Nothing. Yet our people are killed and we are driven from our homeland because of it."

Harper chuckled at the thought of the Indian's ignorance of the value of the precious metal. "Well, Crow, civilized people—"

"Civilized! Killing thousands of Indians, taking away their hunting land, driving them into reservations, and giving them strange tools to grow things from the ground with—is that what you call civilized?"

Inadvertently, Harper had done the exact opposite of what he wanted to do, and instantly, in response to the sudden anger of the young chief, the vision of a crop of kinky hair impaled upon a lance flashed through his mind.

"Now, uh, Crow, just hold on a minute, I didn't mean you weren't civilized. What I meant was, people from my way of life think a little different than you do. Not that it's better, mind," he added, holding up his palms, "just different, that's all. I guess we just think gold's purty and that's why we like to have it."

"You kill for something pretty? I kill because I hate my enemies, be they white, Arapaho, or Sioux. I kill because a warrior is trained to kill, and the more coups I count here, the more horses I will have in the world of the spirits beyond. Pretty? Hah!" Iron Crow spat again. "You can have all the pretty you can carry."

Now a broad grin split Harper's ebony face. "Why, Crow, that's damned decent of you. When this is over, me an' old Aikens'll just unleave your Paha Sapa of a few handfuls of that nasty old purty and be on our way."

Iron Crow shook his head in disgust. "Enough talk of gold. Tell me about this new group of Americans. They are bluelegs, are they not?"

"Yeah, a dragoon company from down south somewhere. Way I understand it from Aikens, they've got a few battles under their belts and they ain't an easy crowd to fool. That's where me and the brass horn come in. Their commanding officer's name is Conway, and the executive officer is Lieutenant Kincaid."

"I have heard of Kincaid."

"I reckon you have, and maybe you've also heard about their chief scout, Windy Mandalian."

"The Snake?"

"Might be."

Iron Crow nodded vigorously and a crafty smile crossed his normally stony face. "There is not a warrior on the plains that hasn't heard of the Snake. His scalp would be the greatest prize of them all."

"Maybe that's because there's only one of 'em and it's purty damned hard to get," Harper offered with a testing smile.

"That is so, for the others. But not for Iron Crow. I am the greatest warrior of all, and when we meet in battle his scalp will hang from my coup belt."

Harper noticed the proud expansion of the Indian's scarred chest and took great comfort in the knowledge that his own scalp was as worthless as tits on a boar hog, as far as Iron Crow was concerned.

"I'm sure the Snake, or whatever he's called, will fall to your rifle," Harper said ingratiatingly. "And when he is gone, the others will fall as well."

Iron Crow had heard what he wanted to hear and he rose abruptly and stalked proudly away, like a rooster strutting a fence rail at dawn.

It was midmorning when Kincaid and Mandalian rode down Deadwood's main street and turned their horses in at the Deadwood Saloon. "If Aikens is the kind of man I think he is," Kincaid said, stepping down to loop his reins over the hitching rail, "then a drinking establishment would be the best place to start looking for him."

"Yup," Windy replied, ducking under the rail, "and maybe the son of a bitch will buy us a drink."

Kincaid pushed the swinging doors aside and stepped in. He was mildly surprised by the size of the crowd for the hour of the day. The room buzzed with conversation, and hostile eyes watched them as they approached the plank.

"What'll it be, fellas?" the harried bartender asked when he finally broke free from the other customers and moved in their direction.

"I'll have a beer, please," Kincaid replied. "How 'bout you, Windy?"

"Beer's for babies what ain't got no mama, Matt. Make mine a double whiskey."

When the drinks were served, the bartender mopped the plank and spoke while he worked. "First damned day on the job and look at this crowd. Hell, I ain't even a bartender, I'm a damned piano player!"

"First day, huh?" Matt said after taking a sip of beer. "Why the big crowd? Some kind of celebration?"

The bartender looked up in surprise. "Ain't you heard?"

"About what?"

"Old Eddie?"

"No, guess not. What about old Eddie?"

"Got killed last night, right outside that back door. Murdered. Stabbed through the heart by some kind of big knife. Hell, it went clear through his chest and out his back."

"That must've been a big knife. Any idea who did it?"

"Nope. Joint was empty, I guess. A couple of fellas left here about eight o'clock and they said old Eddie was breathin' pretty good then. About eight-thirty another fella comes in and Eddie ain't here. He waits awhile, then goes out back lookin' for him. Finds him dead in the alley. Dirty bastard that killed him even had the nerve to wipe his knife off on Eddie's apron. Didn't rob the joint or nothin'. Just killed old Eddie and wiped his knife on his apron."

Kincaid shoved his empty mug across the plank. "That's too bad. Sorry to hear about your friend. Got another beer back there?"

"Seems to be a whole passel of killin' goin' on around here," Windy said in a lowered voice. "Appears they don't know about those miners yet."

Matt held his reply until the beer was served and the bartender moved away in response to a demanding voice farther down the line.

Matt chuckled quietly. "I wouldn't have that bartender's job if it was the last one on earth." Then he turned to Windy. "No, it doesn't seem like they know. Maybe it's best, might keep some other fools from trying the same thing."

"Yeah, but it won't last for long. And when the news breaks, guess who's gonna get the blame."

"I know. The army."

When the bartender managed to work his way in front of

them again, Kincaid asked, "Have you seen an army sergeant in here this morning? Kind of a big guy with a rough-looking face?"

"Friend, he's the only son of a bitch in town that *ain't* been in here. Every other bastard what's big enough to see over this here plank's been in here, and there ain't a damned one of 'em that don't think he's the only customer in the joint. Miserable, disrespectin' sonsabitches," he mumbled, moving again toward another yell for drinks in the opposite direction. "Hold onto your mules, damn you! I'm comin' as fast as I can!"

Since the bartender had forgotten to collect for their drinks, Matt shoved some money to the center of the plank and turned away. "Come on, Windy. There must be more saloons in this town."

As they led their horses in the direction of the Gold Dust Saloon, Windy tilted his hat back and scratched his forehead. "I've been thinkin', Matt, which, as you know, is a chore I usually try to avoid. Anyway, does it strike you strange that a bunch of miners, hard-drinkin' men all, ride off and get themselves butchered and then a bartender gets killed for no apparent reason?"

Kincaid thought about it for a couple of seconds. "No, can't say that it does. Boomtowns like Deadwood are rough places and nobody is exposed to rougher men than a bartender. Maybe whoever killed him just didn't like the fellow."

"Could be, could be. Still, it kinda sticks in my craw. Maybe another whiskey'll wash it out."

"Let's find out," Matt replied, tying his horse and moving toward the batwing doors.

They had just stepped inside when Windy tapped Kincaid's forearm with the back of a hand. "Look over yonder, Matt. At the poker table."

Matt looked and saw the strained material of a blue shirt stretched across broad shoulders. Aikens had his back to them and he held his cards in one hand and a whiskey glass in the other. "Oh yeah. The pride of the cavalry. Get us a couple of drinks, will you, Windy? And one for the sergeant. Meet me at that table over in the corner."

Windy moved toward the bar while Matt walked up behind Aikens and tapped him on the shoulder.

"What the hell you want?" Aikens said, turning. It was

obvious from his slurred speech and red-rimmed eyes that he had been drinking all night and into the next day. "Well!" he added with absolute disrespect. "If it ain't Lieutenant Kincaid."

"In the flesh. Come on, Sergeant. I want to talk to you."

"Talk to me later. I want to finish this hand."

"I said now, Sergeant," Kincaid replied with cold firmness. "And when I say now, I mean *right* now!"

The other players watched in silent anticipation, wondering what the surly sergeant would do. Aikens nodded after several seconds' hesitation, and a dirty smile spread across his unshaven face. "Why, hell yes, *sir*. Ain't every day a poor old sergeant like me gets to talk friendly-like with a high-and-mighty lieutenant. Deal me out of this hand, boys. I'll be back in a minute."

With considerable difficulty, Aikens managed to stand and follow Matt to the table, and they sat down just as Windy arrived with the drinks.

Aikens looked up with a lopsided grin. "Why, hell, and here's Buckskin Bobby from Abba Dabba land."

"You ain't worth the trouble it'd take to knock you off that chair, Aikens. Here, have a drink," Windy said, thumping the glass down in front of the sergeant and spilling some on his shirt front. "Even though you obviously don't need it."

"Now ain't this a sight?" Aikens replied, ignoring the spill and leaning back in his chair. "Old Sergeant Aikens drinkin' with a good *sir* and a civilian half-breed. Can't tell for sure which is worse."

"Don't press your luck, Sergeant," Kincaid said evenly. "I don't care how drunk you are, or where you are, you're still in the army."

"Yes, *sir*!" The mocking tone was obvious in Aiken's voice.

"Where were you yesterday?"

"Right here."

"Can you prove that?"

"Can you prove that I wasn't?"

"No. Not just yet, anyway."

Kincaid looked around to make sure they were out of earshot of the other customers before saying, "Twenty-two miners were killed and scalped by Cheyenne yesterday. Did you know that?"

"That a fact?"

"It's a fact. Did you know about that?"

81

"Didn't before. Do now. Musta been the same ones what got them other two."

"Maybe. And then maybe not. You've been in town a couple of days now. Did you hear talk of any miners going out for revenge against the Cheyenne?"

"Didn't come here to talk to miners, Lieutenant. I came here to get drunk, fuck, and play cards. I got the first two handled and now I'm workin' on the third. Least I was, till you so rudely interrupted."

Windy twirled his drink on the tabletop. "Since you don't know anything about them miners, what do you think of that bartender getting killed down at the Deadwood Saloon?"

Aikens replied expressionlessly, "Luck of the draw, way I see it."

"Pretty shitty hand if it was," Windy replied, watching Aikens' face closely. "Kinda strange, ain't it? Somebody goin' around town carryin' a knife long enough to go plumb through a man's chest and out his back. Seems like folks would've noticed. Kinda hard to keep something like that in a man's front pocket."

"Maybe he had it up his ass, for all I know!" Aikens snarled. "What the hell are you two accusing me of, anyway?"

Windy smiled and sipped his drink. "Mighty uncomfortable place to carry a knife, I'd say. Accuse you? My dear Sergeant, we're only sharin' military secrets with you."

Aikens glowered at the men across from him. "Like hell you are! Now, if you're through with all this chitchat, I've got a poker game to finish."

Aikens kicked his chair back and loomed above the table, holding his clenched fists by his sides, and Kincaid looked up calmly at him.

"Sergeant. You will report back at your post at eight o'clock in the morning. I'd tell you to go back now, but I think you're too drunk to sit a saddle."

"Sorry, Lieutenant, sir, and all that shit. I'm on a three-day pass and this is only the second day. Besides, I take orders from Lieutenant Greggory."

"You take your orders from any officer in the United States Army, soldier, and don't you forget it. Eight o'clock tomorrow morning. Not a minute after or you'll be facing a court-martial and at least three months in the stockade."

The mention of stockade time sobered Aikens slightly. He knew that three months in the stockade for insubordination was very possible, and he also knew it was the last thing he needed. "All right, Lieutenant. I'll be there. But you'll hear from Lieutenant Greggory about this."

"Fine. Love to chat with the man." Kincaid rose slowly to his full height. "And one more thing, Sergeant. You salute when you're dismissed by an officer."

Aikens stood there undecided, and glanced over either shoulder to see how many people were watching, which, by this point, included everyone in the saloon. He hesitated a second longer before saluting with all the enthusiasm of a condemned man taking the final drag from his last cigarette.

"You might work on that a little more, Sergeant," Kincaid said laconically as he returned the salute. "When you get time, that is."

Aikens turned away, jerked his chair back from the poker table, and flopped down. "What're ya lookin' at?" he growled at the other players. "Deal the goddamned cards!"

"That was beautiful, Matt," Windy offered as they stepped from the saloon. "Absolutely beautiful. I don't like the chances of anybody who crosses old Aikens tonight."

"He'll get his, Windy. But right now, what say we get something decent to eat before we go back?"

"Don't know what's decent anymore, Matt. If it don't run over the sides of your plate and drip onto your boots, I'm out of business. Let's give 'er a try anyway. Looks like an eatin' place right over there."

It was an hour later when Matt and Windy left the restaurant and swung onto their saddles. The crowd around the Deadwood Saloon had spilled onto the street by now and Windy said with a smile, "Think a man could get a bartendin' job in there if he was to ask real polite, Matt?"

Kincaid grinned. "I think so, Windy. And name his own wages."

They could see a lathered horse tied to the hitching rail as they approached, and when one of the crowd saw Kincaid's uniform, he shouted to the other, "There's one of 'em now!"

Matt and Windy reined their horses in as the crowd surged toward them while more men spilled from the saloon.

"What the hell we payin' you for, mister?" one man screamed, with his hate-filled face turned up toward Kincaid.

"Would you mind telling me what you're talking about?"

"You know what I'm talking about! What we want to know is what you're gonna do about it!"

"Look, friend, I don't know what you're talking about. But I am willing to listen."

"Hear that?" the man mocked as he turned to the others, who were now standing ten deep in front of their horses and flanking them on both sides. "Army here is willing to listen. Well"—he turned back to Kincaid—"if you don't know about it, then maybe you'd just better give a little listen to a man who does. Floyd! Get up here!"

An elderly man, obviously a buffalo hunter, moved to the front of the crowd and the speaker pulled him forward to face the lieutenant. "Here, Floyd. Tell army what you told us."

"I was out near White Bluffs this mornin'," the hunter began in a surprisingly soft voice, "thinkin' I might scare up a buff or two. What I found was twenty-two dead men—miners they was, by the looks of it—and there wasn't a topknot left on a one of 'em. I hightailed it in here and that's what the ruckus is all about."

Kincaid nodded and said, "Thank you, sir." Then he looked out over the crowd. "I'm Lieutenant Kincaid, Easy Company, United States Army. The man beside me is Windy Mandalian, chief scout for the same army unit. Mr. Mandalian saw the whole thing. Those dead miners were in pursuit of ten Cheyenne, shooting at them, and they would have killed them if they could have. Instead, they got killed themselves. The army is well aware of what happened and we will take the appropriate action at the appropriate time."

An angry murmur rose up and a man from the rear yelled, "We ain't got time to wait for your appropriate action, Lieutenant."

"The ones who got killed didn't have time either, sir," Matt said in a flat tone.

"Aw, to hell with him," another man said. "The Citizens' Committee will damned sure get some action for us."

Kincaid looked at the man. "If I may ask, sir, what Citizens' Committee?"

"The Citizens' Committee what left here about twenty minutes ago to go out to your spankin' new outpost what's supposed to protect us and tell the commanding officer what's supposed to be in charge but what's doin' the world's most shittiest job of protectin' us, that's what Citizens' Committee!"

Matt and Windy glanced at each other, and Windy said just above a whisper, "Greggory ain't gonna love ya, Matt."

"No, I suppose not." Kincaid raised his voice again to be heard above the sullen murmur. "This is an army matter and the army will take care of it. Now stand aside so we can pass through and get back to the post and do the job that needs to be done."

With a show of reluctance the crowd parted, and Kincaid and Mandalian rode down the street to a chorus of jeers.

"Matt," Windy said, pressing his horse to a full run in stride with Kincaid's, "we ain't never run from a fight before."

"I know that, Windy," Kincaid replied over the pounding of their horses' hooves, "but sometimes discretion is the better part of valor. Besides, I think we'll find trouble enough when we get back to the post."

There were at least thirty civilians milling around in front of Lieutenant Greggory's office when Matt and Windy galloped across the parade. Everyone was talking at once, and an exasperated Greggory was standing on his tiptoes, waving his hands for silence and shouting to be heard above the noise of the crowd.

"Just calm down! I promise you, I didn't know a thing about any of this! Just calm down! At daylight tomorrow I'll send a full company into the field. I'll lead it myself, and we'll bring the guilty parties to justice! Now please, just get back on your horses and go home! You'll be protected to the fullest extent possible! Trust me! Go home and I'll take care of everything!"

Amid grumbling and shouted threats of letters to the War Department and demotions for certain officers, the townspeople mounted up and rode away. It was then that Greggory saw Kincaid and turned his withering glare in Matt's direction. "You! Where the hell have you been?"

"In town, Lieutenant," Kincaid said, swinging down. "We're not too popular there, either."

"Popular!" The word exploded from Greggory's mouth. "I've seen friendlier lynch mobs! You're off to town, Captain

Conway's up inspecting work on the bluff, and I'm left holding the goddamned bag!"

"You are the commanding officer, aren't you?"

"Yes I am, dammit, and I'm going to start acting like one." Greggory continued to shout as though he were still addressing the mob. "Tomorrow I'm going to lead my company into the field. Do you know that the Cheyenne killed twenty-two miners yesterday? Twenty-two! If word of this gets back to Washington, I'm done as a—"

"Excuse me, Lieutenant," Kincaid broke in. "First of all, there is absolutely nothing wrong with my hearing, and secondly, I know about the dead miners, and thirdly, don't you think we should discuss this in your office instead of out here for the entire world to hear?"

Greggory's mouth still hung open, and it slowly closed while he lowered his hands to his sides. "Very well, Lieutenant. As you wish. We'll talk in my office."

Greggory stomped inside, and when they stepped to the door, Windy grinned across at Kincaid. "Think I ought to tell him the joke about the Arapaho squaw and the pink-cheeked boy from back East?"

"No, Windy. I don't think he's in a laughing mood. And besides that, it's a shitty joke."

When they passed by the first sergeant's desk, Ritter and Cohen were seated close together and going over another document, which was the only scrap of paper to be seen. Kincaid tapped the desktop.

"Ah, bare wood. Nice to see, Sergeant."

Cohen glanced up with a knowing grin. "We're workin' at it, sir. Besides, it sounds like it's safer in here than out there."

"That it is, Ben, that it is."

Greggory was pacing back and forth behind his desk like a midget on a treadmill, and he looked up sharply when Mandalian closed the door.

"You knew about this, Lieutenant?" he demanded. "Just when did you find out about it?"

Kincaid tossed his gloves on the CO's desk and said offhandedly, "Last night. Windy told me about it. He saw the whole thing. Where do you keep the brandy?"

"Brandy? This is no time for brandy."

"It's the perfect time for brandy. You need it to calm you

86

down. I need it if I'm going to listen to you, and Windy needs it . . . because Windy needs it. Pour us each a glass, if you would, and heed your own advice in the process; just calm down."

The decanter trembled in Greggory's hand, and glass clinked against glass as he filled three goblets and passed them around. "Now, Lieutenant," he said testily, moving again behind his desk, "if you're quite comfortable, I want to get to the bottom of this whole mess. Why wasn't I informed immediately of this disaster? I don't think it needs to be pointed out that I am military commander in charge of this district."

"Not at all, and you're welcome to it. The way you're acting now is precisely the reason why you weren't informed. I wanted to ask a few questions before you stormed out of here, chasing ghosts in the Paha Sapa."

"The what?"

"That's the name the Sioux and Cheyenne have for the Black Hills."

"Oh. I see." Greggory's neck reddened slightly and he clasped his hands behind his back to resume his pacing. "Now, back to our original conversation. If you had questions to ask, why did you go into town to get your answers?"

"Because Sergeant Aikens is there."

"Sergeant Aikens? What could he possibly tell you?"

"That's what I went to find out, but I came up empty. He was the man who found those first two miners, wasn't he?"

"Of course."

"I just wanted to find out if there was a connection. Oh, by the way, he's reporting back for duty at eight o'clock tomorrow morning."

Greggory ceased his pacing and turned with a start.

"He's what?"

"He's needed sober here more than he's needed drunk in town."

"Sir, Sergeant Aikens is my most valuable and trusted non-com in the field. He deserves the pass he was given and I hope he enjoys it to the fullest. All three days of it! And if he chooses not to return per your request, he'll not be punished by me."

"Not bad brandy," Kincaid said, swirling his glass before taking another drink. Then he looked directly at Greggory. "If he's not here, he will be court-martialed. And if you don't wish to press the charges, Captain Conway will be more than happy to do the honors upon the strength of my suggestion."

The tinge of pink that had been embarrassment transformed instantly into a florid look of rage, as though a belt had suddenly been cinched tightly around Greggory's neck. "Now look here, Lieutenant. I've had just about all I can stand of what's been happening here these last two days. My outpost has been damned near completely dismantled and put back together again, my troops are being required to perform menial physical labor, my guard mount is twice what it should he, and now my best noncom is being humiliated by a lieutenant who fell out of the sky at no request of mine. I'm just a little bit sick of it, if you don't mind my saying so."

Kincaid shrugged. "Don't mind at all. And if you're sick, I think you're going to get just a little bit sicker."

A haughty look filled Greggory's face. "I am, am I? And why is that, if I might presume to ask?"

"Because you're not leading any units into the field tomorrow."

"Like hell I'm not!"

"Like hell you are," Kincaid replied without raising his voice. "Not one soldier will leave this compound until Captain Conway deems it completely defensible."

"Need I remind you, Lieutenant, that twenty-two men were killed yesterday? Their killers must be brought to justice."

"Dead men don't count, Lieutenant," Windy offered from where he stood leaning against the back wall. "It's the live ones you gotta keep shittin' regular."

"But I made a promise to those townspeople. I can't go back on my word! Why, you saw them out there. If we don't do something and do it damned quick, they'll have the Inspector General on my ass so damned quick it'll make your head swim."

Kincaid swirled his goblet again and downed the last drop of brandy. "The ride would probably do him good. And as for the townspeople, they don't count either. Every damned one of them was nearly falling-down drunk. Are you going to be dictated to by a bunch of drunk miners, more of the same who rode out and got themselves killed yesterday simply because of hotheadedness?"

"Well, I . . . no . . . I didn't take it that way."

"That's the way *they* took it. You let them start calling the

88

shots for you and you'll never have another minute's peace around here. Our chief priority right now is to complete the fortifications that are the life's blood of this outpost. You'll get your chance to lead in the field, Lieutenant," Matt concluded, taking his gloves and moving toward the door. "But we would like to see you have a chance to lead in the field more than once. Good day, Lieutenant."

Greggory slammed his palms onto the desktop and stared murderously at the closing door. Then, with a sudden enraged sweep of his hand, he sent the piles of paperwork sailing into the air to separate and flutter to the floor. Gritting his teeth, he clenched his hands behind his back again and resumed his calculated pacing.

eight ═══════════════════════

It was exactly eight o'clock in the morning when Sergeant Aikens stomped into the orderly room and Ritter looked up from his work in feigned surprise. "What the hell's this, Sergeant? Never seen you come back early from a three-day pass. You usually show up on the fourth day."

Aikens' cheek was swollen and there was a ring of black under his left eye, and it was obvious he was in no frame of mind for jovial banter. "Don't give me any shit, Ritter. I want to see the CO."

Ritter's hand made a sweeping gesture toward the door. "Be my guest. Your moods should match perfectly. But this time try knocking?"

"Aw, fuck you," Aikens growled, and rapped loudly on the door twice.

"Yes. Who is it?" a disconsolate voice asked from within.

"It's me. Sergeant Aikens. I've gotta talk to you, Lieutenant."

"Just a minute!" Greggory replied, leaping from his desk, scooping the papers from the floor, and stuffing them into the lower drawer of a file cabinet. With a final glance around, he adjusted his tunic and sat behind the desk. "Come in, Sergeant."

Aikens, impatient now as well as mad, threw the door aside, letting it bang against the wall, and crossed the room in two steps to place his knuckles on the desktop and lean forward. "Just what the hell is going on around here, sir?"

Greggory, having taken all the shit he intended to take, waggled a finger toward the door and said in a firm voice, "Please close the door, Sergeant."

Surprised by the lieutenant's tone, the big sergeant closed the door with a thud and turned to resume his original position.

"Just one minute, Sergeant. First, keep your goddamn hands
90

off my desk, and second, isn't it customary to salute your commanding officer?"

Aikens straightened with a weary sigh and offered one of his lackluster salutes. "Can we get on with it now, sir?"

"Certainly. Repeat your original question, please."

"I said, just what the hell is going on around here?"

"One of the finer questions I've heard since taking over this command." Greggory swung back and forth in his chair a couple of times before looking up at the sergeant. "And to answer you bluntly, I haven't got the vaguest idea what's going on around here."

The lieutenant's response exasperated Aikens. A muscle twitched in his cheek. "Okay, let's start over again. Just how long is this goddamned Easy Company outfit going to hang around here poking their noses into our business and telling us what to do?"

"I would say, from my casual observations, apparently until everyone in hell is smitten with a severe, incurable case of frostbite."

"Look, sir," Aikens began again, even though he could see he was getting nowhere, "ain't I your best noncom in the field?"

Greggory leaned back and pressed his fingertips together before his chest. "That is a correct assumption. Go on."

"If any changes needed to be done around here, wouldn't I have told you about them? This goddamned place looks like an army of moles moved in!"

"I'm not entirely sure they haven't."

"We should be in the field chasing those Cheyenne who ambushed that bunch of miners yesterday, not fucking around here doing gardening, for Christsakes!"

"You heard about that?" Greggory asked, arching an eyebrow.

Aikens hesitated, searching for the right words. "Well, of course I did. Everyone in town was talking about it. That's how I got this." He touched his cheek gingerly. "Some wiseass started mouthing off about the army."

"I see. Perhaps you should have bought him a drink and offered to take his wife out dancing. His ass might not have been all that was wise."

Aikens stared at the man whom he had dominated for so long. "Have you been drinking, sir?"

"No, unfortunately, I haven't been." Greggory took up a pencil from his desk which he held between the tips of two fingers and studied in contemplation while he spoke. "Sergeant, this has been an arduous experience for all of us, at best. Now, you've been in the military long enough to know that a lieutenant is outranked by a captain, and a captain by a major, and so on. Well, the point of my story is that I don't happen to be a major and neither do you. But there *is* a captain here who arrived with official orders in his pocket. Now, unless I happen to get promoted within the next day or two, which is not a possibility I personally would wager a lot of money on, we are, one and all, doomed to our fate until that happy day when we see nothing but the backs of Easy Company heading blissfully away to permanently alter the married life, military pride, and digestion of some other poor bastard somewhere in this vast world of ours." He looked up with a condescending smile. "Do I make myself perfectly clear?"

"How 'bout in the field, sir? Will you be in charge in the field?"

Greggory waved his hand listlessly. "What field would you be referring to, Sergeant? The fields presently being cleared around this outpost and apparently being prepared for a crop of rutabaga?"

"I mean in the real field, sir. The one where we're supposed to be, catching and kicking the shit out of a bunch of renegade Cheyenne!"

"Ah, that field. The one often referred to in training manuals as 'any area extraneous of the parent compound and into which troops might be sent to engage in combat.'" Greggory gazed wistfully at Aikens. "Have you seen any fields around here, Sergeant? If you have, you've got one hell of a good imagination. All I've seen are hills, trees, boulders, canyons, creeks, and two porcupines. Captain Conway's field not withstanding, of course."

Aikens shook his head sharply, as if to clear his blurred vision, and leaning toward the lieutenant while being careful not to touch his desk, he said, "If you'll pardon my asking, sir, are you cracking up?"

"Cracking up, Sergeant?" Greggory replied, slowly standing with a wan smile crossing his lips. "Certainly not. But cracking *down*? A very real possibility. From the head down. However, let me tell you one thing," he continued, tucking his hands behind his back and beginning to pace, "I must have pissed God off somewhere along the line or he wouldn't have sent Easy Company here. Now I'm sure it's not a permanent condition, and he did have the good sense to make me a first lieutenant and commanding officer of this unit. I'm equally sure that my not being a captain or a major by now is merely an oversight."

Greggory stopped, face to the wall, then spun with eyes blazing. "And when we *do* finally have every last fucking tree in sight chopped down, potatoes taking root on the roofs, that bluff out there reduced to a tiny pebble, and enough water in that well to float a goddamned Mississippi steamboat, *then* we will go to battle. And when we do, I'll be commanding this company of fighting men and you will be my right-hand man in the conflict. That day, I pray to the God who has forgotten me, will 'come very soon. Unless, of course, Captain Conway decides the entire outpost should be moved to the right three feet and the Indians all die of old age before we get the job done. Do you understand what I'm saying?"

"I think I do, sir," Aikens replied, smiling now. "When we do go into the field, it will be just you and me in charge of our outfit?"

"Precisely. Now, just to make it look good, why don't you go and present yourself to Lieutenant Kincaid and participate in this charade until that final moment when, on a clear day, we can all see Kansas City without an obstruction in sight."

Aikens turned toward the door. "Right, sir. I'm on my way."

"Sergeant? Aren't you forgetting one little formality?"

"What's that, Lieutenant?"

Greggory made a motion toward his forehead with closed fingers.

"Oh. Yeah. That." Aikens replied, saluting. "Seems to slip my mind sometimes."

"Don't worry about it, Sergeant. I'll remind you from time to time. You're dismissed."

When Aikens had left the room, Greggory pulled his saber from its scabbard and pierced the air with a few feints, parries, and thrusts. Satisfied, he replaced the weapon, drew a single sheet of paper from the pile in the file cabinet drawer, and signed it with a flourish, without looking at the document. He placed it carefully to one side, drew out another sheet, which he signed with a similar whirl of the wrist, and placed it neatly on the first. By noon his paperwork was all done and he gently placed the stack on Sergeant Ritter's desk and went home to lunch with a smile on his face.

Across the parade, Captain Conway laid down his fork and touched his lips with a napkin before reaching for his coffee cup. "How deep would you say the water is in the bottom of that well, Matt?"

Kincaid looked up from his lunch. "I'd say at least a good three feet, sir. Waist-high to Private Malone."

"What's the approximate depth of the well?"

"Between twenty-five and thirty feet. I think we hit a pretty good supply."

"Fine. By this time tomorrow we should be through with the clearing outside the walls. The roofs are covered now, and water barrels are in place. Should be able to move against those Cheyenne the following day, don't you think?"

"I think so, sir. We'll reinforce the well this afternoon and tomorrow morning, and the crank standard is already built." Matt pushed his plate away and watched the captain light a cigar. "When we do move against the Cheyenne, according to Windy's calculations we're not going up against just a few young bucks who don't give a damn. He thinks the ones we're dealing with might be members of the Crooked Lance Society."

"Crooked Lance Society? They're supposed to be about as close to suicidal as you can get, aren't they?"

"Not close, Captain. They are."

"What makes him think that, Matt?" Conway asked, leaning back and slowly exhaling a stream of smoke. "Are they known to be in the area?"

"No, they were thought to be in Canada under the leadership of a chief known as Straight Shooter. But, to answer your question more specifically, when Windy was at the scene of the massacre yesterday, he noticed that several of the bodies had been speared with a lance, which was unnecessary. They had already been killed by rifle fire."

Conway took a moment to think while he picked a strand of tobacco from his lip. "Does Windy have any idea how many of them there might be?"

"Somewhere between sixty and eighty, sir."

"Let's say seventy of the finest warriors the Cheyenne ever produced. And fighting in these Black Hills, which they know as well as the backs of their hands. Could get pretty messy before it's over, Matt."

Kincaid pushed his plate aside and took a sip of coffee. "I'm aware of that. They're obviously bent on victory or death, whichever comes first. Kind of tough to fight men who don't care about death but who are highly skilled in the art of killing. A rather poor place to break in a green cavalry unit, I'd say."

"From what I've heard, these cavalry troops think they're the hottest thing since the wheel was invented."

Kincaid smiled knowingly. "Yes, I know they do, and Greggory shares that same view. But they're no different from any other green outfit that hasn't come home with fifteen or twenty dead men strapped across their saddles."

"What about Greggory, Matt?" Conway asked, brushing the ash from his cigar. "How do you think he'll do, commanding under fire?"

"That's one thing you can't predict about anyone, sir, you know that as well as I do. I've seen some of the biggest, bravest bullies drop to their knees and cover their heads with their hands when the shooting starts. Then, on the other hand, a little man whom you would expect to cut and run becomes the hero of the day. Can't tell until the real heat's on. I do think, however, that he should lead his company into battle. It's been kind of rough on him, having us come in here and take over his command, even though it was entirely the right thing to do. His spirit might be bent, but I don't think it's broken, and he should have the chance to prove to his men that he is a capable officer in the field."

"And prove it he shall," Conway agreed. "He hasn't got any choice. Let's keep as close an eye on him as we can, though, because this craving for revenge over what happened to Custer could get him in a hell of a pile of trouble."

"Without a doubt." Matt started to rise, and then sank down again. "Oh, by the way. Sergeant Aikens reported in this morning at eight o'clock as he was ordered to do. He's working out there like the rest of us now. I just wanted to thank you, sir, for offering to back me in the blind like you did."

"Think nothing of it, Matt," Conway replied with a wave of his cigar. "I'll back you a hundred percent on anything you ask for, without question." He paused to stare at the wisp of smoke escaping the moist tobacco, and a sly grin crossed his lips when he looked at Kincaid again. "You remember when we first met Sergeant Aikens and I said I thought I knew him from somewhere?"

"I remember."

"Well, it finally came to me late this morning. When I was serving under General Grant during the War, I was sent by Grant to discuss with Sherman the logistical problems he might have during his March to the Sea. When I got there, a court-martial was in progress and Sherman asked me to sit in. That's why I remember it. How many commanding generals have you ever seen sit in at a sergeant's court-martial?"

Matt shook his head. "None that I can recall, sir."

"Me either. Anyway, Sherman told me a little about the man being tried. While he agreed the fellow wasn't a model soldier, he said he was one of the deadliest, most highly motivated fighting men he had ever seen. Motivated in a way that made the general think he was killing Confederates for sheer bloodlust more than for the cause of the Union. Sherman didn't give a damn about that; he was only concerned about what the man did on the battlefield."

Conway paused to lay his cigar in an ashtray and fold his hands across his flat stomach before continuing. "At any rate, the court-martial centered around this particular sergeant's having taken a Confederate prisoner. After disarming the man, he had slammed his bayonet into the Reb's chest, through his heart and out his back. Others were sickened by it and turned him in, and the sergeant was being tried for murder."

"Did he get off?"

"Hell yes. Sherman didn't think any more of the graybellies than the sergeant did, and he felt their primary purpose was to kill Confederate soldiers anyway, not take them captive. The general intervened and the sergeant got off scot-free."

"Do you remember the sergeant's name?"

Conway smiled again. "I do now. You talked with him this morning. His name was, and apparently still is, Sergeant Frank Aikens."

Kincaid whistled softly between his teeth. "And he's Gregory's right-hand man?"

"Rather have him on my right side than on my backside, Matt," the captain said with a chuckle.

Kincaid sank into thought, his mind going back to the events of the morning. He remembered the details of how the bartender had been murdered, and he was struck by the similarity of that murder to the one the captain had just related. He was so silent and so deeply engrossed in thought that he might have been alone in the room.

Conway leaned forward in his chair. "Matt? Are you all right?"

Kincaid broke from his reverie. "Oh, sorry, Captain. I was just thinking about something that happened in Deadwood last night."

"Is it worth repeating?"

"Yes, I think it is. A bartender was killed last night. Stabbed through the chest, heart, and back in a manner very similar to what you've just described. It was done with an unusually long knife, the kind not often seen on a man's hip. Unless that man happens to belong to a cavalry outfit."

Conway's brows furrowed. "You mean a saber?"

"I mean a saber, sir." Matt pushed away from the table and stood. "Excuse me, Captain, but there's something I want to check out, and the sooner the better. Thanks for the lunch."

"Aren't you going to tell me what you're looking for?" Conway asked, turning in his chair and watching Kincaid stride toward the door.

Matt stopped with his hand on the latch. "Only if I have something conclusive to tell you, sir. Right now it's nothing more than a hunch."

He found Aikens bellowing orders to the men laboring on the land-clearing detail, and the sergeant turned toward him as Kincaid approached.

"I was here at eight o'clock, Lieutenant," Aikens said after a lackadaisical salute. "Ask the CO if you don't believe me."

"I don't have to ask. I was watching the gate when you came in." Kincaid's eyes went to Aikens' narrow waist. The revolver was there, but no saber. "Where's your saber, Sergeant?"

"Don't wear a saber on work detail, Lieutenant."

"You didn't answer my question. I asked, where is your saber?"

Aikens shrugged. "Back in my room. You see, I live in the barracks like the rest of these pigs, but I do have a room to myself. Does that surprise an officer?"

"I'm entirely familiar with the configuration of an army barracks, Sergeant. Let's go have a look at it."

"Why?"

"Because I said so. Those men were doing damned well before you got here; they'll manage without you for a few minutes, I'm sure. Let's go."

As he turned, Kincaid caught a glimpse of Tipton out of the corner of his eye. The private was hooking a chain around a log, but he had been watching both men during the entire conversation and now stared at Matt with a vacant look in his eyes. And when Aikens turned to see what Kincaid was looking at, Tipton glanced away and concentrated on his work.

"That trooper Tipton is quite a worker, Sergeant," Matt said as they walked toward the outpost.

"He ain't got the brains God gave a pissant."

"God? Do you believe in God, Sergeant?"

"Yeah. And I believe in fairies, goblins, witches, and all that shit." Aikens risked a sideways glance at Kincaid. "What the hell, are you a chaplain too?"

"No, just curious, that's all."

"Curiosity killed the cat, Lieutenant. Same could happen to you."

"Is that a threat, Sergeant?"

"No. Just a fact."

Compared to the open barracks, which were sparkling clean, with blankets stretched tight across bunks, the sergeant's room was a complete shambles. Covers draped onto the floor from one side of the bed, clothes littered the room, and three or four whiskey bottles lay where they had been cast.

"Very impressive, Sergeant," Kincaid said, stepping into the small room near the doorway to the building. "Offhand, I'd say we officers are inspecting the wrong quarters."

"I really ain't had time to clean 'er up, Lieutenant. Been kind of busy."

Kincaid glanced at the empty bottles. "I can see that. Would you accept the same kind of answer from one of your privates?"

"Now look here, Lieutenant," Aikens growled. "I ain't a sergeant because I do good housework. I'm a sergeant because, when it comes time to kick ass and take names, I'm the boy that's there."

"All well and good, but I'm still going to put you on report."

"Now look here, dammit!"

"Easy, Sergeant. The stockade fits all sizes, big and little. I'll be back in one hour and I expect to see this room no less spotless than those barracks out there. And when you talk to me, you say either 'lieutenant' or 'sir'. You got that, *Sergeant*?"

Aikens' body was tense, puffed up to full height, and there was hatred in his eyes as he looked down at Kincaid, who was a shade over six feet tall. "Yes, *sir*! Lieutenant!"

"You can't bank 'em, Sergeant, so just use one at a time," Matt said, looking around the room. "Is that your saber hanging from that chair?"

"Sure as hell ain't the cook's."

"Get it and bring it to me. I want to have a look at it."

Aikens swaggered across the room, snatched up the scabbard belt, and thrust it toward Kincaid. "Army issue. Have a look for yourself," he said flatly.

Kincaid pulled the long weapon from its sheath and examined the blade closely. The metal had obviously been recently polished, and Matt could judge through experience that it had been worked over no later than that morning.

"Strange that your saber should be so much cleaner than your room, isn't it, Sergeant?"

"I fight with one, live in the other. Big difference."

"That there is," Kincaid replied, continuing to examine the shiny blade and speaking as though an unseen third party were in the room. "Strange thing about blood, especially human blood. If it isn't cleaned off right away, it will pit and corrode even the finest metal-plating work. Seems to be a lot of acid in it. But," Matt concluded, sheathing the weapon and handing it back to Aikens, "obviously there's no chance of that happening to yours."

"Ain't been no human blood on that one," Aikens replied, then reluctantly added, "sir."

"Maybe you'll have a chance to change that, Sergeant. In a day or two we'll be going after the Cheyenne who killed those miners that you didn't hear about. Then we'll see what kind of fighting man you are in the field."

99

"Just be glad you ain't a Cheyenne, Lieutenant, that's all I gotta say."

"Spare me threats you can't carry out, Sergeant. I'll be back in one hour. If this room isn't up to the standards you expect of men like Tipton, then you'll be minus at least one stripe, maybe more. Be kind of hard for you to function in this outfit as a private, wouldn't it? Now get to it."

Kincaid matched Aikens' glower and knew he was coming ever closer to pushing the sergeant to the breaking point where hatred overruled military discipline.

"Forget the salute, Sergeant," Matt said as he turned and walked away. "You've got a lot of work to do in an hour."

In exactly one hour, Kincaid stood in the open doorway of Sergeant Aikens' quarters. The floor was still wet from the scrub brush, and Aikens was bent over his cot, pulling the blanket to make it drum-tight before tucking it in.

"Your hour is up, Sergeant. Are you ready for inspection?"

Aikens turned away from his cot and stood slope-shouldered before Kincaid. "Ready as I'm ever gonna get, Lieutenant."

"Fine. But you stand at attention when being inspected. I'll overlook that sloppy uniform due to the work at hand, but don't ever let me see you like that again when I inspect your quarters, which will be on a daily basis until I leave here."

Kincaid was actually surprised that Aikens had managed to salvage what he had from the ruins. Neatly spaced, his uniforms hung on his wall locker above boots not shined but brushed clean. His footlocker stood open for inspection; his shaving gear, toothbrush, and other personal-hygiene paraphernalia were arranged in the top tray as outlined in the manual. Lower, in the larger portion of the locker, his underwear, wrinkled but folded, was stacked neatly in a corner and his socks were rolled in accordance with regulations. Overall, the room was acceptable but not perfect, the kind of quarters that would net a private only cancellation of a pass and not extra duty.

Kincaid knew he was making an overly long inspection, but that too was done intentionally. When he finally turned and stood in the doorway, he shook his head as though disappointed. "Not good, Sergeant. Not good at all. However, I am willing to overlook a few things since you are obviously more familiar with being the inspector than the inspected. Return to your detail now, and I'll be back at seven in the morning."

He pointed toward the wall locker while keeping his eyes on the sergeant's face. "Those boots look like they were shined with a stick and mud, not polish and a brush. In the morning I will expect to be able to see my reflection in them well enough to shave if I wanted to. The same goes for your brass. Are there any questions, Sergeant Aikens?"

Aikens made no attempt to disguise the hatred that he felt for the lieutenant. "Nossir," he managed through gritted teeth. "Except one thing."

"I'm listening."

"When you fuck with the bull you get the horn, sir."

"What's that supposed to mean?"

"You're the man with all the answers, Lieutenant. You figure it out."

"Fine, and while I'm doing that, you should have a little time to think as well. This afternoon we're going to start lining the well with rocks. We'll need a big strong man down at the bottom to handle the heavy stuff. Report to well detail in five minutes. And if I have to ask you to salute before I leave, you'll be confined to quarters with an armed guard on the door throughout the entire campaign against the Cheyenne. Your choice, Sergeant."

Uncontrolled rage swept through Aiken's body and his massive fists trembled by his sides. He stood stock-still, as if rigor mortis had set in.

"I'm waiting, Sergeant," Kincaid said. "You've got five seconds."

He might have been lifting a giant weight, so slowly did Aikens' hand move to his forehead. The journey took all of five seconds, and Kincaid smiled when the salute was finally completed.

"Your enthusiasm is overwhelming, Sergeant. I'll be waiting for you beside the well. Dismissed."

It was later that afternoon when Greggory approached Kincaid, who was standing with one foot propped against the edge of the well and watching the flat rocks being lowered down in rope slings.

"Good afternoon, Lieutenant," Greggory said somewhat

stiffly. "You haven't seen Sergeant Aikens by any chance, have you?"

"Afternoon to you, Lieutenant. Yes, I've seen Aikens."

"You have? When and where?"

"I'd say about thirty seconds ago. The last time I peeked over the edge there," Kincaid replied, nodding toward the well.

"What?"

"It seems the sergeant had some anger to work out, and in keeping with the old theory that physical activity soothes the troubled soul, he kind of volunteered to help line your well."

Greggory cast a hesitant look at Kincaid before edging forward to peer down into the black hole. Two big men, wearing nothing but their skivvies, worked silently in the waist-deep water, and the occasional grunts accompanying the placement of stones drifted upward.

"Sergeant Aikens? What the hell are you doing down there?"

Aikens' voice echoed hollowly up the well shaft. "Ask the good *sir* up there, Lieutenant. It's his goddamned idea, not mine."

Greggory straightened as he turned on Kincaid. "What's the meaning of this?"

"Meaning of what?"

"My best sergeant being down in that hole."

"He's keeping Private Malone, my best private, company. One of my men and one of your men. Couldn't ask for anything fairer than that."

"But your man is only a private!"

"And your man is one fuckup away from being the same, Lieutenant."

"This is an outrage, sir!" Greggory fumed. "Sergeants are supposed to be in charge of details, not man them!"

"True. Except when a lieutenant is in charge." Kincaid smiled indulgently. "I happen to be in charge of this one."

"You're pushing me, Lieutenant," Greggory said, backing away with a finger jabbing the air. "You're pushing me too damned far. We'll see what the captain has to say about this!"

Kincaid shrugged and glanced unconcernedly into the well again. "Save yourself a trip. He thinks it's a dandy arrangement."

"Oh sure. The two of you in cahoots against me, is that it?

You can do anything you want to with my men, but I can't do anything to yours?"

"Sure you can, Lieutenant," Kincaid said, bored with the entire conversation. "If you find one of my soldiers out of line, shape him up. You won't have much luck finding one, but knock yourself out. The only fuckup I've got is down in that well with your sergeant."

There was a hesitation before a distinctive Irish brogue drifted up from the bottom of the well. "You wouldn't be meanin' that now, would ya, sir?"

Kincaid chuckled. "No, Malone. You just shit too close to the house, that's all."

Turning away and heading for his office, Greggory called over his shoulder, "My day will come, Lieutenant. Mark me, my day will come."

"I'm sure it will. The day after we have a drink of clear water from this well. And not one minute before."

nine ─────────────────────

The office was dimly illuminated with pale yellow lamplight, and a feeling of tension and animosity permeated the atmosphere. Lieutenant Greggory had taken a seat behind his desk, and Captain Conway sat in a chair against one wall, while Kincaid was seated with his legs crossed against the other. In hard-eyed silence, Sergeant Aikens stood near the lieutenant's desk. Sergeant Gus Olsen leaned against the wall behind Kincaid, and Windy Mandalian stood near the window. Each man held a brandy glass in hand, and Conway raised his and swung it in salute toward the others.

"I propose a toast to a job well done. To you, Lieutenant Greggory, and the men of your command. To you, Matt, and the men of Easy Company. We've worked shoulder-to-shoulder for the last three days, and in my opinion, Outpost Thirteen is totally impregnable by anything less than overwhelming forces."

They all raised their glasses and drank. Greggory took a modest sip while Aikens swilled his down in one gulp before thumping his glass on the lieutenant's desk and continuing to stare, hot-eyed, at Kincaid. Matt watched the sergeant over the rim of his glass and nodded as the brandy touched his lips.

"And now that we have worked shoulder-to-shoulder," the captain continued, "it's time to fight shoulder-to-shoulder. To-morrow morning we move against the Cheyenne. While we've worked here, Windy has been out scouting and he's found the Cheyenne encampment. Windy? Would you care to fill the others in on what you've told me?"

"Sure, Cap'n, be glad to," Windy said, standing away from the wall and turning to face Greggory. "I figure their group numbers from seventy to seventy-five warriors. A sizable war party for any tribe of Indians, but here we're dealing with members of the Crooked Lance Society. They're the best fighters the Cheyenne have got. They take no captives and will not be taken captive themselves. Given the choice, they will fight to the death, and with twenty-four dead miners to their credit in the last four days, I reckon we can figure that they mean to win or die. Yesterday—"

"Excuse me, Mr. Mandalian," Greggory said, lifting his hand apologetically. "Just how do you know we're dealing with members of this Crooked Lance Society, or whatever you called it?"

"There is a lance with a crooked shaft that has been passed down from generation to generation. Only warriors who've counted coup in battle can belong, and then they have to be voted in by the others. The way they elect their leaders is a mite rougher than Republicans and Democrats, and a hell of a lot simpler. The candidates just go out somewhere and fight to the death.

"As I was saying earlier, yesterday I managed to get close enough to their camp to see the traditional lance stuck in the ground near where their night's fire had been. I suspected we were dealing with the Society after I had seen those miners, and now I'm plumb sure of it."

"You say you found their encampment, Mr. Mandalian," Greggory said excitedly. "Then we should have no difficulty engaging them and putting this insurrection to rest. Where are they located?"

"We'd best not put the cart before the horse here, Lieutenant," Windy replied with an indulgent smile. "Finding where they slept last night don't exactly mean the battle is over."

"Come now, Mr. Mandalian. Surely six full platoons of United States—"

"*Six* platoons, Lieutenant?" Conway asked. "Whom did you have in mind to protect the outpost?"

"Well, of course a detachment would be left behind. A couple of squads, maybe."

Conway shook his head. "I don't think so. According to Windy's estimates—which, I might add, have never been far wrong in the past—we are dealing with upwards of seventy well-armed, dedicated fighting men. Should they choose to move against the outpost while we are in the field, two squads and everyone within the walls would be almost entirely at their

105

mercy. It's accepted policy out here that at no time will there be less than one-third of the parent command within the walls for defensive purposes."

"One-third? That seems a trifle overcautious to me."

"Custer learned a little something about caution, Lieutenant," Kincaid offered. "Turned out to be his final lesson."

Greggory sat stiffly in his chair and stared at Kincaid without affection. "My troops are anxious for battle, Lieutenant Kincaid. What happened to Custer plays no small part in their feelings. Cavalry units tend to take care of their own, and we feel an obligation to settle old accounts. We hope to begin that process tomorrow morning."

"Don't you think the Cheyenne feel they have a little settling of accounts to do themselves, Lieutenant Greggory?" Kincaid asked. "There is nothing they would like more than a reenactment of the scene at Little Big Horn, and I'm sure the razing of a cavalry outpost would fit quite nicely into their plans. Captain Conway is right. We should leave at least two platoons of your outfit here to defend against attack."

"Two platoons? That's half of my command, sir! These men came here to fight, and any left behind will be damned well disappointed!"

"How disappointed would they be if they came home from the field and found nothing but a pile of ashes? With your wife and Mrs. Conway most likely raped and killed in the bargain?"

The thought sobered Greggory to a considerable degree. "All right, let's suppose you're right. Then we move with two platoons of cavalry and two platoons of mounted infantry?"

"I think you'd better go with your instincts, sir," Aikens said with a glower at the men from Easy Company. "Obviously this mounted infantry outfit ain't got any stomach for a fight."

"How many times have you gone up against the Cheyenne, Sergeant?" Conway asked without any indication of animosity.

"I've seen my share of battle, Captain," Aikens replied in his usual surly tone. "The Civil War wasn't exactly a Sunday picnic."

"No it wasn't. But the tactics used were as different as night and day when one compares the Georgia campaign to the Dakota Territory. There are no battle lines here, Sergeant. We're dealing with ambush, lightning-quick strikes by some of the world's finest horsemen, and then they are gone."

Conway smiled easily. "And as far as the lieutenant's instincts go, his first instinct had better be to listen to the voice of experience and his second instinct had damned well better be to observe military protocol. Now let's get down to business," he said, looking again at Greggory.

"Two of your platoons will stay here to defend the outpost. All of my men from Easy Company and your two remaining platoons will move out at dawn tomorrow to find and capture, or kill, the renegade Cheyenne." Conway turned once more toward Mandalian. "Windy? Give us a breakdown on what you see as the best way to accomplish that mission."

"I've been studyin' on that since I found their camp, Cap'n, and I'd be right pleased to. They're camped about four miles from the White Bluffs, where they did in those miners, at a place where the prairie kinda meanders into the hills and back out again. They're snuggled up right close to the foothills, so they can skedaddle into the Paha Sapa if they need to, or raid on the open plains, whichever suits 'em best. Now, the way I see it, two platoons should skirt the hills down on the prairie floor, while the other two move out along Eagle's Nest Pass. The outfit on the plains can jump them and send them high-tailing into the hills, where the other outfit will be waiting. If everybody does his job, we should have the Cheyenne flanked and they'll either have to surrender or eat a lead lunch, whichever one they choose. But the outfit on the plains has got to remember they aren't supposed to go chasin' after those bucks like a dog after a rabbit. Their job is to flank the Cheyenne and turn them into the hills. Both outfits will be close enough together to help each other if necessary, and one can hear the bugle calls of the other. As far as the bugle callin' goes, Cap'n, you'll have to work that out for yourself. I ain't much on music."

Conway smiled easily. "That's the first time I've ever heard an army bugler referred to as a musician, Windy. We'll use standard army bugle calls. Advance, retreat, flank left, flank right, charge, attack, and so forth. Are you and the men of your command familiar with such calls to the degree of instant reaction, Lieutenant?"

"Of course. And Sergeant Aikens here will be right by my side throughout, so there will be no chance for confusion."

"Absolutely, sir. The cavalry will do its job. Let's just hope the mounted infantry does the same."

"Were you sent to help us, or were we sent to help you, Sergeant?" Kincaid replied with a cold smile.

"Never thought we needed your help before, Lieutenant. Don't think we need it now."

Conway held up his hand, saying, "That's enough of that. The last thing we need at this point is bickering among ourselves. Lieutenant Greggory? You will take your command along the prairie route as suggested by Windy. I'll take my unit through the pass. Be alert for any kind of trickery that might lead you into an ambush, and remember, your primary goal is to turn the Cheyenne toward us and not to attempt to win the battle singlehandedly. Is that understood?"

"Understood. Remember, I've attended war-game classes myself, Captain," Greggory replied.

"That's fine, I'm sure you have. But you remember, here we're dealing with a different kind of lead than that found in classroom pencils." Conway stood and turned toward the door. "We move out at dawn tomorrow. Have your men prepared for battle."

"Yessir."

No one saw Aikens leave the compound at the midnight change of guard, nor did they see him return. And they couldn't have seen the man to whom he had spoken in the moonlight shadows beyond the treeline, because that man was as black as the shadows themselves.

There was a biting chill in the gray morning air, and the contrast between light and darkness was matched by the contrasting appearance of the two army units mounted and prepared to take to the field. The men of Easy Company, dressed in faded blue-on-blue uniforms, sat their saddles in a relaxed manner like the veterans they were, and gave no indication of excitement or anticipation. Single-shot Springfields hung from spider swivels attached to the front swells of their saddles, and each of them wore a Schofield Smith & Wesson, with its holster flap cut away for easy access. Their horses were calm and totally obedient, as if they too had seen it all before.

On the opposite side of the parade, the cavalry troopers

were dressed in their new, deep blue and brilliant yellow uniforms, and each of them wore a shiny saber scabbard hanging from his left hip. From their saddle spiders hung the newer Spencer five-shot repeaters, and there was about them an air of eagerness and a feeling of tension as they awaited orders to move out for their first combat patrol. Their mounts, as if perceiving the prevailing mood, moved with a restless shifting of weight and arching of necks against tightly held reins.

Conway and Greggory stood talking in the center of the parade, while Matt and Windy waited at the head of Easy Company's twin columns.

Windy glanced across at the cavalry unit. "They look like a Christmas present that somebody forgot to open, huh, Matt?"

Kincaid chuckled. "Yeah, Never thought about it that way, but now that you mention it, I guess they do."

"I wonder what they think they're gonna do with them giant can openers."

"Their sabers?"

"Yeah. Worthless as a drink of water to a drowning man. If you ever get close enough to a Cheyenne warrior to use one of 'em, you've got a problem that ain't gonna be real easy to solve. Hell, you can't shoot it, can't throw it, all you can do with the damned thing is to wear it. One step below ridiculous, in my book."

"I agree. Not worth a damn for anything but parades, and there aren't going to be many bands playing where we're going."

Windy nodded toward the trooper mounted on his horse just behind Aikens. "What's old Greggory doin', specializing in stupidity today?" he asked, indicating the new guidon held in the trooper's hand, its staff wedged in the socket on his right stirrup. "All that thing's gonna do is get the poor bastard holdin' it shot."

"I'm afraid so, but I hope not. You recognize that trooper?"

"Looks like Tipton."

"It is Tipton. Aikens assigned him to carry the guidon."

"That's like assigning a man to kiss a rattlesnake, ain't it?"

"Just about. I tried to talk Greggory out of even taking the thing along, but he's damned proud of it. I told him that it was intended only for show and parades, but he wouldn't change his mind. Went into all that shit about how proud cavalry outfits are, and all that."

"Hell," Windy scoffed. "They all ought to have yellow plumes in their hats, for all the good that pride's gonna do 'em. If Tipton lives through the day—which I doubt—I'll bet they'll never get him to touch that son of a bitch again."

"Strange, isn't it? Out of fifty men, Tipton is the one picked to carry a guidon into battle. And Aikens is the one who picked him?"

"Yeah, real strange. Almost as strange as rain fallin' down instead of up."

They watched the captain and the lieutenant exchange salutes before Greggory walked to his mount and vaulted into the saddle. The cavalry unit moved out ahead of Easy Company and turned left in the clearing with their horses moving at a canter, while Conway led his troops into the hills at an easy walk. The first rays of sunlight were just touching the treetops as the heavy gates to Outpost Thirteen closed and the guards resumed their appointed rounds.

Inside her quarters, Tina Greggory peeked around the edge of the shutter and felt a thrill of pride race through her heart while her husband, handsome and tall, rode at the head of his command.

Across the compound, Flora Conway performed the ritual that had become a habit when her husband left on a combat patrol. She knelt beside her bed, hands clasped before her forehead, and prayed. She preferred to remember him as the strong, gentle, and kind man she knew her husband to be; the outcome of death's game, either giving or receiving, she felt was better left to more capable hands.

Iron Crow studied the sun with a hand shielding his eyes from the intense, midday glare. "You said they were to leave at dawn?" he asked the man standing beside him. "The sun is nearly at its highest point. It should take them less than half a day to get here. They should be near us now."

"That's what Aikens told me last night," Harper replied, glancing once at the brilliant yellow sun in the hard blue sky before looking away and blinking. "He said the cavalry would be coming by way of the prairie, the same way the miners came, and that Easy Company would be working their way

110

through the Paha Sapa from Eagle's Nest Pass on the eastern side."

"And they believe they can close me in a trap?"

"That's what they're thinkin'."

Iron Crow smiled. "Perhaps they might have; it is a good plan. But they won't. I am glad it is the cavalry whom we shall defeat first, and once they are gone, it is only this Easy Company that will be left to destroy. And then we will raid their outpost and the Paha Sapa will be ours to hold and control once again."

"That's the plan," Harper replied. "Frank will be riding beside the lieutenant and just ahead of the trooper carrying the guidon. According to Aikens, the man with the guidon should be your first target."

"He will be. I have told my warriors and they know what your sergeant friend looks like. He will be safe. My men are moving to their places now, and you should do the same. You can see what happens from where you will be hidden in the foothills with your valuable instrument. We go now. The second Battle of the Greasy Grass is about to begin."

The chill of dawn had rapidly given way to the blistering heat of a new day, and on the great expanse of prairie with no shade available, the cavalry unit moved forward at a reduced pace. Traces of sweat glistened across their mounts' chests, while the troopers occasionally mopped their brows with the backward swipe of a sleeve. Their excitement at the prospect of combat had not diminished; they had merely settled into the routine of a long and boring ride. But when the cream-colored rise of chalky bluffs passed off to the right, a murmur passed along the column and Greggory turned to Aikens.

"Is that the White Bluffs, Sergeant?" he asked, having never been that far from the outpost before.

"Yup. Sure is, Lieutenant," Aikens replied with eyes searching the vast expanse of grass and rolling swells before them. "Won't be long now."

"Good. Pass the word back for a weapons check and for all eyes to be on the alert."

"Done, sir," Aikens said, turning in his saddle and speaking to the corporal riding to his left rear. His eyes passed across Tipton, dutifully holding the guidon, which hung limply in the absence of breeze, and Aikens smiled at the thought of what was to come. "Corporal Goldsmith, pass word along for a weapons check. We've got less than an hour to go now."

"Right, Sarge. Weapons check! Breech and muzzle! One round locked home and four in the door!"

The metallic sound of rifle chambers being opened and then clicked shut rose above the gentle creaking of saddle leather and the soft jingle of bit chains. Greggory straightened to his full height, loosened his revolver in its holster, then rode with the reins in one hand while the palm of the other rested on his thigh. There was an unmistakable look of pride on the young officer's face, and his chest swelled with the emotion of the moment. It had finally come, that great day when he would lead his men to glorious victory.

Now they were rounding the final jutting neck of land and turning into the encroaching grassland between the solitary butte and the Black Hills themselves. Aikens suddenly shot up his hand, stopping the column.

"Look there, sir! Off to the right."

Greggory's head snapped in the direction indicated by the sergeant's gloved hand. Nearly two hundred yards distant, fifteen Indians scrambled for their ponies as if they had been caught by surprise. It appeared as if they were having some difficulty mounting their skittish horses.

"Are those Cheyenne, Sergeant?" Greggory asked, barely able to control the excitement in his voice.

"Yes they are, sir! Looks like we jumped 'em at their camp."

"But there couldn't be more than fifteen or twenty of them. I thought that scout said there would be seventy or better."

"Beats me, sir. Maybe he made a mistake. Don't matter. We came here to teach them featherheads a lesson, and I—"

Aikens stopped speaking abruptly, and the call of a solitary bugle wafted across the plains. It seemed to originate somewhere in the foothills, and the piercing notes it was sending were those of an army unit assembling for attack. And then a second call went forth, this time the urgent and commanding signal given for the charge into battle.

The Indians were mounted and disappearing over the distant swell, and Greggory could not stand to lose them. "Sergeant! I think Kincaid has closed with the enemy. I'm sure that was his bugler! I don't want that mounted infantry outfit winning the day! Have Trooper Sloan sound the charge!"

"Right, sir!" Aikens said, turning around in his saddle. "Sloan! Sound the charge!"

The call of the cavalry bugle identically matched that of the one yet drifting down from the foothills, and the horses were instantly pressed to a dead run. The Cheyenne maintained their distance, neither gaining nor falling back as they raced toward the inlet of green arching into the hills at an angle, three hundred yards away to the right.

"I think we're gaining on them, Sergeant!" Greggory yelled.

Aikens didn't respond, but he smiled inwardly at the jubilation in the officer's voice.

Kincaid and Windy looked up at the same time. The two platoons had dismounted and were spread out in an L-shaped firing line, with their horses held by handlers two hundred yards to the rear. Captain Conway was moving among his soldiers to make certain of a full field of fire.

"Now what the hell is that?" Windy asked, cocking his head toward the sound of the first bugle call.

"That's assembly, Windy. Greggory must—"

Then came the first strident notes of the call to charge. "What the hell is he doing?" Matt asked.

"Fuckin' up mostly, I'd say."

Conway was hurrying toward them when the responding call to charge split the air, but this time it came from a different angle, more distant and lacking echo.

"What do you make of it, Matt? That was two different bugles, wasn't it?" Conway asked.

"Sounded like it to me, sir. How 'bout you, Windy?"

"It was either two different bugles, or the guy blowin' it has got the fastest goddamned horse in the territory. If I remember right, Greggory was supposed to flank the Cheyenne and turn them into this pass, not charge the sonsabitches like a bull in a punkin patch."

"Yeah, he was," Kincaid responded hurriedly. "If he had turned them toward us, we should be hearing some hoofbeats by now. Maybe he missed the entrance."

"I don't think so, Matt. There's a box canyon about two ridges over. If he's fallen for a Cheyenne trap like the fool he is, they'll lead him in there sure as hell."

"Your horse is the only one left up here, Windy! Bust on

113

over there and see what the hell's going on. If we hear rifle fire, we'll mount up and ride down the pass to the plains, then cut toward the sound!"

"Good as gone, Matt," Windy said, running toward his horse and leaping onto the saddle. "Goddamned greenhorns anyway!" he snarled as he raced away, sending dirt and chunks of rock flying from his horse's hooves.

To Greggory, the Cheyenne seemed to be losing ground, and he was certain they could catch them within the next few hundred yards, and when they veered to the right he had no doubt that the Indians would soon be within rifle range. He made a motion with his hand and the two columns split apart to form a running firing line. Without hesitation they pounded into the narrow canyon. When they did, those supposedly tired Indian ponies put on a sudden burst of speed and quickly outdistanced the weary army mounts.

When Mandalian's horse plunged down the first ridge, crossed a narrow swale, and galloped up the second, the scout could see immediately what was happening. Two surprised warriors leaped up from where they were hidden behind the rocks and turned their rifles toward the sound of hoofbeats coming up from the rear. Snatching his revolver from its holster, Windy angled his horse straight at the two Cheyenne. The braves scrambled to avoid being run over, and Windy's first shot slammed into one Indian's chest while he whipped the revolver over the horse's neck and squeezed off another quick round. The second warrior went down with a gurgling scream, and by that time Windy was moving down again toward the canyon floor, not a hundred yards away. Rifle fire exploded all around him in a deafening crescendo, and he screamed toward the cavalry unit, whose horses were now breaking stride, with several going down and riders spilling from saddles.

"Go back, you fuckin' idiots!"

Startled, Greggory pulled in his mount and watched Windy break clear of the rocks and boulders to his left and pound toward them across the neck of grass. The completely stunned men of his command hadn't fired a shot while a withering barrage of fire rained down upon them from the surrounding ridges. More horses went down, and screams of pain filled the air. Directionless riders milled about in the confusion, and

114

finally the besieged cavalry unit began returning sporadic fire at unseen targets.

"Sound the retreat, you goddamned idiot!" Windy yelled as he reached the head of the column. "You've ridden into an ambush! Another hundred yards and your entire command will be wiped out!"

Greggory whirled his rearing horse. "Sergeant! Sound the retreat!"

"We can take 'em, sir!" Aikens replied with a frantic look toward the nearest ridge. "We have to charge, not retreat!"

"Like hell you do!" Windy snarled, passing by the sergeant and grabbing the blank-eyed, terrified bugler by the shoulder. "Boy, you sound retreat and blow on that son of a bitch like you've never blown before!"

"Yessir!"

The sound of the bugle call clashed with the roar of exploding weapons and the line of cavalry, ragged and broken, turned to race toward the open plains behind them. Off to his left, Windy saw a dazed young soldier struggle to his feet while groping in the tall grass for the guidon. Tipton's horse had been killed in the first volley fired by the Cheyenne, and now there was a glazed look in his eyes from the shock of the fall.

"Leave that bastard where it is!" Windy shouted, reining his horse toward Tipton and jerking a foot free from his right stirrup. "Get up behind me and let's get the hell out of here!"

Tipton's hand had closed over the guidon and he looked up at Mandalian. "But without colors, sir, we—"

"Fuck your colors! Get up here and do it now!"

Reluctantly, Tipton let the guidon fall and scrambled to swing up behind Windy's saddle. Mandalian punished the horse's flanks with his heels, and they raced away behind the cavalry unit as heavy fire continued to pour down on them from both sides.

Immediately assessing the situation, Kincaid split his two platoons at the entrance to the canyon and they leaped from their saddles to advance along the pair of ridges, taking advantage of the cover and snap-firing at targets of opportunity.

Greggory galloped up to Kincaid; the cavalry officer's face was ashen with shock. "We were ambushed, Lieutenant!"

"No fooling?" Kincaid replied, firing his revolver at a muz-

115

zle flash high up in the rocks. "Dismount your troops and have them advance on foot!"

"We're cavalry, man!" Greggory protested. "We're trained to fight on horseback!"

"You're infantry now, Lieutenant! Get off that damned horse and help us bail you out of this mess!"

"Sergeant Aikens!"

"Forget him and the chain of command. You take care of it!"

Bewildered now, Greggory shouted the necessary commands to the troops milling about him, and they jumped down to join Easy Company in the fierce battle for the ridges. The Cheyenne retreated before them, and in ten minutes all return fire ceased and the warriors were gone, slipping through the timber to mount ponies hidden well beyond the treeline. An eerie silence closed over the canyon, where blue-and-yellow uniforms, lying crumpled in the grass, were interspersed with dead and dying horses.

A mocking laugh drifted down from the timber, followed by the taunting words, "Hear me, Blue Sleeves! You have been beaten by Iron Crow, leader of the Cheyenne! You are no match for us and you all will die! Are you listening, Mandalian, the one called the Snake? You were lucky today, but you will not be so lucky next time we meet! Your scalp will hang from my coup belt!"

The words echoed through the canyon. Then there was silence and the Cheyenne were gone.

ten

Lieutenant Greggory watched the lifeless remains of the men who had trusted his judgment being loaded upon the backs of the horses that had carried them into battle. There were eight of them, and with only four spare horses left alive, the corpses had to be doubled up, and that seemed ignominious in itself. Ten more wounded either sat or lay in the grass while temporary bandages were applied. Greggory couldn't take his eyes off the bloodstains spreading across the shiny new uniforms of which the men had once been so proud.

"Eight dead and ten wounded," the lieutenant said softly. "I honestly feel I should be among the dead ones."

"You would have been, Lieutenant," Conway replied, laying a hand gently on the young officer's shoulder, "if Windy hadn't risked his life to stop you. In another thirty seconds you would have been far enough into this valley to be brought under fire from both the front and the rear. Then it would have been over before Easy Company could do anything to help you, and Iron Crow would have had another Little Big Horn."

Rather than soothing the lieutenant's mind, Conway's words seemed to irritate him. "I accept full responsibility for what happened today, Captain, but I do not accept full blame. Why did your bugler sound the call to charge? Part of our battle plan was to react to each other's signals."

Easy Company's bugler, Red McBride, was standing nearby, and Conway called to him. "Corporal? Come here for a moment, please."

The young ex-Confederate soldier stepped forward smartly and presented himself to his captain. "Yessir?"

"How many times have you blown that bugle of yours today?"

"None, sir."

"What do you mean, none, soldier?" Greggory snapped. "I distinctly heard two calls. One for assembly and the other for the charge."

McBride turned toward the lieutenant, saying, "I'm sorry, sir, but you didn't hear any calls from my bugle. I heard those calls too, sir, but someone else blew them."

Greggory's irritation turned to confusion as he looked at Conway. "If he didn't give those signals, then who the hell did?"

"That is a question of concern to all of us, Lieutenant. Unfortunately, none of us has the answer. We can only assume that someone in league with the Cheyenne has complete knowledge of army signals and the skills necessary to play them on a bugle."

"But why? Why would any white man want to help destroy two platoons of United States Cavalry?"

"Is it necessary that he be white, Lieutenant? Many Crow and Delaware have worked with the army in the past, and there's no reason why any of them couldn't have learned to use a bugle. Not to mention numerous deserters during and after the Civil War, some of them probably buglers."

"It still doesn't make any sense to me," Greggory replied weakly, looking again at the bodies.

"The only thing consistent about fighting the Cheyenne is that nothing ever makes sense," Conway said, watching the lieutenant closely. "And another thing that doesn't make any sense is why you elected to charge the enemy instead of turning their flank, as per our battle plan."

"There wasn't any flank to turn, Captain. I expected to engage their main force, but instead we encountered only fifteen or so."

"And they were decoys, the classic entrapment device of the Cheyenne. Or didn't they teach you that in those war-games classes you took at West Point?"

There was a hurt look in Greggory's eyes as his head reluctantly turned toward Conway. "No they didn't, sir. I was trained to fight in honorable combat."

"This *is* honorable combat, Lieutenant. At least from the Indians' point of view, which is what we're dealing with here. Without pressing you for details, it's my guess that you wanted a victory, which you were afraid Easy Company might steal

118

from you. In accordance with that theory, when you heard that bogus call to charge, you issued your own signal and we are now witnessing the end result." Conway nodded toward the last of the bodies now being lifted from the ground. "If you had been thinking properly, you never would have ridden past the entrance to Eagle's Nest Pass, where you knew my forces were deployed."

"I'm aware of that now, sir, and I am very sorry."

"Sorry only applies to army grub, Lieutenant. It won't make dead men walk again."

Conway realized he was being hard on Greggory, but he also knew that there was a lesson to be learned from the events of the day and a point to be driven home. He noticed the glistening film of tears in the lieutenant's eyes, but he forced himself to ignore them.

"Under other circumstances," the captain continued, "I would personally see that you were removed from command and held accountable for gross violation of orders. However, we have to deal with the situation at hand. In any further campaigns, until this conflict with Iron Crow is settled, our two units will be interspersed with yours; you'll take one platoon of my soldiers and I'll take one of yours. Windy Mandalian will ride with you, and Lieutenant Kincaid with me. Normally I would put Matt in charge of your entire unit, but I feel you need a chance to prove yourself and demonstrate both to yourself and your men that you are a competent officer in the field. Easy Company will be gone from here shortly, and then all command decisions will be entirely up to you. I think you have learned today what the consequences of those decisions might be."

Greggory blinked his eyes and brushed his cheek with the back of a hand. "I understand your feelings, sir, and I accept your decision. You are right, I was anxious for a victory in this battle. Now I will be content with a victory in this war."

"That's the attitude I had hoped for."

"Will we be going after the Cheyenne this afternoon?"

"No. We are going to take your dead and wounded home. Those of your wounded who are able to serve will trade places with the guard detachment, and the healthy ones will join in the field campaign. According to our body count, we killed six Cheyenne today, so our numbers remain roughly even, which is important. Iron Crow has the advantage because he knows what he's going to do, while we can only guess. We have to take that advantage away from him if we are to win this thing with minimal losses on our side."

"How are we going to do that, sir?"

Sergeant Aikens stopped near them and knelt down as though looking for something in the grass, but his head was cocked as though he were listening, like a robin searching for a worm in the ground.

"We'll discuss that later, Lieutenant," Conway replied with a glance at Aikens. "But for now let's get your wounded back to the outpost and proper medical attention."

Trooper Tipton stood some distance away with the guidon in his hand. "Excuse me, sir?" he called to the lieutenant. "I've found our colors, sir. We didn't lose them to the enemy."

Greggory offered a weary smile. "Thank you, Trooper, but I'm afraid we did, symbolically at least. They were abandoned on the field of combat. We won't be bringing them with us on future patrols, and they will never be displayed again until we have defeated Iron Crow."

"We have the dead and wounded loaded, Captain," Kincaid said as he helped the last injured man into the saddle. "The troops are mounted and prepared to move out."

"Very good, Lieutenant," Conway returned. "Let's go, then. It's going to be a long ride home."

The outpost was bathed in the pink glow of sunset when the combined company crossed the wide clearing that now surrounded the log walls. Even without the difference in uniforms, one could easily have differentiated the men of one outfit from those of the other. The soldiers of Easy Company rode in as they had ridden out, showing no outward emotion and appearing to have just returned from a routine escort patrol.

On the other hand, the cavalry troopers slouched in their saddles and defeat was written on their faces while the boots of eight of their comrades bobbed silently in rhythm with the movement of horses' hooves. Gone was the exhilaration of anticipated victory, and there was the look about them of beaten stepchildren.

When the columns moved through the main gates, Flora Conway's hand stopped on the crank above the well and she

120

looked first at the lead rider to make sure her husband had returned, then ran toward Tina Greggory's quarters with skirts clutched about her thighs.

"Tina?" she called, rapping on the door. "We've got some wounded men out here! Please come and give me a hand!"

The door flew open and Tina rushed out to stand by Flora. There was a frantic look in her eyes as she searched out the troops riding slowly by, and then relief flooded her face when she found Lieutenant Greggory at the head of his unit. She offered a tiny wave, but Greggory didn't look at her and his face was cold, like chiseled stone.

"Get whatever containers you have, Tina, anything that will hold water," Flora said, touching the small of the young woman's back. "Fill them and bring them to the dispensary. We'll be needed there to help clean and bind the wounds."

Tina hesitated momentarily before returning to her quarters, while Flora ran toward the makeshift room that was used primarily for the dispensing of pills and minor medicines. Those troopers who couldn't walk were carried into the building, and those who could walked from their mounts with grimaces of silent pain.

Flora set immediately to stripping blood-soaked uniforms away, moving from man to man to determine the most serious injuries. When Tina entered, carrying a cauldron of water, Flora's hands were probing a young trooper's thigh; a large chunk of muscle had been blown away. The wound hung open like a gaping red yawn, with bits of uniform imbedded in the mutilated flesh. Flora glanced quickly over her shoulder.

"Let's start with him, Tina," she said. "Set that water down here on the table and then get me some clean cloths."

Tina stood transfixed, staring at the ugliness, clutching the cauldron before her like a forgotten watermelon.

Flora watched her and knew what was going through her mind; she remembered her first such experience. "Put the water down here, Tina," she repeated gently.

Still Tina did not comply, and her eyes were filled with horror while her head turned slowly from side to side. Her mouth closed as if to speak, but she only swallowed dryly and no words came forth.

"This man is badly hurt, Tina. He needs help and he needs

help now," Flora said more firmly. "If you can't contribute, then make room for someone who can."

Flora's words might as well not have been said, because the young woman appeared to have been stricken deaf as well as dumb. Stepping forward, Flora took the cauldron from Tina's hands, but the younger woman seemed not to notice. Then she turned and ran from the room, nearly colliding with the two cooks now stepping through the doorway to aid with the medical attention.

Two hours later, when all the wounded had been cared for, Flora walked slowly across the parade in the direction of Tina Greggory's darkened quarters. There was blood on the front of her dress and she was exhausted from urgency and strain, but her weariness was put aside through concern for the lieutenant's lady. Without knocking, Flora walked into the living room and heard sobbing coming from the bedroom. After finding a match, she lit a lamp and moved toward the rear of the quarters, the yellow lamp globe carving a circular hole in the darkness.

"Who is it?" a weak, strained voice called from within.

"It's me. Flora."

"Go away! I don't want to talk to anybody!"

"You haven't got any choice, Tina. I'm here and you are going to talk to me."

The young woman was stretched across the bed with her face buried in a pillow. Flora placed the lamp on a nightstand before sitting down on the edge of the bed. With motherly tenderness, she gently rubbed Tina's shoulders and trailed her fingers through her hair.

"You have beautiful hair, Tina," Flora said softly.

Tina shook her head. "No I don't. Nothing about me is beautiful."

"You're wrong. You're a beautiful person in a way that has nothing to do with appearance."

"No I'm not. I'm an ugly weakling."

"You mean because of what happened tonight?"

"Yes!"

"That wasn't weakness. That was shock. Have you ever seen a man who had been shot before?"

There was a moment's hesitation. "N-no."

122

"It's a terrible thing. I reacted almost the same way as you did when I first saw it."

Now Tina rolled over and sat upright. "You did? I can't believe that. You were so . . . so strong and unaffected by it all."

"It hasn't always been that way," Flora said with a smile. "I had to be slapped to bring me out of it the first time."

"Who slapped you?"

"The strongest, bravest woman I've ever known. Maggie Cohen, Sergeant Cohen's wife. I'll admit it was a little worse than what you saw tonight, but my reaction was the same. A young soldier had been shot in the stomach and Maggie was trying to stop the bleeding with a compression bandage when I came into the room. She asked for another bandage and I just stood there staring, just like you did tonight, as if I were in a trance or something, which I guess I was. Maggie asked me a second time but I didn't respond. That's when she slapped me and told me either to go to work or get out. I guess the slap did some good because I snapped out of it." Flora's voice became distant with the memory relived. "The soldier died, but he died with his head in my hands and in all the comfort we could give him."

Tina looked down and toyed with the edge of the bedspread. "It's all so terrible, Flora. I've seen animals shot and killed, and even though I hated it, I could deal with it. But tonight, to see a human being mutilated the way that poor man was, by another human being no less, was more than I could take. Something snapped in me and all I could see was Steven lying there. I don't want him to die or be hurt, and suddenly I hated the army and everything it stands for." She brushed the tears from her cheeks and looked at Flora. "Can you understand that?"

Flora nodded and the weak smile returned. "Certainly I can. I've experienced that feeling myself. Being an army wife isn't easy, especially when your husband is in command. Every time he rides out through that front gate you have to be prepared never to see him again. Alive, that is. But you have to understand that his is the business of killing in the defense of the rights and property of others. He owns nothing and is often despised, but it's the life he chose and no one forced him to make that decision."

123

Flora paused to pat Tina's thigh gently. "And no one forced us to marry them. We made that choice knowing they were soldiers and what the possible consequences might be. And maybe that's the reason we love them more than other women might their husbands. Because we know we could lose them any day and can do nothing but pray for their safe return. Tomorrow will be another patrol, another journey into combat, and we must be strong in the belief that they will not be the ones to get hit. And when they come home, we must be prepared to help the wives of those men who have not been so fortunate, because someday we might need the help ourselves."

Tina suddenly reached out and hugged the captain's wife, with her damp cheek pressing against Flora's. "I love you, Flora. Thank you for coming to talk to me. I'll be all right now, and I think I'll be able to handle it better next time."

"I'm sure you will, but let's hope the futile hope that there won't be a next time."

Tina nodded and watched in silence as Flora left the room.

Lieutenant Kincaid and Windy Mandalian were walking toward Greggory's office, but they stopped when they noticed a single lamp burning in the stable and saw a soldier grooming his mount with concentrated strokes.

"What are you doing here this late at night, Tipton?" Kincaid asked, walking up to lay a hand on the horse's flank.

Tipton glanced up, then back to the brush. "Grooming a new mount, sir. Mine got shot today."

"I know that. Why do you think you were chosen to carry the guidon into battle?"

"Don't know, sir. Somebody has to do it, I guess."

"No they don't. That's like painting a bulls-eye across your chest and turning it toward the enemy."

"I know that, sir," Tipton replied in a soft voice. "But Sergeant Aikens ordered me to do it and I didn't have any choice."

Kincaid studied the young trooper closely. "Why do you think the sergeant wants to see you killed?"

A troubled look crossed Tipton's face, and the first hint of a twitch began at the corner of his mouth. "I don't have any idea, sir."

"You don't have any idea, Trooper, or is it just something you can't or don't want to talk about?"

"Maybe both, Lieutenant."

"Is Aikens threatening you in some way? If he is, tell me about it and I'll put a stop to whatever he's doing."

Tipton glanced nervously around the stable and saw Windy standing in the door. "I got nothin' to say, Lieutenant, except thanks to Mr. Mandalian there for saving my life."

"No thanks needed, Tipton," Windy replied, moving inside. "You showed a lot of grit out there today. Not many men would have done what you did."

"And there aren't any that would have done what you did. You risked your life to save ours."

"That's part of the bargain, Tipton," Windy replied, breaking off a chew of tobacco before offering the cut to the young man. "Care for a chaw?"

"No thanks, sir," Tipton said with a nervous laugh. "Never touch the stuff."

Windy shrugged and stuffed the plug into a breast pocket, saying, "Should try it sometime. Keeps the worms down."

"Tipton," Kincaid began again, circling the horse, "I know something is going on between you and Sergeant Aikens. Now, I can't order you to tell me, but I would if I could. Somebody tipped Iron Crow and his bugler off about today's mission, and that same scoundrel could very well get your entire outfit killed if he isn't stopped. If you know anything, you owe it to your buddies to tell me."

The twitching increased and Tipton worked in silence while the other two men watched him. "Like I said, sir," he muttered finally, "I don't know anything. I just want to keep my nose clean, finish this hitch, and get out of the army."

"All right, however you want it, but the offer I made before still stands. If you ever want to talk, I'm ready to listen. Let's go, Windy. The captain is waiting for us."

When they left the stable, they didn't hear the rustling movement in the hay loft, nor did they see Sergeant Aikens climb down the ladder with a revolver in his hand.

"You done good, kid," he said as he walked past Tipton while holstering the revolver. "Like I said, you're going to be watched all the time and you'll be as dead as a turd in a milk bucket if you even so much as *look* like you're going to talk."

125

"I haven't said anything, Sergeant," Tipton replied almost under his breath.

"Just see you keep it that way, Trooper. It's a little early in life for you to suddenly go bald."

Tipton watched the sergeant swagger from the stable, then slumped onto a stool and stared at the hay-strewn floor beneath his boots.

"Why isn't Sergeant Aikens here, Captain?" Greggory asked as he looked about the room at Kincaid and Mandalian. "He should know about the plans for tomorrow's action the same as the rest of us."

"I'm not sure about that, Lieutenant. We have reason to believe that the sergeant isn't all you think he might be."

"What do you mean by that?"

Conway turned toward Mandalian. "Windy?"

The tall scout finished pruning a fingernail with the big knife in his right hand, and sheathed the weapon as he turned. "Do you remember what the sergeant said when I headed you off in that box canyon?"

Greggory searched his mind. "No," he said with a shake of his head. "There was so much confusion that I can't remember much of anything."

"I'll refresh your memory, then. When I told you to sound the retreat he advised you to continue the charge. Ain't that a fact?"

"Yeah, I guess so. Like I said, with all that incoming fire and my men going down all around me, I don't remember a hell of a lot of conversation."

"It's a fact, trust me. Now why would he want you to continue on into a trap that would mean the virtual annihilation of your command?"

Greggory shrugged and looked up at the scout with a hint of disdain. "Beats me, but I don't believe he did. He was just as confused as I was."

"I don't think so. The captain here knows him from the Civil War, and it ain't a particularly fond memory. Aikens had been under fire numerous times with General Sherman, and he wouldn't lose his head like some tenderfoot—no offense intended, of course."

Whether intended or not, offense was taken by the lieutenant. "I resent that, sir. I made a mistake, but that won't happen again."

"Resent it all you want, Lieutenant," Windy replied, resting a foot on the lower rung of a chair, "but facts are facts. At dawn tomorrow morning there will be eight fresh graves outside the walls of this outpost. I believe that if Aikens has his way, that will be just the beginning." Mandalian smiled as he continued. "That's why we're not going to let him have his way."

"Just what exactly are you people accusing my best sergeant of, anyway? There is not a seditious bone in his body." Greggory glared at each of the three men in turn, and there was no doubt that he was angry. "I have accepted the mistakes I made today and your attendant criticism, but I do not intend to tolerate your spurious remarks about my senior noncom. I am a fairly competent judge of character, and while Sergeant Aikens is a little rough at times, he is totally dedicated to our purpose here. As a matter of fact he volunteered for this assignment, just for your information."

"That's marvelous," Kincaid replied dryly. "We consider ourselves duly informed. That still doesn't change the situation. Windy, the captain, and I had a little talk before we came here tonight, and we would like to present an idea to you. We think you have a collaborator in your midst, and if you agree with our proposal and cooperate fully, we should be able to smoke him out."

"I'm listening," Greggory replied firmly.

Kincaid nodded. "That's good, because we feel your entire command is at stake. The Cheyenne have obviously been tipped off on two different occasions, first with the miners, and second, before your unfortunate battle with them today. Now we're not accusing anybody, but it's imperative that we find out who stands to gain the most from the annihilation of your command.

"At any rate, tomorrow we move against the Cheyenne again, but this time with a different set of rules. When our bugler sounds the call for a move to the left flank, it will mean the right flank in actuality. When he blows retreat, it will mean charge. When he blows the call for 'enemy in sight,' it will mean 'no contact made.' In short, every signal given will mean just the opposite. Obviously they have someone who understands the calls, and he will relay their meanings to Iron Crow.

Further, if any other bugle calls are heard in another attempt to confuse us, they will have no effect because our people will react totally differently from what the Cheyenne expect. If they blow the call to charge, we should retreat, and so forth."

"This is preposterous!"

"Maybe so, but it will work if those in command understand exactly what they are supposed to do. Our forces were confused today with artificial calls, and we intend to turn the tables on them. But since we feel we have cause to suspect Sergeant Aikens' loyalty to our cause, you are not to tell him of this plan."

As was his habit, Greggory picked up a pencil and examined it while he thought. "I can give you my complete personal assurance, Lieutenant Kincaid, that no one in my command, with particular emphasis on Sergeant Aikens, is serving as a spy in our midst. I repeat, *no one*. Anything that has happened in the past has been purely circumstantial, not intentional." Greggory looked up with a smug look of defiance. "Now, if *I* can be made privy to classified information, what has your brain trust of three come up with in terms of a method of operation for tomorrow?"

"I'll answer that, Matt," Conway broke in with a wave of his hand. "In Windy's judgment, the Cheyenne go for the unique but never the obvious. That is to say, they will probably use the bugle trick again, but not the attempt to lure any of our forces into a trap similar to the one you experienced today. They are confident and cocky now, due to the victory they feel they have under their belts, and they will be more prone to engage in a face-to-face conflict. Again, in Windy's learned opinion, Iron Crow will quit his encampment on the plains now that we know where it is, and move into Whitefish Valley, deep in the Paha Sapa and located on Whitefish Creek. It is the homesite of his tribal ancestors and the place where he would go to celebrate a victory over the United States Cavalry. We will jump him there tomorrow, but we will attack exactly at dusk, when he least suspects it. You are to take your troops into the valley via the creek, and I will cut off their escape and we will close on them from the flanks. Since we have farther to ride than you do, we will leave at ten o'clock in the morning and you leave exactly at noon. Again, remember the bugle signals when we attack precisely at five o'clock. You do exactly

128

the opposite of what the call says you should do. Is that understood?"

Greggory smiled coldly. "While I may not be a military genius like the three of you, Captain, I am not a total dunce. I'll remember what the signals mean."

"Good. As I said earlier today, Windy will be with you just in case of any problems. Let's all get some sleep now and be ready to move out tomorrow."

Greggory said good night to the men from Easy Company and waited behind his desk for more than ten minutes after the trio had gone. Then he rose and hurriedly went into the orderly room and called the sergeant of the guard.

"Sergeant!"

"Yessir," the acting buck sergeant replied as he scrambled from behind the desk in the guardroom. "You called me?"

"I certainly did. Go find Sergeant Aikens and bring him here immediately."

"Yessir!" the sergeant replied, pulling on his hat and trotting toward the door.

Greggory was drumming his fingers on his desktop and staring into space with an absentminded grin on his face when he heard the familiar rapping on his door. "Come in, Sergeant. Come in."

Aikens stepped inside, closed the door, and saluted with what, to him, was military crispness. "You sent for me, sir?"

"Yes, yes I did, Sergeant. Have a seat if you like."

Aikens drew up a chair and sat down with a quizzical look at his commanding officer. "What's on your mind, sir?"

"What's on my mind? The role one must play when dealing with supercilious oafs." Now he looked directly at Aikens. "Have you ever supported, initiated, or intended any harm to this command?"

Aikens looked shocked. "Why, no, sir. I've always tried to serve you and this man's army the best I know how, sir."

Greggory pursed his lips and nodded. "I personally have never doubted that, Sergeant. But for reasons I cannot specify, it was necessary for me to make that inquiry of you. It seems that Kincaid, Conway, and Mandalian share another view, but I think they are using you to make a spectacle of me."

"In what way, sir?"

"To undermine my confidence in my command. To make

me subservient to them, as they already have with their ridiculous alterations around here, and to put me in a position where I will appear incompetent. They seem to have some innate desire to show me up and thereby, I assume, have me relieved of my command, to be replaced by some officer of the mounted infantry. Well, I'm not going for it."

"As well you shouldn't, sir."

"I knew you would see it my way," Greggory said, nodding. "But we'll have to go along with them until this campaign is over. But you, as my most trusted advisor, should be informed of the circumstances as they stand. Tomorrow we move against the Cheyenne again, and God praise the day when this is over and that damned Easy Company exits our region and returns to purgatory, where it belongs."

"I agree, sir. We don't need no outside help."

"I'm glad to hear that, Sergeant, and that's why I called you here tonight, to talk with someone who is just as sick of this as I am. Let me tell you about their latest harebrained scheme. We are going to use false bugle calls tomorrow. Everything will be exactly the opposite of what it is supposed to mean. We are to attack the Cheyenne in Whitefish Valley, wherever that is, at dusk, at precisely five o'clock as a matter of fact, instead of during daylight, and I am to lead my unit into battle through the valley while Easy Company attacks from the hills to the rear. I'm having a hard time trying to figure out whether all this is merely ridiculous or just plain stupid. Why don't we find the Cheyenne, close with them in combat, defeat them as we both know we can, and be done with it?"

The smile crossing Aikens' face was something closer to relief than pleasure. "I don't know, sir. But like you said, we'll have to go along with it."

"Yes, I suppose so." Greggory sighed. "These have been the longest four goddamn days of my life." He glanced quizzically at Aikens and said, "I just can't figure it out."

"Figure out what, Lieutenant?"

"Why they have chosen you as the one person on this post not to be trusted."

Now Aikens smiled more broadly, and the gap between his yellow front teeth was a strip of blackness in the dim lamplight. "I guess it's 'cause I bucked 'em from the beginning. Didn't kiss their ass, and told 'em a cavalry outfit didn't need no help from the mounted infantry."

Greggory thought about Aikens' response and nodded. "Yes, that sounds logical. But what they don't seem to realize is that by attempting to undermine my trust in you, they are only weakening the overall strength of this command. You and I have to work together for a long time after they're gone, and that's why we must have absolute faith in each other."

"I agree, sir. You just listen to old Sergeant Aikens when we're in the field and away from the others. I'd never let you down."

"Thank you, Sergeant. I'll just have to go along with all this hocus-pocus about mixed-up bugle calls and the rest for the time being. My day will come."

Standing, Aikens moved to the doorway and turned with his hand on the latch. "It certainly will, Lieutenant. Maybe even sooner than you suspect. 'Night."

Long after Aikens had gone, Greggory sat in his office and stared silently into the gloom. For the first time in his married life, he dreaded going home to his wife. Failure was the last thing he ever wanted to admit to Tina, and he knew deep in his heart that he had failed miserably that day. He was glad for the conversation with Aikens because he had needed to feel he was in command, and the sergeant's expression of displeasure with the officers of Easy Company had given him a brief respite from his mental torment. But he knew he had to go to his quarters sometime, and after nearly an hour he blew out the lamp and trudged wearily homeward.

Even if he had been looking, Greggory wouldn't have seen the tall man in buckskin clothing who had been standing in the night shadows and watching the lieutenant's office. Aikens hadn't seen the man either, and when he slipped away from the post for his midnight rendezvous, he was absolutely confident of total secrecy.

eleven

Iron Crow's chest swelled with pride as he looked around the lush valley, whose tall grass took on an even deeper shade of green in the settling twilight. Whitefish Creek murmured and gurgled as it meandered its way down from the surrounding hills with their dark pines looming upward as though they were sentinels warding off the closing darkness. The valley itself was of a bowllike configuration, enclosed to the rear and on both sides by sharply rising ground, while to the east there was a sloping meadow that followed the course of the creek.

Strips of venison were being cooked over several small fires, and the Cheyenne warriors squatted around them with roasting sticks in hand. There was a sense of tranquility about the setting that pleased Iron Crow, but did not soothe him. Earlier that day he had nearly achieved the first portion of his goal, that being the complete annihilation of the cavalry unit, and he was anxious to resume the battle. He had no doubt that victory would be his, but he was propelled by something beyond that. He had felt a powerful, all-encompassing thrill at the sight of bullets slamming home into those brilliant blue-and-yellow uniforms, and he wanted to experience that sensation again, to kill white soldiers and leave their bodies strewn across the plains. As a boy he had delighted in seeing a rabbit or deer fall to his arrows, and had known at that time that his love for hunting was not merely for sport or food, but instead to watch something die as a victim of his skill and cunning. And when his father, a great warrior in earlier times, had found him stabbing the lifeless carcass of a dead buck with his knife, even he had expressed concern for the boy's mental stability.

Iron Crow had been unconcerned about that then, as he was now. His unquestioned courage, brutal deadliness, and insatiable lust for killing had gained him immediate acceptance into the Crooked Lance Society, and he had risen quickly within the organization to become one of its most respected and feared members. And now, as his gaze drifted over the other warriors, he knew he was finally their chief and unchallenged leader.

White Claw was seated beside him, staring deeply into the coals, his snake stick in hand, and the flickering light gave his splotched face a ghostlike, ethereal aspect. Iron Crow touched the medicine man's shoulder as he rose, and spoke to his warriors in a strong, clear voice.

"Hear me, my brothers! We had another great victory over the white men today. Yellow-legs fell to our rifles, and the others ran like frightened children. If it had not been for the Snake, they all would have died. Tomorrow we will have complete victory and I will personally kill the Snake with my own hands and drive the sacred spear though his evil heart. We have returned to Whitefish Valley, home of our fathers, and we will never be driven from this land again."

He paused, looking down at White Claw and tapping him lightly on the shoulder. "White Claw has spoken with Manitou, and was told of our powerful medicine. He has given us this power through the snake stick, and White Claw will show us of its presence now. It will give us the strength and courage to defeat the white men, to burn their outpost and take their women. We will be feared and respected and live forever in the Paha Sapa."

Eyes glazed, White Claw rose and began to chant in a high-pitched voice while his feathered legs rose and fell in a shuffling dance. The other warriors watched in silence, and all eyes were locked on the magic stick in his hand, which had been anointed with great power from the gods. Over the course of nearly five minutes, the volume and rapidity of the chant increased in direct proportion to the pumping of White Claw's legs. Then, with one sharp motion, he thrust the snake stick at the fire, threw his head and shoulders back, and stared straight up at the sky.

As if a lightning bolt had struck, the fire exploded in a flash of bluish white light and the flames shot skyward to burn with searing intensity for several seconds. The brilliant light danced across the deformed medicine man's emaciated body and drove the shadows from his face. His pink eye glowed in the white side of his face as if it were a coal from the fire, and hushed murmurs of awe drifted around him. And then he was gone, moving alone toward the surrounding timber.

Iron Crow watched his warriors and was pleased with their reaction. Only he and White Claw knew where the snake stick got its magical power, and he also knew why no one else was allowed to touch the mighty instrument of the gods.

"Manitou has spoken to us again! Believe in the medicine he has given us. He has told us to kill the white soldiers, and we must obey him. Eat now and rest. Tomorrow we kill for Manitou!"

After a second murmur had died, the warriors turned again to their roasting sticks. Iron Crow called to the two braves nearest him, as he sank to his haunches beside the fire. "Black Wing! Running Horse! Come, we must talk."

The two warriors moved over to sit beside their chief.

"Black Devil has gone for his meeting with the Blue Sleeve sergeant, and he will be back just before dawn. After we have heard what he has learned, I want you two to go to the Blue Sleeves' outpost. Take the long way around back through the hills, so there can be no chance of your being seen. I want you to watch the outpost from the bluff and tell me how many guards they have there to defend against attack."

"Can we not fight with you in the battle tomorrow, Iron Crow?" Running Horse asked. "We want Manitou to smile down on us like the others."

Iron Crow smiled and clapped the warrior on the shoulder. "You will be doing as Manitou wishes, Running Horse. You will have your chance to fight after we have defeated the Blue Sleeves. Your job is an important one. We will raid and burn the outpost after we have won our victory, but I will need to know how many soldiers are there, where the guards are posted, and when they change defenders."

"We will do as you say, Iron Crow," Black Wing replied. "You will know the workings of the outpost like you know these hills of the Paha Sapa."

"Good. Join the others now to eat and rest. You will leave in the morning."

The air was cold in that final chill just before dawn, and the fires had gone out late in the night. With the exception of the guards, all the warriors lay wrapped in their blankets and continued to sleep the sleep of contented men, but Iron Crow sprang up from his blanket at the first sounds of a horse's hooves moving through the grass.

Willy Harper smiled when he saw the Indian move toward him through the darkness, and he swung down to clasp his arms around his chest and clap his hands against his shoulders to warm them.

"Damn, it's cold," he said when the chief moved up to grasp his horse's bridle. "How the hell can you stand it without a shirt on?"

"I need no shirt. I am warmed by the thought of killing the Long Knives. What have you learned from your sergeant friend?"

Harper's smile widened. "Everything we need to know. They've planned some trickery, but it's goin' to backfire on 'em, just like yesterday. They will attack us here this evening, right at sundown. Half of 'em will come up that valley there," he said, nodding toward the meadow, "and the other half will come down through the trees to try and get behind us. They'll use reversed bugle calls to try and confuse us, but I'll blow the ones we want them to hear. They think we don't know about their plan, so when we want them to charge into our trap, I will blow retreat. You will have a complete victory and count coup on their entire command."

"You have done well, Black Devil. You and the sergeant will be well rewarded. Since they won't attack until the sun falls, we will have much time to rest our ponies and prepare for battle." Iron Crow nodded his thanks before turning to trot soundlessly over to where two warriors slept near his blanket.

"Running Horse! Black Wing!" he said in a harsh whisper, while shaking a shoulder with either hand. "It is time to go."

The two Cheyenne were instantly awake and on their feet. "Go to your ponies now, and watch with the eyes of the hawk. The Blue Sleeves are coming to us when the sun falls this evening. We will be waiting for them, and their scalps will be ours. Then we will come to you and warm ourselves by the fire that once was their outpost."

The two braves nodded and moved quickly away, and Iron Crow sank to his blanket again with the smile of a pleased fox on his face.

It was four o'clock in the morning when Reb McBride walked to the center of the parade and raised his bugle to his lips. The clear, almost frantic sound of reveille shattered the silence. He sounded the call three times in succession, and the sound of feet stamping into boots and equipment being hastily buckled into place could be heard over the clear notes drifting into the heavens.

"What the hell!" Greggory exclaimed, tearing himself away from the arms of his wife, which were wrapped tightly around his chest, and sitting upright.

"What is it, honey?" Tina asked in a sleepy voice, pushing the hair back from her eyes and watching her husband leap from bed.

Greggory was struggling into his uniform and trying to pull his boots on at the same time. "Beats the hell out of me! But I know for a fact that if Easy Company doesn't get the hell out of here damned quick, you're going to have a crazy man on your hands. It's so dark a goddamned owl couldn't find his way around, and they're out there blowing reveille, for Christ's sake!"

"How do you know it's them?"

"Who the hell else would it be?" Greggory snapped, tucking in his shirt and reaching for his revolver and saber. "It's either them or some ghost who's having trouble getting to sleep. About the only thing they *haven't* done around here until now is sound reveille at four in the goddamned morning. They must've just become aware of the oversight."

"Do you think everything is all right?" Tina asked, stifling a yawn with the back of her hand.

Greggory arranged his hat on his head and pulled his saber away from his crotch and around to the side, where it was supposed to be. "No, I don't *think* everything is all right. I *know* everything is *not* all right and never will be until Easy Company has used up every last second of their squatters' rights. Go back to sleep now, Tina. I'll go out and see what the hell's going on."

Tina squirmed beneath the sheets and pulled the comforter up around her chin as Gregory headed for the door.

"Steven?"

"Yes?" he replied with a hint of impatience.

"Do you love me?"

"Yes, Tina. I love you more than you know."

"Last night was good, wasn't it?"

"Look, Tina. I've got to go." A fourth repetition of reveille rattled off the window panes. "And if that bastard plays one more note on that damned thing, I'm going to throw him and it down Kincaid's well!"

A pouty tone came into Tina's voice. "Don't cuss so much, Steven. It seems like you could just tell me if it was good, yes or no?"

"Yes, Tina. It was good. I was tired but it was good. Now I'm even more tired and this isn't good. I've got to go."

"Be careful!" Tina called over the slamming of the door, but Greggory didn't respond.

Soldiers were spilling from their barracks and tents like bees from an overturned hive, and scrambling onto the parade to line up in formation. McBride lowered his bugle, drew in a deep breath, and was raising the instrument to his lips again when Greggory strode up to his side and jerked his arm down.

"What's the meaning of this, Corporal?" he demanded.

"Not my idea, sir. Ask Lieutenant Kincaid. But please let go of my arm, sir. He told me I had to play it at least five times. I've only done four."

"I'm aware of that, soldier. I've heard every damned one. Carry on if you must."

The bugle's call broke the air again, and Greggory grimaced as he set out to find Kincaid. He found the lieutenant standing just inside the doors of the stable and directing a detachment of men who were in the process of saddling mounts. "Keep it movin', boys. We haven't any time to waste."

"Lieutenant Kincaid?"

Matt turned at the sound of the stern voice behind him, and he smiled when he saw the hot-eyed Lieutenant Greggory.

"Mornin', Lieutenant."

"Mornin', my ass! What's the meaning of this?"

"That bugle call? Means it's time to get up."

"I know what it means," Greggory snapped with no small amount of exasperation in his voice. "What I don't know is, what the hell are we getting up in the middle of the damned night for?"

"This isn't the middle of the night, Lieutenant," Kincaid

replied cheerily. "It's four in the morning, best time of the day."

"I thank you and all the roosters in the goddamned world for that little tidbit of information," Greggory replied acidly. "I demand to know what the hell's going on."

"There's been a change of plans, Lieutenant. We're going to move against the Cheyenne this morning. We leave in exactly a half-hour."

"But why?"

Kincaid shrugged. "Captain's orders. Also, we will be using standard bugle calls. Charge means charge, retreat means retreat." Kincaid couldn't resist another grin. "And reveille means boots on the floor and race toward the door."

The look on Greggory's face was a mixture of confusion and anger. "What the hell happened to the strategy we discussed last night?"

"Like I said, change of plans. Oh, and two more things. You will not advance up the valley as planned. You will wait in the timber and charge down only if the Cheyenne try to escape. The main battle will be fought on foot, like most Indian fights are. Your men are to leave their sabers here. We want a minimum of noise, and they always seem to be banging against something or other. My second platoon, along with Windy Mandalian and Sergeant Olsen, will be riding with you while I'll be taking your first. Better get cracking, Lieutenant. Like I said, we move out in half an hour."

"But . . . but we had planned to bury our dead this morning!"

"They're not going anywhere, Lieutenant. We'll do that when we get back, and that way maybe we can handle the whole deal with just one ceremony. Excuse me now, I want to make sure these horses get saddled as quickly as possible."

Greggory turned and stalked out the door, only to run straight into Captain Conway. "Good morning, Lieutenant. Have you talked with Lieutenant Kincaid?"

"Morning, sir. Yes I have."

Conway's eyes went to Greggory's hips, "I see you're still wearing your saber. Didn't he tell you about that?"

"Yes he did, Captain," Greggory replied weakly. "I just haven't had time to take it off."

"See that you do, and the rest of your men as well. Did he fill you in on the other changes of plan?"

"Yes, sir."

"Standard bugle calls, attack from the hills instead of the valley, all of that?"

"Yes, sir."

"Good. Pass the order about the sabers along to your men and be ready to ride in less than half an hour."

"I will, sir. But can I ask you one question?"

"Certainly, Lieutenant."

"What the hell's going on, sir?"

"You'll find out exactly why we're doing this after the battle. For now, let's just say it's a necessary precaution. Get your troops squared away, Lieutenant. We've got work to do."

Conway disappeared inside the stable and Greggory stopped the salute halfway to his forehead and dropped his arm. He watched the vacant door for several seconds before spinning on his heel and striding toward his assembled troops. The first man he met was Sergeant Aikens.

"What the hell is going on here, sir?" Aikens demanded.

Greggory smiled without warmth. "I have asked that question half a dozen times this morning without a definitive answer, Sergeant. Do you expect a great deal of luck on your first try?"

"What?"

"Briefly stated, Sergeant Aikens, I am equally as well informed as to what's happening in Pittsburgh at this present hour as I am regarding current events around here." A grimace flashed across Greggory's face. "I have been receiving orders, not giving them, Sergeant. To wit: the troops are to leave their sabers here; we move against the Cheyenne this morning instead of this evening; we use standard bugle calls instead of bogus ones; and we attack from the foothills instead of advancing up the valley. Our second platoon goes with Kincaid, and his first, along with Mandalian and some Sergeant Olsen, goes with us. Is that all understood?"

"Goddammit, sir!" Aikens bellowed. "The attack was planned for this evening! How much longer are you going to take this shit from those people? You're the commanding officer around here, not Conway!"

Greggory reached up and slowly tapped the silver bar on his shoulder strap. "How many of these do you see on my uniform, Sergeant?"

"One, but—"

"Precisely. Now go find Captain Conway and count his, if you wish. You'll find two, I'm sure, and therein lies your answer as to how long I intend to take all this shit. Now please pass the instructions about the sabers along to the men. We move out in half an hour."

Even in the darkness, an ashen look of desperation was visible on Aikens' face. He stood there staring at the Lieutenant but not seeing him, while a myriad of thoughts sprayed through his brain.

"Was there something else, Sergeant? You don't look well."

"Huh?" Greggory's words finally registered and Aikens touched his stomach gingerly. "You're right, sir. I don't feel good at all. Must be something I ate. Maybe I'd better report to sick call."

"Nonsense, Sergeant. Report to sick call and miss all the action? No way. We've been wanting to get this Indian matter settled for a long time. I don't give a damn if it's morning, noon or goddamned midnight, we're going to see that it gets done. You'll feel better after an hour or two in the saddle. Now pass the revised plan along to the troops and prepare to move out."

"This fucked-up outfit," Aikens growled, turning away without the "sir" to which Greggory had become accustomed, or even Aikens' usual lackadaisical salute.

Greggory shrugged and started toward his quarters, but he stopped when Windy Mandalian stepped in his path.

"Mornin', Lieutenant."

"I'm glad you didn't say *good* morning, Mr. Mandalian. May I help you?"

"Naw, not really. I was just watchin' to make sure Aikens goes along with us this mornin'. Wouldn't want to see him miss the fun."

"He'll be there, Mr. Mandalian."

"I know he will, because I plan to make damned sure he is."

"Well, actually he's not feeling well, but—"

"He's gonna be feelin' a lot worse before the day's out, and I'm gonna be in his hip pocket like a mouse turd in a sack of grain until that time. Me and Gus'll be ridin' with you this mornin'. Guess you knew that."

"I'm aware of the current plans, Mr. Mandalian. I'm afraid

140

I would have to be three men to keep up with the constant changes, but I am in grasp of the present situation for however long it lasts."

"That's fine, Lieutenant. Mighty fine," Windy said with a grin. "You just hang in there and the wash'll be on the line before you know it."

"I'm not familiar with your frontier jargon, Mr. Mandalian, but 'hang in there' is the one thing I intend to do. Now if you'll excuse me, I must return my saber to my quarters."

Windy stepped to one side. "By all means. If you're waitin' for me, you're backin' up."

Greggory shook his head and marched toward his quarters. When he stepped inside, a sleepy voice called from the bedroom, "Is that you, Steven?"

"Whom did you expect, sweetheart?"

"Steven!"

Greggory didn't reply, unbuckling his saber with concentrated effort while he walked toward the bedroom.

"Is everything all right?" Tina asked, propping herself up on one elbow.

"Whether everything is all right or not, Tina, is a relative question. If being manipulated beyond all common sense is all right, then everything is all right."

"What do you mean by that, and why are you taking off your saber?"

"What I mean by that is the reason why I'm taking off my saber."

"Steven? Are you all right?"

"Dandy. Just peachy dandy," Greggory replied, throwing the scabbard onto the floor with a rattling crash. "I wonder if that shipping clerk's job is still open back in New York."

"What?"

"Never mind. We're moving against the Cheyenne this morning," he said, leaning over and kissing his wife's cheek. "Go back to sleep now, and I'll see you when this whole mess is settled."

"Steven? Please be careful."

"Careful? I'll have to check with Lieutenant Kincaid to see if that is in accordance with plan number four hundred and goddamn sixty-five. I have to go now."

"Please promise to be careful."

"I promise to try and endure this present ordeal, honey. If that constitutes being careful, then I'll be so damned careful I couldn't get a broken fingernail in a rockslide. See you sometime tonight."

"Steven?" Tina called as Greggory headed for the door.

"What is it, Tina?" he asked with exaggerated patience.

"I love you."

"You've already told me that this morning, sweetheart. I love you too, and the birds and the bees in the sycamore trees and every goddamned captain and lieutenant in the whole fucking army. Goodbye."

The door slammed and Tina sat up in bed. She would remain there, staring at the closed door, until long after sunrise.

Even though there were guards on the walls, the outpost seemed abandoned to Flora Conway as she crossed the parade in the direction of Tina Greggory's quarters. With the main command on combat patrol, she knew there would be a need for more bandages, and she thought that if Tina were to help roll them, it might take her mind off her husband's chances of death or injury. After knocking on the door twice and receiving no reply, she carefully opened the door and stepped inside. Seeing no one in the living room, she tiptoed into the bedroom, but it too was vacant. The bed was unmade and the lieutenant's saber lay where it had been thrown. Flora hesitated, wondering, and then she left the quarters and angled toward the stable.

"Good morning, Corporal. Have you seen Mrs. Greggory this morning?" she asked the soldier standing guard beside the door.

His arm was in a sling bandage and there was a spot of red showing where he had been shot in the shoulder. He remembered Flora from her having doctored him the previous day, and he smiled cordially while sweeping the hat from his head. "Good morning, Mrs. Conway. This is the first chance I've had to thank you for helping me yesterday."

"You're welcome, Corporal. Come to the dispensary later this afternoon and we'll change that bandage. You shouldn't even be on your feet yet."

"I'm sorry, but you're wrong, ma'am. I should be doing whatever I can do for the good of this command. I can't serve in the field but I can serve here."

"Very commendable," Flora said with genuine appreciation. "Have you seen Mrs. Greggory this morning?"

The corporal glanced down. It was obvious he had been given instructions that ran contrary to his inner feeling. "I'm sorry, ma'am, but I was asked not to say anything."

"Did she leave the outpost?"

"Ma'am, like I said, I'm sorry but—"

"Look, soldier, Mrs. Greggory's life may be at stake here, just like yours was yesterday. Sometimes things happen, as they did to you, that we don't plan on. Now, I don't know that Mrs. Greggory is in any danger, but she was told never to leave the outpost by herself. If she is gone," Flora's voice was stern now, "I want to know when she left and where she said she was going."

The corporal looked away with a pained expression. "She left about half an hour ago. Hartford saddled her horse for her. She didn't say where she was going, but it's general knowledge that she goes to the wild strawberry patch up on the left of the bluff. Lots of us have seen her there, lying in a glade and just staring up at the sky. Kinda strange, some of us think."

"Thank you, Corporal. Have Hartford saddle my horse for me while I change into my riding habit. I'll be back in ten minutes, and don't you forget to have that bandage changed this afternoon. You hear me?"

"I hear you, ma'am. I'll be there." The corporal turned toward the musky dampness behind him. "Hartford! Saddle Mrs. Conway's horse! Have it ready in five minutes!"

"Yeah, Corporal," came a sleepy voice from the back. "I'll get a saddle on the damned thing. What is this around here this morning, a riding academy?"

"Don't you sass me, soldier! There's a lady present out here and you better darned well mind what you say!"

"Yes, Corporal!"

"That's better," the corporal said, turning to Flora. "Sorry, Mrs. Conway. Sometimes Hartford don't put his mind to working before his lips start to flap."

"I'm not offended, Corporal. Thanks for the help. Mrs. Greggory will never know where I got my information."

"Thankin' ya, ma'am. I 'preciate that. Your horse will be waitin' in front of your quarters when you're ready for it."

"Thank you," Flora replied, turning and walking quickly toward her room.

In less than ten minutes, Flora had her clothes changed and was heading for the door. Then she hesitated. Her husband's words of warning flashed through her brain. *Don't ever leave the outpost unless you are armed, no matter how innocent your purposes are.* She gazed at the dresser beside the bed and her mind was made up. Pulling out the top drawer, she took a pearl-handled derringer from beneath her neatly stacked clothes. Pulling up her skirt, she tucked the over-and-under, forty-four-caliber "hideaway" into her boot top. Then, once again remembering Conway's warning, she took the weapon out and checked it for rounds before lowering her skirt to cover the pistol.

As promised, the horse was tied to a post in front of her quarters. Mounting sidesaddle, Flora headed for the main gate.

"Excuse me, Mrs. Conway," the guard called down from his position atop the wall, "but may I ask where you're going?"

"I'm going for a ride near the bluff. If I'm not back in one hour, send a squad to look for me."

"Do you think you should go alone, ma'am?"

"This time, yes. Any other time, no. Give me one hour and then alert the sergeant of the guard."

"Yes, ma'am. Have a nice ride."

"Thank you," Flora replied, clucking her horse forward and moving across the clearing and into the trees.

Concealed by a low outcropping of rock, Running Horse and Black Wing lay on their stomachs in the pine needles and watched the beautiful white woman who was no more than twenty yards down the slope from them. They had watched her dismount and tie her horse to a tree and then wander across the glade, stooping occasionally to pick a tiny strawberry and nibble it with a dainty but sensual movement of her lips. Often she would glance up at the cloudless sky and they could hear strange words coming from her in a singsong voice, like music, but spoken rather than sung.

When Tina opened the top two buttons on her blouse and pulled the light material back to expose her lower neck and upper chest, the two warriors grinned at each other. She turned to find a comfortable place to sit, and when she bent down to

144

brush some small pebbles away, her blouse sagged and they could see the firm roundness of her breasts.

She held a small book in one hand, and when she finally sat with her back to the slope, she opened the tiny volume and began to ready aloud.

Touching one finger to his lips for silence, Black Wing nodded, touched his chest with his other hand, and pointed toward the woman. Running Horse returned the nod. He could feel the heat building in his loins. Neither of them had ever seen such a beautiful woman before, and their inner excitement was even greater than they had experienced when waiting in ambush for the army patrol.

Without a sound, Black Wing rose up from behind the outcropping, crouched slightly, then sprang down the slope like a mountain cat falling on its prey, with Running Horse not five steps behind.

Tina looked up at the last second with a startled gasp, but the alarm in her brain had sounded too late. Black Wing's hand sealed off her mouth while his other hand went inside her blouse and closed over her left breast. Tina stared up in stark terror at the grinning warrior above her, and attempted to break away, but strong arms held her. Walking around to the front, Running Horse gazed down at Tina for several seconds before stooping and ripping her blouse apart with a sudden flip of his wrists. Buttons popped in all directions, and one white breast was exposed, with its pink nipple hard and erect, while the other was covered with a large brownish-red hand that worked in a massaging motion.

"What a prize we have here, Black Wing," Running Horse said with a cruel smile. "She will keep our beds warm for a thousand nights."

Tina jerked her head from side to side and tried to scream, but it was to no avail. Her eyes, large in her head, rolled in horror.

"Do not struggle, little fawn, it will do no good," Black Wing said, increasing his grip slightly while he glanced up at his companion. "That is what we will call her, Little Fawn."

"A good name. A very good name. Lay her on her back and let's see what the rest of Little Fawn looks like. Then let's see what she feels like. You know if we take her back, she will belong to Iron Crow. It is the chief's right. If we are to fill her with ourselves, we must do it now."

Nodding his agreement, Black Wing lowered Tina to the pine needles while Running Horse immobilized her thrashing legs with his knees, grasped the waist of her skirt, and ripped it away. Then, with excited grunts, he began to work her bloomers down over her hips. Just when the first hint of dark brown pubic hair could be seen, Running Horse froze with an ear cocked toward the forest. He heard the sharp, metallic sound of a shod hoof striking stone. With a nod toward Black Wing, he picked Tina up and carried her to the outcropping and pressed her to the ground, out of sight.

Seconds later, Flora's horse walked into the sunlight and she reined in when she saw Tina's mount. "Tina?" she called, sliding from the saddle. Seeing the volume of poetry spread open on the needles, she picked it up and glanced at it quizzically before turning to search the glade.

"Tina?"

There was no response, and Flora began to walk slowly up the hill, searching all around her for some sign of the young woman.

The two warriors looked at each other in pleasant surprise. There, below them and approaching, was an even more beautiful woman than the one they held in their grasp. Her shoulder-length blond hair captured the sunlight and sparkled like a mantle of diamonds, and her breasts bulged enticingly beneath the bodice of her riding habit.

Flora stopped about twenty yards below the outcropping and tapped her thigh with the tiny book while searching around her again.

"Tina?"

Running Horse sprang up and bounded across the opening in two huge strides before lunging at Flora in a flying dive. Flora turned in the same instant and ducked away, but the warrior's shoulder hit her side and she rolled down the slope. Running Horse leaped to his feet and dove at Flora again, before she could stand. Her nails dug deeply into the Indian's face as she twisted beneath him. Carried by his own momentum, Running Horse tumbled over her and when he regained his feet they stood no more than ten feet apart.

"You have spirit, Yellow Hair. You are worthy of a warrior

of the Crooked Lance Society. You will give me children with great medicine." He was crouched with his arms spread wide, panting slightly, not so much from exertion as from sexual excitement. "I will play with you for a while," he said with a grin, before lunging forward again.

Flora danced to one side and her eyes blazed in anger. Backing away now, her heel caught on an exposed rock and she stumbled. Running Horse was upon her before she could regain her balance, and he knocked her to the ground with his body upon hers. Even though she was no match for the warrior, Flora struggled mightily while one of Running Horse's hands covered her mouth and the other moved up her ribcage toward her left breast. Flora's right arm was free, however. Raising her right leg as if in an attempt to use leverage, her hand closed around the derringer in her boot top.

Running Horse was breathing heavily and his hand began to caress the firm mound of flesh in the same moment that Flora's thumb drew back the hammer. As she twisted the weapon in her hand, she could smell bear-grease warpaint, the smoke from a recent fire, and the odor of a body not recently washed. With the muzzle of the derringer barely four inches from Running Horse's ribcage, she pulled the trigger and there was a muffled explosion, combined with the thump of a bullet against flesh.

A startled look filled the warrior's eyes while the force of the blast lifted his body slightly and he toppled to one side.

"Flora! Watch out!"

Hearing Tina's scream, Flora came to her knees and turned to face uphill. Black Wing had crossed half the distance between them, and sunlight flashed off the long blade of the knife in his hand. He was in full stride and nearly on top of her before Flora could raise the derringer and aim. The little gun spat flame and the slug caught Black Wing in the throat, just beneath his Adam's apple. The Indian's knees buckled, his upper body bent over backward, and he flopped onto the needles to stare upward with surprised, sightless eyes.

"Oh God, Flora," Tina sobbed, running down the hill to throw her arms around Flora and help her to her feet. Tears streamed down her cheeks and her shoulders shook uncontrollably. "Oh God! That was horrible! Just horrible! They were going to rape me, Flora!" The young woman's arms closed tightly around Flora as though she were the last stable object on earth, and she pressed her cheek against Flora's shoulder. "Thank God you came when you did!"

"Yes, I think we both have a lot to thank God for," Flora replied in a trembling voice. She put her arms around Tina and patted her back with one hand while the empty derringer dangled in the other. "But I'd rather thank Him inside the walls of the outpost than out here. Did you see any others?"

Unable to speak, Tina shook her head and continued to cry.

"It's over now, Tina. It's over. At least I hope it is. Quickly now, get your horse and let's get back where it's safe. More of them might show up at any moment."

A squad of troopers were pounding across the clearing as Flora and Tina broke from the trees with their horses at a dead run. The soldiers and the women reined in and Flora pointed over the rear of her horse, while Tina pulled what remained of her blouse tightly across her chest. "Two Indians!" Flora said, unable to control the fright in her voice. "Two Indians tried to kill us!"

"You're safe now, ma'am," the corporal said, searching the trees. "We heard shots. How many Indians were there?"

"I don't know. I shot two of them. I don't know if they're dead or not."

"Come on, ma'am. We'll escort you back to the post and then we'll check it out."

Side by side, Flora and Tina walked their horses toward the gates, with the squad of soldiers surrounding them. Tina glanced across and offered a weary smile. "I'll never leave the outpost again like that, Flora. I owe you my life and you have my promise on that. I can't thank you enough."

"Once is enough, Tina. I'm just glad we both got back safe."

"God, but that was horrible! Here I go around trying to act tough and look tough, and what do I do? I almost get both of us raped and killed."

Flora smiled and reached over to pat Tina's hand. "That's the strange thing about being an army wife, Tina. You don't have to act tough or look tough. You just have to *be* tough." She looked at the gate drawing near, and a shudder ran down her spine. "All I want right now is to hear those gates close

148

behind me and then sink down in a hot bath."

"I agree. But what I think I need most is a good stiff drink."

"I forgot that. First the gates, then the drink, then the bath. We must keep our priorities in order. Care to join me in my quarters?"

Tina smiled her assent.

twelve ──────────

With Conway and Kincaid leading the first two platoons, and Greggory and Windy Mandalian leading the second pair, the combined company wound its way into the Black Hills throughout the long morning. Mandalian had noticed the taut look on Sergeant Aikens' face and the shifting, nervous motion of his eyes, like a man seeing a trap close around him.

At one point Mandalian had turned and said, "What's the matter, Sergeant? You've waited a long time to turn the tables on those Cheyenne, so why so glum? I figured you'd be whistling and humming like a brand-new groom on his way to the bridal suite."

Aikens had glared at Windy and replied, "You go to hell, Mandalian. You'll get yours."

Windy laughed and turned forward in his saddle. "I mean to, Aikens," he said, breaking off a chew of tobacco. "But not for a while yet."

Now, with the morning nearing eleven o'clock, Conway held up his hand and signaled for Windy to come forward. "Is this about right, Windy?" he asked as the scout pulled up by his side.

The scout studied the surrounding hills. "I'd say so, Cap'n. We're about half an hour, maybe forty-five minutes from the Whitefish. By coming up the backside like we have, any guards Iron Crow might have posted can't see us due to the ridge of hills surrounding the valley. Now's as good a time as any to pay a little visit to those guards."

"How many do you think he'll have out, Windy?" Kincaid asked.

"If our hunch is right, he ain't expecting us till suppertime. I'd say probably two, one on each side."

"How do you want to work it?"

150

"We'll take 'em together, you and me, just like we talked about last night."

"Fine. Is Aikens going to stay put back there?"

"Old Gus is sittin' right there by his side and watchin' him like a cat watches a birdcage. He ain't goin' nowhere. Let's head on out and see if we can't take the Crow's eyes away from him. We'll take the one on this side first. In about an hour, Cap'n, you bring the company up to the lee of that line of hills surrounding the valley. When me and Matt get back, we'll have to close in mighty fast."

"Consider it done, Windy. You and Matt be damned careful, hear?"

"Careful as a pregnant lady on ice skates. Let's go, Matt."

A half-hour later, Kincaid and the scout were off their horses and moving soundlessly through the thick timber. Suddenly, Windy grabbed Matt's forearm and pulled him into an even lower crouch.

"See him there, Matt?" Windy asked in a whisper, pointing upward and off to the right.

"Yeah, I see him," Matt replied, focusing his eyes on the warrior standing in the sun atop a bald rock.

"Good. Now you give me five minutes to get in place, then you step out and show yourself." Windy pulled his bowie knife from its sheath and tested the blade for sharpness with his thumb. "You take care of that little chore and I'll do the rest."

Matt could feel his heart thumping in his chest while he counted off exactly five minutes. Windy had disappeared into the timber like the snake the Indians considered him to be, and Matt hoped he had given the scout enough time. If he hadn't, he knew he would be killed and the mission would be off. He waited another thirty seconds, drew in a deep breath, and stepped into the clearing.

The flash of blue caught the warrior's eye and he turned immediately, sinking into a crouch and raising his rifle to his shoulder. It was the last movement he ever made. With the warrior's full attention on Kincaid, Windy rose up from behind and was on the boulder in two strides. His hand closed over the Indian's mouth while his knife slammed hilt-deep into the warrior's throat. Catching the warrior's rifle to keep it from clattering on the rock, Windy dragged the dead man down to the trees, out of sight.

"Nice work," Kincaid said when Windy trotted up to him.

"That old boy thought he was gonna get himself an easy piece of army blue. Instead, he got a free ticket to the Happy Hunting Ground. Let's go get the other one. Hate to see a feller travel alone."

According to Conway's pocket watch, it was half past twelve when Windy and Matt rode through the trees and stopped before him.

"All I've got to say, Captain," Matt offered as they reined in, "is that I'm glad the old bastard is on our side."

Windy worked the tobacco in his jaw and spat a brown stream. "Couldn't have done it without you, Matt. You make a dandy target." Then his face became serious and he looked at Conway. "We'd better move now, before they change the guard and find out there ain't none to be changed."

"Right. Everybody knows what they're supposed to do. I've already split three of our four platoons into two equal halves of platoon-and-a-half strength. Matt, you take your half around to the other side, dismount, and advance on foot. How much time will you need?"

"Better make it forty-five minutes, sir."

"Fine. I'll take the other half and move in from this side. We'll all spread out in the trees and assume prone firing positions. Windy, Greggory, and Olsen will take the remaining platoon to the edge of the meadow. You are to stay on your mounts until after I've given them a chance to surrender. If they refuse—"

"They will," Windy said dryly.

"All right, when they do, have Reb blow the call to charge, then you and your platoon seal off any escape down the meadow. Now remember, if at any time during the fight they decide to surrender, have Reb blow the cease-fire and allow them to do so. If not, we have no choice but to continue firing until . . . well, you know the rest of it.

"Windy? Tipton is going to be with your unit, and so is Aikens. If he has a reason to kill Tipton, as we assume he does, he'll go for him when the fighting gets thick and blame it on the Cheyenne. Keep an eye on both of them and by no means allow Aikens to escape."

"Cap'n, you sound like you're askin' me a favor. Hell, I'd pay ten dollars and swim through a mile of shit just to have the job."

The two officers grinned. "I'm kind of glad he's on our side too, Matt," Conway said. "Very well, the company is broken into the three sections I described. Take your men and move out, Matt. We'll give you exactly forty-five minutes. Windy, you take your unit and move into position beside the meadow. Good luck."

Kincaid waved and moved to the head of his column. Windy spat while turning his horse toward the other platoon, farther down the line. When Windy rode up to Greggory, he thought he could detect relief on the lieutenant's face, as if he were glad not to have the burden of decision on his shoulders. Aikens' face was pale and drawn, and he stared straight ahead with an apprehensive look in his eyes.

By the time half an hour had passed, Conway's men were dismounted and crawling toward the crest of the hill on their stomachs, with the captain in the lead. While handlers held their horses below them, they inched forward with rifles thrust out in front, and in fifteen minutes they lay in wait, with the Cheyenne encampment spread out below them and exposed to a full field of fire.

Conway looked down upon what appeared to be an entirely peaceful scene. Picketed ponies grazed in the meadow while the warriors sat in groups, talking among themselves. Several braves were sleeping on their blankets in the warm sunlight. Three men stood off to one side. One was tall and muscular, and the captain knew that he was looking at Iron Crow for the first time. His eyes went to the second man and he could distinguish the black face, the blue coat, and the shiny brass object in his hand. The third man, an Indian, looked strange even from that distance. A whitish, clawlike hand hung by his side and he held a long stick in the other.

Rolling onto his side, Conway checked his watch one last time. Forty-seven minutes had passed. He cupped a hand to his mouth and raised his head slightly.

"Iron Crow!" The captain's booming voice rolled across the narrow valley. "You are under arrest by the United States

153

Army! We have you surrounded! Throw down your weapons, raise your hands above your heads, and surrender!"

Iron Crow spun toward the sound of the voice and his body sank into a wary crouch. He glanced once over his shoulder at the black man behind him, who had an equally shocked look on his face. Then he looked back to where the voice had come from, while his warriors grabbed their rifles and sprang to their feet.

"You have thirty seconds to get those hands up or we open fire!"

"Hear me!" Spotted Crow yelled, snatching the crooked lance from the ground and brandishing it over his head. "The Crooked Lance Society will never surrender! You will die, Blue Sleeves!"

With those words, the Cheyenne broke for their mounts, jerking hackamores from pegs in the ground and leaping onto their ponies' backs.

"Fire!" Conway said, but there was no enthusiasm in his voice.

There was a terrific ripping noise as twenty-five rifles fired simultaneously and an echoing thunder rolled across the valley, to be answered by the first volley from Kincaid's position. Nearly all the warriors were mounted now, with only a few still trying to swing onto rearing horses. Several Indians spun from their horses' backs and flopped in the deep grass while those remaining fired at the puffs of smoke rising in the trees. With their horses at a full run and the warriors leaning low to their necks, Iron Crow led his braves down the valley and toward the narrow opening leading to the meadow.

A shrill bugle call split the air, the call to charge, and Greggory's unit burst from the trees and onto the lush grass. Undaunted, Iron Crow whirled his pony and headed back into the valley and they came under rifle fire from the hills again.

Willy Harper had finally gotten into his saddle, and confused thoughts raced through his brain. *They blew the charge and they charged! What the hell? That was supposed to have been retreat!* The bugle moved toward his lips. *Now if I blow retreat, what the hell's going to happen?* The bugle touched his mouth. *Maybe I should blow . . .*

He had no more time to ponder. A bullet ripped the bugle

from his hand while a second slammed into his chest, throwing him over the horse's rump.

More Cheyenne spilled from their milling horses and a pall of smoke drifted across the valley. Each time Iron Crow led his braves in a charge toward a possible escape, they were met with withering fire from the surrounding hills and forced to turn back. Wounded horses went down, and those without riders raced back and forth, adding to the confusion of the wild melee.

As Greggory's mounted unit moved forward, Windy eased his horse to the rear of the platoon. He could see Aikens firing into the Indians just as the others were doing, and he knew what was on the sergeant's mind. If all the Cheyenne were dead, including the black bugler who was already stretched out motionless in the grass, then that would leave only Tipton to implicate him for his actions.

The private, with no lack of courage, was firing his Spencer and totally concentrating on the firefight. In the excitement of battle, he had forgotten about Sergeant Aikens, who was now angling his mount off to one side. To the left, a lone warrior was breaking for the trees at the edge of the meadow, and Windy looked away from Aikens long enough to raise his long-barreled Sharps and blast the Indian from his pony's back.

Aikens glanced quickly around. There were no eyes on him. He raised his rifle and snapped off a quick shot at Tipton. The young trooper pitched forward against his horse's neck and slid slowly from the saddle. Windy looked back an instant too late. He saw Tipton fall and his eyes jumped to Aikens, who still had his rifle to his shoulder and aimed in Tipton's direction.

"You son of a bitch, Aikens!" Windy screamed.

Aikens' head jerked toward the sound of his name, and he jacked in another shell as he swung his rifle barrel toward Mandalian. The Sharps came up and belched flame, and in that same instant Aikens' head seemed to explode from his shoulders. He slammed backward across his horse's rump and the rearing animal, its front hooves flailing the air, toppled over backwards as well.

Ahead and to the left, a bullet ripped into Greggory's left arm and he was almost knocked from the saddle, but he recovered and raised his revolver to continue firing. Nodding in satisfaction, Windy began to search in earnest for Iron Crow, who now had no more than thirty of his braves left alive. The chief screamed his war cry and charged toward the mounted unit, knowing his only chance of survival was to break through to the meadow. With weapons ablaze, they crashed their ponies into the army mounts, and as guns went empty they were used as clubs. The army held its ground and fought hand to hand while a squad each from Conway and Kincaid's flanking forces ran down the hill, leaped upon their horses, and raced toward the meadow in a pincers move.

With horses rearing and bodies falling all around him, Mandalian tried to urge his horse through the mass of flesh to get to Iron Crow, but he was unsuccessful. He could see White Claw lashing out with his deformed hand and swinging the snake stick with deadly accuracy. Windy raised his rifle and fired at the disfigured Indian.

White Claw's great medicine didn't save him.

One pony broke through the wild struggle and Windy turned to see Iron Crow racing away while the two flanking squads converged and threw much-needed muscle into the defenders' sagging effort.

Again the Sharps came up, and with one well-aimed shot, Mandalian placed a slug through the left front shoulder of Iron Crow's mount, now nearly a hundred yards distant. The pony pitched forward and Iron Crow sailed over its head to land on his side in a tumbling roll before staggering dazedly to his feet. Windy wheeled his horse and closed on the chief, standing alone in the meadow and shaking his head to clear his vision.

Windy slowed the horse to a walk as he drew near, and leveled his rifle at Iron Crow's heaving chest. "So, Iron Crow, we finally meet face to face. I've been kind of lookin' forward to this. I'll give you one chance—do you want to surrender to me?"

There was an eerie wildness in the Indian's eyes, the look of a man gone totally mad. He shook his head and his lips curled back in hatred. "I will never surrender, Snake," he snarled. "Not to you or anyone else. Shoot me now and get it over with."

"I'll go you one better than that," Windy replied, stepping down with the rifle still trained on the warrior. "You said a while back that you wanted to lift my scalp. Strange thing about me and challenges. I just can't seem to walk away from 'em. Tell you what I'll do. I see you've got a knife there, just like I have. What say I lay this old Sharps here aside and we'll settle it between us, man to man?"

A wary look came into Iron Crow's eyes. "You mean you want to fight me to the death with knives?"

The rifle fire behind him had diminished and grown sporadic now, and Windy knew the battle was nearly over. "That's what I mean, Iron Crow. If a man makes a brag he ought to live up to it, don't you reckon?"

"Yes. I will never get away from here alive, but it will be a pleasure to kill you before I die."

"Come on now, Iron Crow. I can't see no pleasure in that at all," Windy replied, laying his rifle in the grass. "The only pleasure you're going to get is in having the chance to try."

Both men snatched knives from their belts and began to circle each other in crouched, wide-legged stances. Iron Crow made the first move, lunging forward to slash downward with his blade at Windy's knife hand. The scout adroitly sidestepped the flashing weapon and brought his own knife across the line of his own movement. The blade sliced into the upper portion of Iron Crow's forearm and blood ran down his wrist.

The warrior gave no sign that he felt any pain as he continued to circle. His eyes were locked on Windy's and he crouched even lower in preparation for another lunge. They moved around each other for nearly a minute before Iron Crow thought he saw another opening. Again he lunged forward and his blade slashed the outer edge of Windy's hand.

Iron Crow smiled at the sight of Windy's blood. "So, the Snake bleeds just like the rest of us? That's good to see." Then his face turned cold. "And he will die just like the rest of us!" he spat as he leaped forward with his knife blade aimed at Windy's heart.

Windy brought his free hand down across Iron Crow's wrist with a smashing blow, while thrusting his own knife forward with all his might. The razor-sharp blade slammed home in the pit of the Indian's stomach, and Iron Crow's eyes went glassy. The knife fell from his hand and he hung on Windy's blade for several seconds before stumbling backward and sprawling in the grass.

Without looking at the blood-red blade, Windy sprang forward to press the tip of his knife against Iron Crow's throat.

"I don't think you'll be takin' any scalps today, Crow," he said softly.

Iron Crow closed his eyes against the pain before slowly opening them again. "No, but there is no loss of honor in being beaten by the best, is there?"

"All depends on how you look at it, I guess. Why was Aikens trying to help you?"

The Indian smiled weakly. "Because he was foolish and greedy, as all white men are. He wanted the yellow metal. He and Black Devil were to have all they could take after we won against you."

"Gold," Windy snorted in obvious disgust. "It can buy nothing but misery."

Iron Crow's eyes had closed again and he opened them with a hesitant flutter. "I see we agree on one thing at least. As one warrior to another, can I ask you to do something for me?"

"You can ask."

"Kill me now. Don't let me be taken captive."

"No, I can't do that, Crow."

The Cheyenne's eyelids were even heavier than before. "Why?"

"Because you're dying anyway. And that's the only reason." It appeared as though Iron Crow were trying to smile again, but his lips wouldn't move and his head slowly tilted to one side.

With the exception of a wounded horse whinnying in the distance, the valley was deathly quiet. The acrid smell of gunpowder hung in the still air, and soldiers moved through the grass, searching out the fallen Cheyenne to confirm death. Windy led his horse up to where Greggory, heedless of his own wound, was kneeling over Tipton.

"How bad is he hit, Lieutenant?"

"Pretty bad," Greggory replied without looking up. "Took a slug through the outer right side of his stomach. Something is strange here though, because it looks like the bullet came out the front. He must have been shot from behind, and there weren't any Cheyenne back there that I know of."

"Aikens shot him," Windy said bluntly.

"Aikens?" Greggory asked incredulously, glancing up at Windy.

"Yes, Aikens. I saw him do it. I killed Aikens myself."

"But why? Why would he shoot Tipton?"

"Because he wanted him dead."

Tipton opened his eyes and grimaced in pain. "Mr. Mandalian is right, sir. I knew he would try to kill me."

"For what reason?"

"Because I saw him kill those two miners."

"Then why in heaven's name didn't you come to me and tell me that?"

"Because I also saw him take their scalps, sir. He said he had somebody watching me who would do the same thing to me if I talked. I...I...know he was lying now. There ...wasn't anybody else, he just made me believe there... was."

"He's getting weaker, Lieutenant," Windy said, kneeling down to take Tipton's bandanna from around his neck, wad it in a ball, and then tie it against the wound as a compression bandage. "Let him rest now," he continued as he worked, "and maybe we can save him. Aikens had a deal workin' with the Cheyenne. If he helped them wipe out your command, he got all the gold he could carry out of here. He would have been clean because the army would think all of you had died in the battle. That colored feller over there was in on it with him, and he's the one who blew the false bugle calls the other day. I'm sure Aikens and his pal are the ones who set those miners up for the slaughter as well."

Greggory leaned back and stared up at the sky. "Oh Christ! What a fool I've been!"

"That's pretty much the way I see it myself, Lieutenant," Windy replied, patting Tipton on the shoulder. "Relax, son. We'll get you back to the outpost and you'll likely live to fight again another day."

When Kincaid walked up, Windy was squatting beside White Claw and looking at the snake stick, which had been nearly broken in half during the battle.

"I didn't find Iron Crow among the dead, Windy. Think he got away?"

"Nope. He's layin' down there in the meadow. I killed him," Windy replied calmly, while he continued to examine the stick, and Matt saw his blood-encrusted right hand.

"You've been hit, Windy. Here, let me take a look at it."

"Naw, it's just a little nick, Matt. It'll heal like all the rest of

159

'em have. Ever heard of White Claw?" he asked, waving the stick toward the Indian at his feet.

"No, can't say I have. Why?"

"That's him there. Kind of a pathetic-lookin' creature, ain't he?"

Matt looked at the grotesquely deformed hand, twisted in death and reaching almost ironically toward the sky. "Yeah, he is. What about him?"

"He was a medicine man, supposed to have great power with this snake stick here. He'd jump around the fire, talk to the chief tom-toms up there in the sky for a few minutes, and *whoosh!* down came the information and up went the flames. Scared the shit out of a lot of Indians that way."

"How in hell did he do that?" Kincaid asked, staring at the stick wrapped in snakeskin.

"Pretty simple, once you have a look at it. This stick here is hollow and it's filled with gunpowder. Just pull this little thong here and the door on the end opens up. Throw it once at the fire, and like I said, *whoosh!* Another message received from the Big Fellers up there."

"And the Indians believed in him? He was nothing more than a two-bit preacher at best."

"Right you are. But you would have been impressed too, if you believed in the same spirits that they do." Windy rose and said, "Let's go have a look at Aikens."

"Where is he?" Matt asked, looking around.

"Where he should be. Dead. He shot Tipton and I killed him."

"How's Tipton?"

"He might live. Before Iron Crow died, he told me about his deal with Aikens. Aikens sold us out for gold."

Kincaid followed the scout to where Aikens lay, most of his head a pulpy red mass. Windy reached into the neck of Aikens' shirt and pulled out a little brown leather sack attached to a thong tied around the dead man's neck. He cut the thong with his bowie knife and stood up, emptying the contents of the sack into his hand. He gave a little snort of laughter and shook his head.

"Guess what, Matt."

"What?"

"This here's fool's gold."

"Fool's gold?"

"Yeah. Iron pyrite. Not worth a plugged nickel."

Windy tossed the nuggets aside and stood wearily. He looked around at the gory scene with a slow turn of his head, and there was heavy sadness written upon his face.

"Let's load up the dead and wounded and get the hell out of here, Matt. I'm sick of this damned place. And besides, I'm needin' a drink awful bad."

thirteen ⸺⸺⸺⸺

Straining his eyes to see through the deepening twilight shadows, the guard on the wall beside the main gate watched the first horses emerge from the trees. The silhouettes of several riderless mounts with ominous-looking bundles across their backs was more easily discernible than the white bandages on several of the soldiers, but the guard knew immediately that the company had suffered casualties.

"Open the main gates!" he shouted down to the men below. "They're on their way in and it looks like several dead and wounded!"

Tina Greggory heard the guard's shout through her open window, and her face went pale. *It can't be him,* her mind screamed. *Please, God, don't let him be one of the dead!*

Rushing to the door, she watched the lead riders of the combined command move through the gates and she saw Conway, Kincaid, and Mandalian, but not her husband. Her hands clutched at the apron around her waist and she twisted the cloth nervously. *He can't be dead, please, let him be alive. Please.*

Then she saw him at the head of the cavalry unit, with his arm strapped to his side and a reddened bandage wrapped around his upper bicep. She started to run to him, then hesitated and veered toward the well instead.

When Flora entered the dispensary, Tina was already pouring water into waiting containers inside the building, with medicines and bandages stacked on the table beside her.

"You've done it, Tina," she said with a soft smile. "You're going to make it fine now."

Tina looked up from her work with a shy smile. "If you can't contribute, Flora, then make room for someone who can."

"Seems like I've heard those words someplace before," she replied, giving Tina an affectionate little hug and then turning at the sound of boots approaching. Tipton was the first man to be carried in, and Flora pushed the medicine aside.

"Here, lay him on the table."

Tipton's face was white and he gritted his teeth against the flash of pain as he was lifted upward. Immediately, Flora cut his shirt away while men with lesser wounds walked or hobbled inside. She saw Tina move forward without hesitation to begin inspecting their injuries. Flora smiled inwardly and removed the compression bandage from Tipton's stomach. It was an ugly wound, but fairly clean, with no bits of intestine showing and none of the pinkish blood that would indicate a punctured lung.

"I think it looks worse than it really is, soldier," she said with a comforting pat on Tipton's thigh. "I'll clean it up a little, than apply clean bandages, and you'll be just fine until a regular doctor can be brought here to take proper care of you."

Tipton's eyes opened reluctantly. "Thank . . . thank you, ma'am. It hurts a mite, but I can . . . stand that."

"I'm sure it does. I'll be as gentle as possible. Just relax as best you can."

Lieutenant Greggory stepped inside and his eyes went immediately to Tipton. He moved to the trooper's side. "Is he going to be all right, Mrs. Conway?"

At the sound of her husband's voice, Tina turned and crossed the room to touch his wounded arm. "You've been hurt, Steven. Here, let me take a look at it."

"No. Take care of the others first, Tina. When you're done with them, you can have a shot at me." He smiled weakly. "No pun intended," he said, and looked again at Flora. "How is he, Mrs. Conway?"

"I think he'll be just fine," Flora replied, dabbing a damp cloth gingerly around the torn hole. "It's a fairly clean wound, but a real doctor should have a look at it as quickly as possible. Where's the nearest one?"

"Back at regimental headquarters. I'll have a rested trooper on a fresh horse heading that way in half an hour."

"Good."

Greggory looked down at the young soldier. "Tipton, it took a lot of guts to go into battle knowing one of your own men intended to shoot you. Why did you do it?"

Tipton opened his eyes again. "Because I had to, sir. Even

163

if it meant getting killed myself." He hesitated and glanced down before looking at his commanding officer again. "I know I'm the one responsible for the deaths of those miners," he said in a voice just above a whisper.

"Why do you say that?"

"Because if I had come forward sooner, Aikens could have been stopped. I heard Windy tell you that Aikens was the one who suckered those poor fellows into that trap. That's why I had to go into battle today, to prove to myself that I wasn't a coward. I'm glad I did now, 'cause maybe I helped settle the score with those Indians for my stupid mistake."

Greggory squeezed Tipton's forearm gently. "I know something about stupid mistakes, Trooper. Believe me, I could write the book on stupid mistakes. You're not the only one who had to prove he wasn't a coward out there today. Maybe we both proved it."

"Thank you, sir. I think we did."

"He'd better rest now, Lieutenant," Flora said. "I'm going to have to turn him over on his back to look at the other side."

"Sure, Mrs. Conway. Take good care of him, hear? He means a lot to me."

"I'll do my best, Lieutenant."

"I'm sure you will, ma'am, and thanks."

When all the other wounded men had been cared for, Tina turned to her husband and removed the bandages from his arm. It was a nasty, jagged wound that had torn a trough nearly an inch deep through the outside flesh of his lower shoulder. Showing no sign of queasiness or discomfort, Tina began cleaning the wound.

"Say, you're pretty good at that," Greggory offered, watching Tina work.

"No I'm not, but I am learning. I didn't realize you would be one of my first patients."

Greggory grinned. "Before you continue, would you mind if I ask how many patients you've lost?"

"Not at all. None."

"Good. Keep working."

When Tina reached for a clean cloth and dabbed it into the basin, she looked at her husband with deep tenderness.

"Steven?"

"Yes?"

"Do you remember the other day, when you asked me for a promise?"

Greggory pursed his lips in thought. "You mean about not going outside the gates alone?"

"That's what I mean."

"Then I remember. What about it?"

"Well, that 'maybe' I gave you is now an absolute, one-hundred-percent, nonbreakable promise. I learned a lesson to-day that I'll never forget for the rest of my life."

"Glad to hear it. What lesson was that?"

"No, you won't be glad to hear it, but I've got to tell you about it anyway. Tonight, after we get home."

"Why not now?" Greggory asked with a shrug. "You'll never have a more captive audience."

Tina grinned impishly. "Because this is a hospital, sweetie. Can't you see that? We've got work to do here, and I can't spend all my time with one patient."

Greggory glanced around the room, which was empty of soldiers except for Tipton, who was asleep on the table. "Yeah, I can see your point. Looks like you've got your work cut out for you. Could be a long night for the angels of mercy."

After breakfast the following morning, the soldiers of Easy Company were mounted once again and prepared for the long ride home. Conway, Kincaid, and Windy Mandalian were inside Greggory's office. The lieutenant sat behind his desk, with one arm free of his tunic and dangling in a white sling. Each man held a brandy glass in his hand, and Conway raised his as if to propose a toast.

"I would say, 'here's to a successful campaign,' but I don't really feel that way about our victory over Iron Crow. Some-how, winning from ambush leaves me a little cold. On the other hand, he did try to do the same thing to us."

"And he would have been successful, Captain," Greggory replied, "if it hadn't been for the courage of your scout here. I thank you from the bottom of my heart, Mr. Mandalian."

"No thanks needed, Lieutenant. I didn't have anything to do with it. When you're sittin' on a runaway horse, you go where it goes."

Conway continued to hold his glass aloft while the laughter subsided. "Let's drink to the future of Outpost Thirteen and your success in your military career, Lieutenant. You showed your mettle today and I have no doubt that you will go far."

"Hear, hear," Kincaid said, taking a sip from his drink along with the others.

When the glasses were lowered again, Greggory said, "I'm not going to propose a matching toast, because I think what you should have from me is both an apology and my thanks. First the apology. I am extremely sorry for my pigheadedness with regard to Sergeant Aikens. I guess I felt a little envious of you and was blinded by his overtures at the same time. I understand now why you set me up last night and then changed the battle plan this morning. You couldn't trust me and I don't blame you. I couldn't trust myself enough to keep your plan a secret. I've learned a great deal from the three of you, and things will be different in the future around here.

"Now the thanks. If it hadn't been for you, this outpost would have been entirely susceptible to attack and most likely would have been burned to the ground by this time. I thank you for putting up with my foot-dragging attitude and less than appreciative mien. I owe everything—Tina's life, the safety of my command, and the future of my military career—to you."

Greggory paused and raised his glass. "Gentlemen? Here's to you. All I can say is a simple thanks."

"Accepted in full, Lieutenant. Glad to be of some help."

Their glasses were on the way down when knuckles rapped on the door. "Lieutenant?"

"Yes, Sergeant Ritter? What is it?"

"Sorry to bother you, sir, but there's a man here to see you. He's the marshal from Deadwood. Says his name's Hickok."

"Send him in."

The door opened and a tall, angular man of spare build walked in, wearing a black, pinstriped suit, a white shirt, and a string tie. The sloping, broad-brimmed black hat and expressionless eyes, in combination with a drooping mustache, gave him the appearance of a man who had sent many men to hell and was prepared to go himself. A young boy about twelve years old was being scooted before Hickok.

"Which of you is in charge here?" the marshal asked.

"I am," Greggory said without hesitation.

"Good, then you're the man I want to talk to," Hickok replied, his leonine head swinging toward the lieutenant. "You and one of your soldiers, that is. Little Tommy Edwards here—" he indicated the boy with a sweep of his hand past the heavy revolver sagging from his hip—"came to me with some information today that he should have come to me with a long time before. A bartender was killed in town a few nights ago, and since there was no robbery, I was kind of up a tree as to who did it and the reason why."

Hickok paused to tousle the frightened boy's hair. "This little rascal here is the first one to come forward with anything that I could work with. The reason he hung back is 'cause he was afraid his pa would take a board to his backside. Seems he snuck out of his room that night to meet some of his buddies, and he was going down the alley at the same time the bartender came out the back door. He hid behind some crates so he wouldn't be seen, but he continued to watch what was going on. He says a second man came out, a soldier dressed in his uniform, and stabbed the bartender with his saber, then took off down the alley in the other direction. I guess Tommy was having a nightmare about the whole thing one night, 'cause his pa heard him talking in his sleep and brought him to me."

The marshal looked at Greggory and there was a hard glint in his steely eyes. "I checked the registers of all the hotels in Deadwood, and only one soldier had been checked in that night, just like he was the only one seen drinkin' in town. His name is Sergeant Frank Aikens. I came here to have a little chat with him."

"If that were possible, you would have my complete co-operation, Marshal," Greggory said. "But unfortunately it isn't."

"Why isn't it?"

"Because the sergeant is dead. He was killed in a battle with the Cheyenne yesterday. These men will confirm that."

Conway looked up and nodded. "It was witnessed by all of us, Marshal. We also have strong reason to believe that he's the one who lured those miners to their deaths. The Indians responsible for that massacre are also dead, so that unfortunate situation is cleared up as well. We would appreciate it if you would pass that information along to the citizens of Deadwood."

"Thank you, gentlemen. I'll take your word for it and I appreciate your cooperation. And I certainly will let the townspeople know that the army has matters well in hand," Hickok replied, looking down and touching the boy's shoulder. "Come on, Tommy. If we hurry fast enough, you still might be able to catch the last half-day of school."

"Aw, come on, Marshal, please? Can't we just forget that for today?" the little boy pleaded, looking up at the towering marshal. "I'd like to stay with you."

"No, we can't forget it. I've got a poker game to play and you've got to go to school so you'll have more sense than to play poker when you grow up. Scat now, or I'll throw you in jail for obstructing justice."

Riding on the playful swat on his rump delivered by Hickok, the boy ran from the room and the marshal turned with a pleasant smile, which seemed alien to his craggy face. "Nice talkin' to you gentlemen. Good day."

After the marshal had left, Windy gazed into his glass and asked in a musing voice, "Any of you fellers ever heard of him?"

"I haven't, Windy," Kincaid replied. "You, Captain?"

"Me neither. What about him, Windy? He's just another town marshal, isn't he?"

Windy laughed and shook his head, then said, "You know, I think maybe I did Aikens a favor yesterday. Hickok would have personally put a noose around his neck and pulled the trap handle himself. If Aikens lived long enough to get that far, which I doubt."

Rising, Conway replied, "Speaking of getting far, we'd better do the same. Lieutenant? Sorry if we caused you some confusion and a few angry moments."

Conway offered his hand, which Greggory grasped with a surprisingly strong grip. "Every bit of it deserved, Captain. Thank you once again for your patience with me."

After shaking hands all around, Greggory followed them to the head of the column and waited while they stepped into their saddles. Mounted sidesaddle and positioned beside Sergeant Cohen in the center of the command, Flora was the picture of elegance. She smiled politely at the Lieutenant.

Greggory glanced over his shoulder in the direction of his quarters. His wife was nowhere to be seen. He felt panic building in his chest until finally the door opened and Tina stepped out. Her hair fell in ringlets around her pretty face and she

168

wore a beautiful lavender dress, ruffled at the shoulders and highlighted by tiny white flowers. Clutching a sparkling white handkerchief in her hand, she walked daintily across the parade and directly toward Flora.

"My, but you look absolutely divine, Tina!" Flora exclaimed when the young woman stopped beside her horse. "I was hoping we would have a chance to say goodbye."

Tears glistened in Tina's eyes as she looked up. "I'm sorry I'm so late, but I wanted to look nice for you this last time. You've taught me a lot, especially about being a lady, and I'll always love you for that."

"I didn't teach you anything that you didn't already know, Tina," Flora replied with a soft smile. "I only reminded you of what you did know."

"Whatever you did, I can't thank you enough. Please don't forget me."

Flora laughed. "I don't think there's much chance of that, dear. If you get to feeling lonely, as all of us out here do, just write. I love to answer letters."

"Forrrrrrwarrrrd . . . *hhhooooooo!*" Kincaid yelled with a sweeping motion of his arm, and the two platoons moved through the gates while Greggory walked over to place his arm around Tina's waist. Just before she passed from view, Flora turned in her saddle and waved.

Tina returned the gesture while nibbling her lower lip. Then Easy Company was gone and the heavy gates closed behind them.

"It's a strange thing," Greggory said in a wistful voice. "All the time they were here I was wishing they would leave, and now that they're gone, I find myself wishing they could have stayed longer."

Tears ran freely down Tina's cheeks now. "I know. You never appreciate what you have until it's gone." She looked up at her husband and her long lashes were filmed with moisture. "I'm afraid I was beginning to feel and act the same way toward you."

Greggory squeezed her more tightly to his side. "I know, and I'm just as guilty of the same thing. But now we're going to make it, Tina," he said, reaching down and tilting her face up to him. "Do you understand that? We've both made some mistakes, but they're behind us now. We are going to make it."

Tina tried to smile, but failed. "I know we will, Steven. I'll try my best to be the woman you deserve," she said, pulling away and walking toward their quarters.

Greggory watched her until she disappeared from view, and then turned to see a guard leaning on his rifle upon the wall.

"You, trooper!"

"Yessir?" the startled guard called down.

"You stand tall and walk your post in a military manner. If I ever see you leaning on your weapon again you will be standing before my desk and looking a court-martial straight in the eye. Do you understand that?"

"Yessir!"

"You damned well better! This is an army outpost, not an old folks' home! You've just been given your last second chance!"

"I understand, sir!" the guard said, shouldering his rifle smartly and resuming the patrol of his post.

Greggory glanced around one more time before stalking toward his office. His shoulders were thrown back and there was a look of determination in his eyes.

"Sergeant Ritter," he said, stepping into the orderly room, "we are starting tomorrow today. You handle the small stuff and pass on to me anything that needs my attention."

Ritter looked up with a pleased expression on his face as the CO passed by. "Yessir!"

Greggory closed the door to his office and sat behind the desk. He looked around, and for the first time since he had come West, he felt like he was actually in command.

SPECIAL PREVIEW

Here are the opening scenes
from

*EASY COMPANY ON
THE BITTER TRAIL*

the next novel in Jove's exciting
High Plains adventure series

EASY COMPANY

coming in September!

one

They moved slowly across the sloping stretch of broken ground, stooping low and occasionally kneeling to turn a rock over in search of insects or to snatch a handful of berries from the scattered brush. There were ten of them, six men and four women, and each of them carried a digging stick, approximately eighteen inches long, blunt on one end and sharp on the other, with the sharp end turned coal-black from fire hardening.

At certain selected bushes they would work their hands down to the base of the stem, test with their fingers, and then scrape the dirt away to expose tender white roots spreading beneath the soil in search of water. After the dirt was wiped away, some of the roots were eaten as they were drawn from the ground, while others were stacked in layered rows in wicker baskets by their sides. In the main, they were a pathetic-looking group, with their emaciated physical features covered by comical mixtures of clothing consisting of tanned leather contrasting with cast-off white men's garments.

But there was one young woman, in the lead and at the center of the group, who stood out from the others. She wore only traditional Indian clothing made from tanned antelope skin, which was fawn-colored and decorated at the neck and waist by rows of multicolored beads. Her dress was nearly ankle length, fringed from elbow to wrist, with the soft leather clinging to her shapely figure, especially against her well-rounded buttocks when she bent down to thrust her digging stick skillfully into the ground. Her long black hair, parted in the center and dangling past either shoulder in a twist of braids, took on a sheen in the lowering sun, and her lean, high-cheek-boned face was radiant with health and beauty. Her breasts, while not extravagant, were firm and full and their size was

173

accented by the narrowness of her waist. She worked silently with the others, apparently as oblivious to her natural attributes as she was to the eyes watching her from above.

There was a whiskey smell about him that reinforced the sullen ugliness of a face that might otherwise have been moderately attractive, were it not for the cruel, cold smile on his lips. Taking another drink from the bottle in his hand, he passed it back to his companions behind him and wiped his twisted lips with the backward swipe of a naked forearm. Mounted on a dun-colored horse, he was the picture of ferocity, his broad chest covered only by a leather vest, which touched the loincloth around his waist. The fringed leather leggings he wore clung tightly to the horse's ribs, and across his thighs lay a Remington repeater. The seven warriors behind him were similarly armed, each of them wearing a silver badge attached above the right breast. The shiny black hair of each man was adorned with a single feather.

A smaller Indian, perhaps three inches shorter than the lead warrior and boasting a ragged scar running from the bridge of his nose to the point of his chin, nudged his horse and moved up beside the warrior staring intently at the woman below.

"There she is, Wokana," he said with a leering grin and a gesture of the bottle toward the low land. "Dark Star is waiting for you."

"I have waited long enough for her to come to me, Hunting Dog. I will wait no longer." Wokana took the bottle from Hunting Dog's hand and took a long drink before waving it with a drunken gesture toward the Indians below. "Look at them! Their men scratching the ground like birds looking for worms and working with women like they were women themselves, instead of hunting for meat like men. If they weren't so ugly, we would take them for our pleasure as we will take their women."

Hunting Dog laughed cruelly. "Remember, Wokana, they are nothing more than Paiutes, to be hunted and killed for sport instead of game. They do not fight to live, they *beg* to live. They deserve nothing but death at the hands of Bannock warriors, and their women's bellies should be filled with Bannock children to give some spirit to their blood."

Wokana continued to stare at Dark Star, whose entire concentration was given to the job at hand as she moved from bush

174

to bush. There was a hunger in his eyes, which were slightly filmed with moisture from the effects of strong liquor. "The words you say are true, Hunting Dog," he said in a distant voice. "But Dark Star is mine. You can have the others."

A tight smile crossed Hunting Dog's lips, and when he spoke there was a taunting tone to his words. "She will not be able to refuse you this time, will she, Wokana? Like she has done so many times in the past?"

Wokana glanced sharply at his companion. "She has refused me only because she is blinded by that weakling Red Hand. After she has felt the power of a Bannock warrior, she will never again allow a Paiute to touch her."

"And Red Hand isn't here," Hunting Dog replied, his gaze drifting to search the lowland for the Paiute chieftain. "Black Bear will not be pleased. We were sent here to kill Red Hand, not the others."

"There is plenty of time to get him," Wokana said, raising the bottle and draining it before tossing it aside. "Right now I want only his woman." He turned on the blanket spread across his horse's back and looked at the warriors behind him. "Ride them down and kill them silently. Do what you want to their women, but leave Dark Star to me. When we have finished we will ride to the trading post and buy more whiskey. We have been paid for our work at the agency and I told Black Bear we would not return for one day. We deserve three. But first we will have our pleasure."

Wokana turned back, pressed his knees against the horse's sides, and sent the mount plunging down the slope at a gallop, with the others following close behind. Rocks clattered beneath their horses' churning hooves and dust rose in their wake.

The Paiutes looked up with fear-filled eyes as they recognized the agency police, Bannock warriors notorious for their brutality in enforcing their powers at the Sand Ridge Reservation. Leaving their baskets behind, they fled down the slope in a futile attempt to elude their pursuers, with women clutching skirts around their thighs and men ignoring fallen hats. The horses quickly closed on them and rifles were swung like clubs, sending the elderly Paiute men sprawling on the ground with crushed skulls or broken necks. There was a chorus of excited yips and yells as the Bannock turned their mounts on the fleeing women and the warriors slipped from their mounts to drag the women down into the sparse grass.

Clothing was quickly stripped away while the warriors, working in pairs, held the women spread-eagled on the ground. Excited, muffled grunts rose in the still evening air as the Bannock took their turns mounting the women, and the occasional scream escaped from between hard fingers pressed over mouths.

Only one had not fled, and she watched the scene below her with a cold look of hatred and disgust before turning to stare contemptuously at Wokana, whose horse had stopped some five yards away. Dark Star's hate-filled eyes shone like obsidian in her tanned face, and she betrayed no fear as she suddenly raised her digging stick and threw it at Wokana's head.

The warrior ducked an instant before the sharpened point of the stick sailed past where his head had been and clattered harmlessly on the rocks behind him. He grinned and edged his horse closer.

"So?" he said, raising an eyebrow quizzically and glancing toward the warrior beside him. "The Paiute woman has more fight in her than her men do, Hunting Dog."

"And so does a crippled bird, Wokana," Hunting Dog replied with a scornful laugh.

"That's true, but this bird is not crippled. She is a beautiful woman who deserves to have a proud warrior lie beside her." Wokana looked closely at Dark Star. "Why did you not run with the others?"

Dark Star's eyes were riveted on Wokana's face and they never wavered. "Because I have no fear of you, Wokana. Just as I have no fear of other cowardly animals."

"Cowardly animals? You are talking to Wokana, the mightiest warrior of the Bannock tribe and chief of the agency police."

"I am talking to Wokana, coward, murderer and taker of women because he can get them no other way."

Wokana flinched involuntarily and his eyes became black slits. "You will pay for those words, Dark Star. I will show you what Wokana does with women and you will never forget it. You will never be satisfied with Red Hand again."

"Kah!" Dark Star replied, spitting at Wokana's horse. "After you touch me I will never sleep with Red Hand again

176

because I will be filled with your filth and my shame. Red Hand is a proud man who does not need to *take* women. Women come willingly to him."

"Enough, woman!" Wokana snarled, leaping from his horse and stepping forward to slap Dark Star with the back of his hand. "I will hear no more!"

Dark Star staggered backward under the force of the blow, but she did not fall, even though her cheek quickly turned crimson where Wokana's knuckles had landed. "You have not even enough power to knock a Paiute woman down, Wokana," she challenged. "How do you ever hope to satisfy one in bed?"

Wokana's face filled with rage and he lashed out again, striking the other cheek with an even more forceful blow. This time Dark Star went to her knees, and Wokana was on her instantly while her fingernails tore into his face and neck.

"Hunting Dog! Grab her hands and hold her down!"

The second warrior's powerful hands closed around Dark Star's wrists and he howled in pain as her teeth sank into his forearm. But he had control of her now and one hand went over her mouth while the other pinned her hands to the ground behind her head. Dark Star thrashed and kicked with her legs as Wokana ripped her dress up past her waist with one hand and worked his loin cloth down with the other. Firm, well-proportioned thighs were exposed to him now, and when his hand touched the patch of soft black hair between them, a moaning grunt escaped his lips. He could smell the gentle hint of muskiness coming from her and could feel the smooth warmth of her skin as he lowered himself to take her. Their eyes were locked on each other, one set hating and defiant, the other set blurring and opaque with sexual excitement. And while he worked over her, his breathing came in sharp gasps and the pace of his thrusts became more rapid. Finally a shudder ran through his body and he lay still for several seconds before standing and rearranging his loincloth. There was a cruel smile of satisfaction on his lips as he looked down at Dark Star, motionless now and offering no resistance.

"You see how satisfied she is, Hunting Dog?" he said with a tone of triumph. "She lies there quietly and relives the pleasure."

The excitement on Hunting Dog's face caused the torn scar to take on a deep red hue and his hand trembled over Dark

Star's mouth. His eyes remained fixed on her pubic region, and there was a quiver in his voice when he spoke. "She deserves two Bannock warriors, Wokana. I will be the second."

"No!" Wokana said sharply. "She is mine. Take one of the others if you wish, but Dark Star is mine."

A hurt look filled Hunting Dog's eyes as he tore them from the damp hair and looked up. "She is nothing but a Paiute, Wokana. Why—"

"Because I said she is mine! Go now!" Wokana snapped, glancing toward the other warriors, now finishing with their victims. "The others have had their fill. Take what you want and then we leave."

After a moment's hesitation, Hunting Dog stood and trotted to the nearest woman, then dropped to his knees with a frantic tugging at his loincloth. Dark Star's eyes had followed him, but she looked away, rolling her head to stare up at Wokana once more.

"You and the others are filthy cowards, Wokana," she said, her voice surprisingly calm. "You are nothing more than dogs, not warriors. Red Hand will kill you for what you've done."

"Red Hand? Kill *me*?" he said with a cold laugh. "I would not be as kind to him as I was to you, Dark Star. I will kill him slowly and with great pain. You are my woman now. Tell him how much you enjoyed the feel of a Bannock warrior and he will cry great tears like the weakling he is. He is not a warrior, he's only a Paiute and no match for me." He paused and smiled down. "Once he is dead, you will have what a beautiful maiden deserves. A proud warrior to give you children."

"I would kill myself first."

"No, Dark Star, you wouldn't do that. If you did, I would kill every Paiute on the Sand Ridge. You would be taking their lives as well as your own." Wokana glanced toward the lower ground and saw Hunting Dog stand and straighten his loincloth. "Hunting Dog! We go now! We have far to ride and much whiskey to drink!"

Wokana started toward his horse, then stopped and turned back. "I have never felt a woman like you, Dark Star. I will take you for my own." Then he stepped to his mount, swung onto its back and spun the horse around with a jerk of the hackamore.

Dark Star struggled to a sitting position and pulled the torn dress around her thighs before covering her face with her hands in shame.

The other warriors were mounted as well, and just as they started to leave, one of the elderly Paiute men who had been knocked unconscious attempted to struggle to his feet. The rearmost Bannock warrior raised his rifle and fired one shot, and the old man sprawled onto his back with a crimson hole torn in his chest. Then the Bannock rode away, and their exultant yells and cries drifted back to the silent patch of ground where the Paiute women were slowly crawling toward the three dead men.

Red Hand's head jerked up sharply at the distant crack of a rifle shot. The adobe jar in his hands was underwater behind the tiny dam he had made to capture the trickle of water seeping from the spring, and he cocked his head in the direction from which the sound had come. Two other jars filled with water lay beside his knees, and his keen eyes searched the distant hills. Seeing seven tiny specks galloping over the broken ground, he sprang to his feet, grabbed the jars and loped on foot toward where the others had been working.

He ran with well-paced, ground-eating strides, and his lean, lithe body showed not one ounce of fat. Bronzed skin was stretched tightly over sinewy muscle, and his shoulders spanned widely above a broad chest that tapered down to a narrow waist. He was nearly six feet in height, with raven-black hair tied in a single braid trailing down his back; his countenance was regal, and the snugly fitted leather leggings and breast cover made him appear even taller than he actually was. His high cheekbones and prominent nose gave an intensity to his dark eyes, and there was a wild handsomeness about him that few men could match.

At twenty-seven years old, Red Hand was the accepted leader of the Southern Paiute tribe assigned to the Sand Ridge Reservation, located on the western side of the southern tip of the Rocky Mountains. It had been a tremendous ordeal, being relocated into an unfamiliar region that was not suitable to the food-gathering lifestyle of his people, but Red Hand had obeyed the decision of the White Fathers and was trying to provide his tribe with the kind of leadership that would ensure their survival against overwhelming odds. Pinyon nuts, which were a staple of their diet and which grew in abundance in their home region of the Great Basin, were nowhere to be found. Sagebrush and juniper were also absent, along with the small game and insects that had sustained his people for so many generations. Oriented as they were to a water-scarce life on the fringes of the desert, the Southern Paiutes were a horseless tribe who lived a nomadic life in the constant quest of food.

But now, as Red Hand ran, he thought of only one thing: Dark Star and the safety of the tribespeople he had left behind to find water for their long journey back to the reservation. When he had heard the shot, he was more than a mile from the band. He crossed that distance in less than seven minutes. And when he slowed at the crest of ground above the swale and looked down, his breath rate was only slightly above that of a man who might have walked the same distance. He could hear the death chant rising on the shrill voices of women wailing over their dead husbands, and could see the four lifeless bodies stretched out on the ground. His eyes darted from woman to woman until he found Dark Star, clutching an elderly woman's shoulders and rocking back and forth in grief. Red Hand trotted toward her. There was a grim set to his tight lips, and the blank look on his face was that of a man who knew what he would find, but was desperately hoping he was wrong.

Placing the water containers carefully on the ground, he knelt beside Dark Star and gently touched her shoulder.

"What happened, little one?"

Dark Star's eyes had been closed and her cheek was pressed against the other woman's graying hair. When she opened them, there was a flood of tenderness and relief at the sight of Red Hand.

"I'm glad you're safe, Red Hand. Wokana and some of his warriors found us. They killed the men and . . . and . . ." She looked down, unable to speak anymore.

For the first time, Red Hand noticed the torn dress hanging loose across Dark Star's legs, and he could see a crimson spot of blood below her waist. He turned her face up to him tenderly and touched her cheek gently with his other hand.

"Don't tell me about it, little one. I think no differently about you now than I did before I left to find water." Then his

180

voice turned as cold as the expression on his face. "But I want to know which of them did this to you. Was it Wokana?"

Dark Star gazed deeply into his eyes before biting her lip and glancing away with a weak nod of her head.

"Was there anyone else?"

"No," Dark Star replied, her voice just above a whisper. "Wokana was the only one. He said I was his now."

"You will never be his, and he will never touch you again. Believe that, little one." Red Hand picked up one of the containers and held it to Dark Star's lips. "I have fresh water. Drink now, you and the others, then wash yourselves clean. I will turn away while you do so and then I must cover the dead. When I am finished, I will take you back to the reservation."

Dark Star accepted a drink and then took the container from his hands while searching his face with darting eyes. "Do you think the agent will punish them for what they have done, Red Hand? Will he make them leave us alone and let us live in peace as the White Father promised?"

Red Hand gazed at her for long seconds before shaking his head with sad resignation. "No, he will not. They are his police and the white men cannot be trusted any more than the Bannock can. We can never live in peace here as they promised. Peace is only a dream, just like the food and clothing we were supposed to have. I have never wanted war, but now I have no choice. I must lead our people away from here, to a new land and a new hope, and when I do they will come after us. But we will fight them now, both the whites and the Bannock, and if we must die, we will die with our heads held high in pride."

Red Hand squeezed her shoulders tenderly and stood. "Clean yourself and help the others," he said, moving away. "I will be waiting on the ridge until you have finished."

Red Hand climbed slowly up to the crest and stood there, a lone figure silhouetted against the darkening sky. The golden rays of the setting sun washed across his body and he stared at the gigantic mountain range to the northeast, glowing red in the distance. He could see the indentation known as South Pass, where the Iron Horse crossed the narrow divide, and instinctively he knew what he must do. And he knew as he stood there that many of his people would not survive, especially the elderly and injured, but he also knew he had no other choice. Escape into an unknown land dominated by whites was the only choice they had, and even if it meant certain death, he had no other alternative. In that moment of solitude he longed for his desert home while the harsh chill of the coming night closed about him. But he felt certain that he would never see his native land again. Many minutes had passed before he heard Dark Star call to him, and he turned wearily to retrace his steps and begin covering the bodies of the slain with rocks.